AN
ORDINARY
EXPLOSION

AN
ORDINARY
EXPLOSION

Q. R. Stuve

OSEL BOOKS
San Rafael

ISBN: 978-1-940121-03-1

Cover photo by David Carlier, davidcarlierphotography.com.
Back cover photo by Wikih101, permission CC BY-SA 3.0.

Osel Books
Published by Urtext Media LLC
San Rafael, CA 94901
www.urtext.us

Printed in the United States of America

PART 1

CHAPTER 1

The nitric acid triester of glycerol, also called nitroglycerin, increases the flow of blood to the heart, but it decomposes with explosive violence when jarred or heated. The mathematics which describe the initial state of the forces binding it, the heat required to upset the balance, and the energy released as the atoms seek other accommodations are well enough known for munitions designers to make a good living. The rest of us know the results, and that's good enough for us.

We know the results of love too, but we're more interested in the process. Songwriters and poets and playwrights describe it but no chemist has yet found equations that predict the outcome. Our math can barely count how much and how long and what happened next. We're atoms who only dimly see the molecules we're part of. Add a little heat, excite us out of our orbit and oop! what happens next no one knows.

Alan Donner's initial state held two grade school kids he deeply loved and a wife who had stopped having sex and wouldn't talk about why. Heat came from Olive Lo, a vivacious colleague whose eyes widened perceptibly whenever she smiled at him. He sensed potential as an electron feels a positive charge. He'd sensed it the first time they met, and when she mentioned that she'd just gotten married he felt regret that they hadn't met before.

Soon afterwards, when he was hired by her office, she was pregnant. He assumed her marital bond was as strong as his—though his own was no longer reinforced by much affection—but her warmth toward him seemed to go beyond her flirtatious way with other men.

For weeks the office had talked about skiing together. In the end only Alan, Olive, Mike and Mike's wife Dorothy went, which was fine with Alan as it sort of paired him with Olive. Alone together, how warm would she be? He was apprehensive, but he felt like being seduced and wanted to seduce her. But where and when could consummation possibly take place? And what if it did? What would it do to their marriages and families? Did he dare? By the time they met at Mike and Dorothy's for the drive to Tahoe, he had decided to add some heat of his own and see where it went.

Her nearness in the back seat made him jittery. He didn't know how to flirt. A frank avowal of infatuation having sometimes been successful and being at least honest, he had an urge to lean over and quietly say, "I have a crush on you." If she shrank away he'd feel like an ass and try to laugh it off, oh ho ho what a funny boy am I. But if she didn't shrink, what could they say next with Mike and Dorothy sitting in front? Calm down, boy, we have a day together. Wait until we're alone. "The Chinese are returning," he said.

"They are? You're not going there again?"

"You went to China?" Dorothy asked.

Olive laughed. "Oh, he help some poor ignorant peasants build a first-class laboratory animal building."

"Art Laguna, you know, the animal facility director, took me to Harbin three years ago to consult on a project at a veterinary research institute. Olive met them a year before that when they came here."

"Alan ask me for his name in Chinese," Olive said brightly. She was drawing attention to a connection between them.

"I wanted some bilingual business cards." It had been a pretext to have lunch with her.

"I named him Confucius of the Southern Calculator because he's one smart engineer," she laughed. She was flirting. He smiled and she widened her eyes at him.

"I spent a week explaining how to design a mechanical

system and then realized they could never do it themselves, so I did it for them."

"I hope they paid you well," said Mike.

"Tell you the truth," said Olive, "I think maybe they take advantage of you. I hope they know what a good deal they got, free design entirely."

"I'm glad to help. They're nice people, and I got two free trips to China. Actually, Olive, you should've come instead of my wife. You'd have been a better interpreter than Chen, remember Chen? And we could've had some fun." She giggled. "Listen, will you join us when they arrive? They want to review the design."

"I'll be the dumb interpreter, huh?"

"Well, they know you, you understand design and construction, and I'll buy you lunch afterwards."

"Okay," she laughed. He'd made a date, two dates. He'd nudged it along.

Mike and Dorothy quit skiing after lunch, and alone with her he nudged again. "You're a very graceful skier."

"But you're an expert!"

She was nudging back but he was too shy to go further. "Don't you think skiing's a metaphor for life? You bounce around, hit bumps, make mistakes, all the while trying to do it with grace. Your spirit reacts to events like your body to the hill. You always get to the bottom, but the goal's to have fun on the way, and that takes control and discipline."

"I'll say. If all I do is fall down, I'll quit." She nodded toward the shirtless young man who helped them onto the lift. "I wish I was eighteen again."

"Why?"

"He is so good looking! I'm too old. When Daniel's born my body stopped being young and taut." She crinkled her eyes.

All right, let's flirt. "No, you look better now. A deeper, more mature beauty."

She smiled.

Mm, your smile is enchanting. "Isn't everything enchanting today? The sun, the snow…"

"It's too cold. I think I'll join Dorothy and Mike at the bar."

He'd lost his chance. He should have dared more. Or maybe not. Maybe she wasn't as attracted to him as he to her—she could have stayed but hadn't. But if he'd pressed, maybe she would have. Damn. How do you seduce a woman?

He skied a last run alone and went to the lodge. Olive smiled and waved a glass from across the room.

"This is my second," she giggled. "I like my wine as much as my skiing."

Great, drink up, my dear. Get loose. He had a glass himself and concentrated on making her laugh.

At the car he said, "I'm going to change my pants."

"Here in the parking lot?"

"Why, sure, they're wet. Do you want to see my red underwear?"

She and Dorothy laughed harder than the joke was worth, which he took to mean he'd reached some boundary, so he didn't change after all and rode back in damp pants.

Mike groused about work. "That son of a bitch Theodore. For the first time in years this university has decent project management and what do they do? They fire the whole damned staff and make us apply for our own jobs. What bullshit!"

"Now, Mike," said Dorothy, "you know the tax laws give him no choice."

"Bullshit. He could convert the contracts without posting the positions."

"I tell you," said Olive, "I'm more angry he's taking our offices. It's a slap in the face."

"You think so?" Alan turned to her. "I'd want my directors close to me, too. It's just our bad luck we have the best offices when we're lower on the totem pole."

"I wonder if he's circumcised."

"You what?" Mike roared with laughter.

"Well, he's Italian, right? So maybe he's not."

She was ribald, yes, but was it only talk? How far did she go, had she gone, would she go, with whom, with him?

"I didn't have Daniel circumcised," she went on. "Chinese parents don't and I couldn't see the reason. Are American men circumcised? I have very small experience, apart from Paul."

Very small meant some? "Susan and I didn't have Philip circumcised either. It'll give some lucky woman more to play with."

She laughed and leaned toward him and punched his shoulder. "Isn't it beautiful? I love natural places so much."

The sun setting through brown haze above an oily estuary crossed by power lines wasn't his idea of natural beauty although her face at that moment was. The mood was right. But there were Mike and Dorothy. Okay, I'll make my avowal when we say goodbye. Last chance.

Dorothy said, "Why don't you stay for dinner?"

"Oh yes!" they both exclaimed.

They drank wine and made pasta. He showered and changed and announced, "Now I have on black underwear."

"Don't show us," Olive laughed. "Have another glass of wine. Oh, I think I'm drunk a lot."

"Why don't you sleep here?" Dorothy suggested.

"Good idea. I'll call Paul."

"I'm drunk too," said Alan while Olive was on the phone. "Maybe I should stay too."

"We have plenty of room."

The coast was clearing. He called Susan, fearing she'd be grumpy after a day of tending the kids. "I'm at Mike's for dinner and we've drunk so much I probably shouldn't drive into the city, so they invited me to spend the night."

"Why don't you?"

"How are you doing with the kids?"

"We're having a good time."

"You're not feeling put upon?"

"No, I'm fine. I'll see you in the morning."

He hung up with a smile. What next. Ah, the piano.

"Oh, I love piano music!" said Olive. She beamed while he stumbled through a prelude.

"I'm playing like a drunken pig. Some other time I'll

knock your pants off."

"You're very good," she said warmly. "Play another."

They drank more wine with dinner and laughed hilariously at Mike's off-color jokes though for a change Olive wasn't telling any herself. Now and then he glanced at her and caught her glancing away. Was the approach of bedtime and its possibilities on her mind? Or was he imagining things? Careful now, no nudge now, don't make her shy away—if desire was dawning, let it wait until they were alone, when it would be harder to deny.

"I'm going to bed," she said. "I'm too drunk."

I should go too... No, not this soon, act like nothing's on my mind. He helped clear the table and wash the dishes until finally Dorothy said, "Let's go to bed."

Good, yes, but is it too late now? He undressed to his underpants and looked at his face in the mirror. Shall I go to her? I'll kick myself later if I don't try... I'm too drunk to know. Oh, better to have loved and lost than... That is, better to have ventured and nothing gained... He caught his breath and stepped into the hallway, would proceed to the bathroom if Mike or Dorothy came out, quietly cracked her door, slipped through the darkness to the bed and said softly, "Olive."

She didn't answer.

She was asleep.

Damn. How do you seduce a sleeping woman?

Leave now, you idiot.

Wake her up. "Olive."

"What," came a drowsy reply.

"It's Alan. Do you want to sleep together?"

"I don't know," she drawled tentatively as if asking a question.

He bent and delicately kissed her on the lips. Her lips pressed back. He sat down and she opened her mouth and her tongue pushed into his. She tasted like wine. After a while he lay down, pulled down the blankets and slowly drew up her nightgown, marveling in the dark at how firm she was, how small and compact, how unlike the flabby body he'd lain beside for so many years that he'd forgotten what a woman's body could be. His hand slid down her back, under her small, thin underpants, into the taut valley between her buttocks. The tips of his fingers touched a wonderful wet slickness and the back of his hand felt the coarse fabric of a sanitary pad. Their tongues slid together. She grew slicker.

"Let's make love."

"I don't know..." she drawled.

A moment of silence. "I've had a vasectomy..." A moment of suspense.

"Oh, I'm not worried about that..." She held him closer. "I have my period."

"I don't care if you don't care..."

"Will Dorothy and Mike hear us?"

"No, there's a bathroom in between."

She kissed him.

He pushed the nightgown above her breasts and she drew it over her head while he pulled off his famous underpants, wishing it wasn't so dark, wanting to see her: crawled between her open legs and nudged blindly: she reached down and guided him inside: in he slipped: so long since he had done this, the ancient and familiar conversation of two bodies: question and quick answer, liquid loss and recovery dissolved in discovery...

She climaxed. His wine-dulled senses relaxed with her, his excitement ebbed. Should he try to come? No, let's not insist: if that's all, it's all: and what a joy it was! She would with him, she had with him! He lay inside her for a while in contentment. His turmoil had vanished. "All day long I was going to tell you I loved you."

"Really?"

"I was too shy."

"I liked you the first time we met."

"You drove us around to see the animal facilities. Do you remember how close our knees were? I was tingling. You talked about your wedding and I was thinking too bad I'm married, too bad she's married."

"I told Dorothy what an attractive engineer I just met. She laughed and said, watch out! We used to joke about the men in the office. Jose's good looking but he thinks too much of himself, Harry is lots of fun but he'd tell afterwards. Later I said you're a noble person, and she agreed."

"How sweet." How many she had gone how far with no longer mattered.

"I liked you so much when you asked me for your Chinese name."

"I still have the paper you wrote it on."

She kissed him. "There's a Chinese tradition that what you dream New Year's Eve will come true that year. I dreamed about you."

He laughed happily. "I wish I'd dreamed about you. I was miserable. We went skiing but there was no snow and Susan was taking her foul mood out on me. I got so upset that I told her I'd had it, she was on her own, I'd take the bus home, and I got out of the car. She drove alongside yelling at me to get back in. I only did because the kids were crying."

"Poor boy. Do you remember when we walked in the rain that time under your umbrella and talked about music?"

"I felt proud and protective and I wanted to kiss you. Here it is, finally." He kissed her.

"Mmm."

"Do you remember our lunch at Slocum Stew's before you had Daniel?"

"I was so unattractive, so fat."

"You were beautiful. I was happy for you—I thought being a mother would round you out."

She hugged him and they chatted in the calm about her dreams of traveling, his dream of writing, the meaning of life, things new lovers share, until their silences grew longer and he began drifting off. "Can't you sleep?" he murmured.

"No, I'm too nervous," she whispered. "I'm afraid they'll find us."

"Do you want to make love again?"

She found his lips with hers.

Again he couldn't climax. After she did he kissed her goodbye, silently closed the door, went to the bathroom to wash off her blood, and then passed out in his own bed.

At dawn he quietly went back. She met him at the door and whispered, "Dorothy and Mike will be getting up."

"They won't hear us."

"No…"

He returned to his room with full loins and tried to make himself come but was still too numbed by wine. He gave up and went downstairs.

"How did you sleep?" asked Dorothy.

"Not so well. I drank too much last night. Hello, Olive, how are you?"

"I'm tired."

"It was a late night, wasn't it?" She nodded and smiled without meeting his eyes. They ate a bowl of cereal and had a cup of coffee, then everyone said goodbye, that was fun, thank you for everything, see you on Monday. He stole a brief kiss at her car and she followed him to the freeway where he waved and she waved back.

Hoo boy, now I've done it, what now, now what happens?

CHAPTER 2

The weekend was a haze. Was she thinking of him? What would happen at work—would she ignore him and pretend nothing had happened? Was this a beginning or had it already ended? What would happen with Susan?

Hope for nothing. What had happened was nothing necessarily special—two people, a man and a woman who liked each other spent a night together... the same old thing, happens all the time.

Then why this hope, this sense of wonder?

They gazed uncertainly at each other in her office until Steve came in and broke the silence. They talked about skiing and dinner and how much wine they drank. As Alan left, Jose passed and smirked, "I hear you and Olive had a great time at Mike's all night long."

"I wish," he grinned.

"Well, it's your fault if you didn't."

Others had and anyone could? He didn't think so.

Mike leaned into Harry's door. "You should have heard Olive and Alan going at it Friday night."

"Oh yeah?" Harry laughed.

"Oh, they made quite a racket!"

"Sure," said Alan, "I wish." Had they been noisier than he thought? No, they'd been quiet as mice.

Olive came by later. "Jose told me Mike told him we broke the bed after the ski trip."

"What did you say?"

"I just laughed."

"They couldn't have heard. And if they did, he wouldn't say anything. He's making a joke."

"Yes, he likes to joke."

He couldn't concentrate. He went to the copier, the bathroom, the coffee station, anything to pass Olive's office. Each time he smiled and she smiled back. Otherwise he avoided her.

At the end of the day they walked downstairs together. "What a strange day," he said.

"Yes. How do you feel?"

"Mixed up. What about you?"

"Yes." They smiled awkwardly and said good night.

The next morning he said, "I'd like to talk."

"Me too."

"Shall we have lunch together?"

"I can't. I have lunch with my architect until one-thirty. Can you meet me then?"

"Where?"

"Somewhere we won't see anybody we know. China Beach Cafe."

She wasn't in the cafe or at the bar when he arrived, so he walked outside along the bay pretending interest in the boatyard next door. The bartender glanced at him when he went back and looked around. He sauntered back and forth on the esplanade wondering if he looked like someone being stood up. When he finally saw her arrive he went to meet her and they walked a foot apart to the cafe. He wanted to touch her, but there is a difference between fucking in a drunken stupor and holding someone's hand, and he wasn't sure he'd advanced that far. The bartender smiled. Alan smiled.

"Let's sit on the deck. It's a nice day." It was actually windy and cool, but he was edgy and wanted to be away from people.

"How do you feel?" she asked.

"I can't sleep. I can't eat. I can't concentrate."

"Me too. I can't do my work at all or think about anything.

What are we doing?"

"Are we falling in love?"

"How can we? You're married, you have two children. I'm married. I love my husband. I love my son."

"And I love my family. But I love you too. I think."

"We can't."

"I know. But I think I do."

"In China there's a tradition of the man who falls in love with a woman and never loves anyone else, gives his life and writes poems for her, but that's all."

Is that what you want me to do? "The troubadours of Provence supposedly loved like that too, but don't you think it's unlikely?"

"My mother told me about an old man in Taipei who loved the married woman next door. All his life he loved her, he never went out with anyone else, and they never went out together. Everyone knew, even her husband. Finally when they're very old her husband died."

"And they got together?"

"No. I guess it didn't matter by then."

He laughed. "Gabriel Garcia Marquez wrote a similar story, but they got together in the end. *Love in the Time of Cholera.* I'll loan it to you." He finally dared to put his arm around her shoulder. She nestled closer, turned to him and they kissed. After a while he said, "I don't think people live like that anymore. People nowadays aren't satisfied with mere devotion."

"Maybe... but this happen in my own mother's lifetime."

"But life can be richer than that. Two people can love each other and also their spouses and children, raise their kids, continue their normal lives."

"How?"

"Get together when they can, be patient when they can't, take only the opportunities that arise naturally. Be mature, relaxed, with no demands on each other. Control themselves, like we do when we ski, discipline their passion."

"It would have to be like that."

It wasn't quite acquiescence, but it wasn't no. "This looks

like Shanghai, lighters and tenders and barges going up and down, ships anchored in the river."

"Before I marry Paul I traveled a lot." She paused. "I tell you something nobody knows except Steve. I was married before Paul, a horrible three years. I was too young, just out of high school." She caressed his cheek. "Please don't tell anyone."

He rejoiced. She trusted him with her secrets!

"Only good part was all we did is travel, but I never went to China. I'd like to go there with you."

"Let's do!"

"Alan." She took his face in her hands. The scent of her warm, perfumed skin filled his nostrils. A strand of hair slipped between their tongues. He exulted.

He made an appointment to be tested for AIDS. Four years before an old girlfriend had visited and invited him to bed. Though he'd been negative when he donated blood a few months later, the rare case did appear after some years and now he wanted certainty.

In the evening while Susan was away teaching, he helped Philip and Claire with homework. His thoughts drifted to Olive's face, her cheek, her odor... Philip repeated a question. He answered vaguely and sank back into reverie. Startled by a question from Claire, he jumped to help, wondering how to fit these commonplaces into his exploding universe.

He'd slept alone for months because Susan said his snoring kept her awake. He thought her own snoring woke her up, but this way at least he could masturbate in peace. He would buy a girlie magazine and turn the pages with exquisite pleasure. On following nights the stimulation waned as the models became familiar. He would scrutinize the pictures until a curve, a hip, a glance, or the texture of vaginal flesh provoked his orgasm. He explored a woman's erotic range by imagining her clothed, half disrobed, nude, costumed, made up, different haircuts and skin colors, with men, women, men and women, sometimes ignoring and other times playing to the camera. He wanted dozens of pages, a volume, thousands of photos, each pose minutely changing to the next, each instant succeeding the last, a lifetime of shots, adolescent, mature, pregnant, swollen nursing breasts, and finally old and careworn and lined.

Or he imagined the model's motives. A few quick bucks for an easy gig, have some fun, why not? She knew what men would do with her pictures—she accepted, invited, flirted with the lens and photographer, abandoned herself and grew excited—her complaisance encouraged his pleasure.

And when the glossy magazines dulled he would look at medical textbooks with line drawings of the corpora cavernosa and spongiosum in flaccidity, engorgement and erection, read the clinical narration of arousal, flush, spasm—it authenticated and intensified the proceedings.

But this week all the tricks were stale. His yearning for a woman, for love, for Olive, vitiated the carefully erected structure of his solitary evenings. He kept at it obstinately for an hour but found no release and after that didn't bother to try. Instead, he read until exhaustion deepened to collapse, woke around three, alone, empty arms aching and groping for Olive, turned out the light and drifted between sleep and yearning until he finally gave up and dressed, drank coffee and went to the office to kill time until she arrived and the day began.

He gave her *Love in the Time of Cholera.* "And try this one, *Hadrian's Memoirs.* He believed we create our own gods, and the most important one is love."

The week went by. They began calling each other from their offices to chat for a minute, and he called from pay phones when he drove to campus. They began to know each other's whereabouts hour by hour.

She gave him a compact disk. "This is music themes from movies I like. I marked my favorites. I hope you won't think it's bad. I have simple tastes, not like you."

He didn't care if it was bagpipe music. "Listen, do you want to have lunch? Otherwise we won't see each other until Monday."

"Yes, but I have a meeting on campus. Maybe Monday."

"That's such a long time off…"

"Yes…"

She'd been working four days a week since she returned from maternity leave a year ago. He wandered around unable to concentrate, wishing she worked Fridays, too.

The phone rang. "Surprise! Daniel's taking his nap and I miss you. What are you doing?"

"Mostly thinking about you. I listened to the music last night."

"Did you like it?"

He detested Puccini and string arrangements of otherwise good music. "I like the Strauss most. Did you see *The Year of Living Dangerously?* The girl's dying–"

"It's so sad."

"Yeah." He was so happy.

"Alan, I just don't know what to do about us. I don't know what to do about Paul. How can I do this to him?"

"I don't know either. Let's don't do anything until we sort ourselves out."

The next day was spring workday at the kids' school. He climbed onto a flat gray roof and mindlessly smeared goop into cracks. Overcome by exhaustion, away from the rush of events and questions, soothed by the featureless calm of the roof and the empty sky, he lay down and drifted to sleep and dreamed of her face.

That evening he and Susan went to the symphony. Susan strode ahead in her forthright way and he hastened to keep up, head down, contemplating the sidewalk disappearing into the fog like a path into vague contradictions. One pace behind, he stepped off the curb to cross an alley. Imprinted in the concrete was OLIVE. He gasped and almost stumbled. He stopped stock still. OLIVE. He turned his head rapidly round and saw only a blurred foggy cocoon and a street sign marked OLIVE on a light pole. My god, I am enveloped by her. Has the world reconfigured itself or have I gone crazy? An alley named Olive? Where am I? Is this still San Francisco? Susan had forged on and he hurried to catch up.

LOVE LETTER

I see only your face, your shining lips trembling in a smile, your bright eyes on mine, black sparks in your alert, smiling face. Eyes closed or open I see your face and your shining hair and feel it tangled between our tongues, your hot cheekbone against my own, your hair and contoured ear against my lips, your firm lips firmly pressed to mine, your intoxicating scent expanding in my face. A hungry pit opens in my gut—I am hollow and no longer sleep. I no longer know if I wake or sleep, my judgment is shot, my perspective is askew, parallel lines diverge and cross.

Maybe we suspected or half-consciously toyed with our attraction to each other, but we were unprepared for this sudden exorbitant passion. It's like stepping from the calm dark night into a roaring circus tent. What a surprise. What do we do?

What are our choices? For all our talking we've found only three:

We stop and return to normal. We ignore our feelings for each other and learn to ignore the pain of being businesslike again.

We run away together.

We grope along as we have this week, afraid to continue but unwilling to stop.

Anything else? Discovery. Spouses find out. People at work find out. Disaster and destruction.

The Greeks named three kinds of love: passion (eros), friendship (philia), and selfless love (agape). They remarked that as passion cools affection warms. (If this passion would wane, I'd be able to get a good night's sleep and you'd be able to catch up on work. (Ah, but, the happy couple objects, our extraordinary passion won't cool. (Ah, but, what's so special about us?)))

Listen, Olive, we have a rare opportunity to have a passion that doesn't cool. We have friendship and selfless love at home. Homes are broken by partners who find erotic distraction outside. Our faithfulness to each other will protect our homes, and our time apart will stimulate our passion. (Oh, I love my love with an e and a p, erotically and philially.) We will create happiness for our families as well as ourselves. It will require cheerful acceptance of the unknown, living with a certain amount of risk, patience when we're apart, pure love for our families... We are mature enough to do this.

I'm less concerned about Susan than you are about Paul. She recently said she no longer objects to extramarital sex though she doesn't want to know if I do. I'm not suggesting I have a license to philander but am explaining why I don't feel I'm betraying her. Of course, it could turn out to have been easier for her to say than tolerate, and I'd just as soon spare her the consternation of finding out about us. Who knows? Maybe one day she and Paul too will see that love doesn't have to be limited to one person.

Look at it another way: Our hearts go pitter-pat and our knees wobble, we sigh and stutter. It means a lot to you and me, but where does it fall in the grand scheme of things? What is passion? A biological function that interferes with commerce... What's the big deal? We can handle it.

Let's make love. It would clarify things—its simple limpidity is so soothing.

I've always thought all the men are a little in love with you, but maybe that's because I have always been. What if I had said out of the blue: I love you. What would you have done?

I love you.

CHAPTER 3

Should he give her the letter? He had listed her worries and fears—all of which he shared though in his own case he was willing to risk everything and deal with consequences later—because he hoped to increase her sense of their affinity and reiterate his suggestions for overcoming her scruples. Then too, avowing his passion wouldn't hurt. If she liked it they advanced one square, and if not, if elucidation of their perplexity caused her to end things, well, better sooner than later. He left it on her desk.

She came by later. "Do you want to have lunch?"

"China Beach Cafe?"

"Too many people."

"Slocum Stew's?"

"I'll meet you at your car at eleven-thirty."

Good. She still wanted to see him. And eleven-thirty was well before their colleagues got together for lunch, and they never went to Slocum Stew's.

"What are we going to do?" she sighed.

"Don't you think we can love each other and our families too?"

"I don't see how." She sighed again. "My sister Fern came home from shopping and found her husband in bed with one of his students. He was her history teacher in high school and they got married when she graduated. He has a problem, but tell you the truth, he's not the only blameful one—she had a hard time leaving our family and still stays with our parents two three days sometimes. Also, she says they didn't make love much. She was very frustrated and wanted to see a counselor but he wouldn't go. He still doesn't see why he should change anything so she's going to move out. She's having a rough time."

"It's hard to give up stability even if it's bad."

"Yes. My first marriage was a nightmare but it was hard to end."

"What happened?"

"After we moved here from Taipei I was popular and attractive, had my choice of boys. All the girls want the handsome football player, so I chose him."

"You're still popular and attractive," he laughed.

"I don't think you'd like me then. I was very demanding. If a boy liked me I made him obey me."

"So you made him marry you?"

"No. In the summer after high school I met the Chinese boy from Indonesia, conceited and arrogant. My parents and sisters didn't like him and at first I couldn't stand him."

"Why did you marry him?"

"I was so naive. After we make love it was end of the world for me—you're a bad woman if you do that."

"I know what you mean. I grew up Catholic."

"From the very beginning we fight like cats and dog, yell and throw things, always screaming. He was very spoiled, wealthy family, always got what he wants."

Why had these girls thrown themselves at the first men they met? Rebellion against strict parents? Were they wealthy and spoiled themselves? He remembered that when they'd been here the time before, before she'd had Daniel, he'd thought she was self-indulgent, the only unattractive trait he saw in her, and wondered if motherhood might cure it. "You must have been miserable."

"It was a nightmare. We traveled a lot. When we're low on money, he call his parents and they send a thousand dollars. We lived with his aunt in Indonesia one summer and I can tell you *The Year of Living Dangerously* is accurate. It affected me deeply, especially the Strauss music."

"Isn't that funny? I was following the news about Sukarno, and the movie and music touched me too."

"I was there then."

"Is that why I was interested?"

She smiled and touched his cheek. "After two years I know I have to get out of the marriage and support myself, so I went to architecture school. I filed for divorce my senior year. And I put it out of my mind for years. This is the first I talk about it in a long time."

"Does it hurt to talk about?"

"Oh no, it's just a long ago bad dream. I don't think about it. I will not."

"Olive, the strangest thing happened Saturday night. I saw your name imprinted in concrete near the symphony—" Her laughter startled him. "I'm not kidding! It's the name of an alley."

"When I was sixteen my father told us we're moving to America and we should choose American names so people won't think we're strange. He gave us a book of names but my sisters and I can't find anything we like. The sounds are queer and we don't know what they mean. Chinese names mean something, you know. My name is Mei Li, means beautiful."

"Good choice. You are."

She smiled. "He also gave us a San Francisco map. We read the streets—Heather, Olive, Fern, Rose, I don't know what else. We saw in the book they're girls' names. Heather and Fern chose those. There were olive trees at my school, so I chose Olive."

"There's one in my back yard!"

"One what?"

"Olive tree. See, this was all arranged long ago."

"It's fate!"

They walked back to the car hand in hand. He drew her to him and they kissed on the sidewalk.

"Mmm," she said. "I keep remembering everything we

did that night. I was so turned on!"

"It was wonderful, but I was so drunk it wasn't as good as it could have been."

"How could it be better?"

"I was afraid you were disappointed that I didn't come."

"It doesn't matter."

"Do you want to make love now?"

"Where?"

"My house."

"What about Susan?"

"She's at work. She teaches from noon to four."

She hesitated, then exclaimed, "No, no, not your house, not in her bed! I couldn't relax, I have to be relaxed."

They had advanced a square.

He brought a camera to the office and took everyone's picture. He started with Olive, had her take his, snapped another when she walked by, and ended with her. Later they drove to campus together and she asked, "Why are you taking pictures?"

"I told everybody it's to remember our old offices, but it was really a pretext for getting some of you."

"You better not show all the ones of me or people will wonder. Give me a copy of yours." She grasped his hand. "Oh, I don't know what to do! There must be some rules. Do you leave the office together? Do you go places in your own car?"

"How much can people know you're together before they start wondering?"

"Can we go out with Paul and Susan?"

"That's a good one. Do we want to?"

"Maybe Mike knows what to do. He and Dorothy fell in love while she was married. Maybe we should ask for advice."

"We need a guidebook. *Dos and Don'ts for Office Affairs—How to Love Successfully and Avoid Scandal.*"

"You should write it."

He laughed. "We'd make a fortune."

"I want you to teach me about music."

"I don't know much about it. I only play piano."

"I think you know very much. Did you take lessons as a child?"

"No, I wanted to play the accordion. I bought one a few years ago over Susan's objections. After a couple months she said I had to choose between her and the accordion. Well, I missed my chance: I said what about piano instead?"

"When do you find time to practice?"

"After I put the kids to bed."

"Daniel doesn't go to bed before ten and Paul doesn't come home until eight sometimes."

"You must not see each other very much."

"No, just on weekends, and often we do things by ourselves. He's very good about letting me do what I want."

"Does he like music?"

"No. We went to the opera with Steve and Sharon and he said he would rather clean dog shit out of the yard."

He and Susan had bumped into them at the symphony once and asked if they were enjoying the program. Paul said he was having a nice nap which he couldn't do at the opera because the screeching kept him awake. Afterwards Susan said she felt sorry for Olive because she was so vivacious and Paul was so dull; she could have done better. Alan agreed, but now all he said was, "Too bad. He's missing a lot."

To his surprise, she turned onto a cross street and stopped. "Kiss me," she said. She clutched him and tongued him vehemently. He broke for a moment and smiled into her almond eyes, and then her hungry mouth blinded him again.

"Okay," she said. She squeezed his hand. "Let's have lunch tomorrow."

"Why have you fallen for me?" he asked. "You seem happily married."

"I like Paul very much, I suppose I love him, but he has his shortcomings. He's insensitive. He doesn't think life is special. I ask him once, don't you want to travel, don't you want to do something great? No, he thinks life is doing a good job, raising a family, celebrating birthdays. Tell you the truth, I didn't want to marry him but he kept on staying around. Now I guess I'm used to his shortcomings. We get along fine and if I don't like twenty percent of him, well, the rest is okay."

"Weren't you ever crazy about him?" If the attraction had never been strong, then all Alan had to overcome was the inertia of habit.

"I worked with him just out of college, Steve too. All us young designers had lunch and drinks together. Tell the truth, I thought he was uncaring. Once my father was very ill, I'm afraid he's going to die and I'm crying, everybody's sympathetic except Paul 'What's the matter, Olive?' he said. 'Having boyfriend trouble?'"

"Oh dear. So why'd you go out with him?"

"I don't know anymore. I always thought he's not the right person, we'll break up. Even after we live together I never thought we'll keep on going."

"Why did you?"

"He sold his house and said he wants to buy the new one in both our names. I said I can't share the down payment, are you sure? He said if we're going to live together he wants us to share everything. I was touched, he really cared about me."

"He's pretty smart. For a few thousand dollars, he got a wonderful wife."

She laughed. "Now tell me about you and Susan."

He wondered what the woman and girl at the next table were making of this. "Well, I never loved her wildly either. I wanted to settle down and have a family. Like Paul, she wasn't everything I wanted but we were comfortable and I thought it would last. My father said nothing's perfect, eighty percent is pretty good and if you wait for perfection you'll never get married."

"He's right."

"She's a good person and a good mother, but our sex life has always been rotten."

"It is?"

"We make love twice a year."

"I think after people are married a long time they don't do it so often."

"She never liked it. On our very wedding day she was too tired for it. I thought, uh oh, is this an omen?"

"Oh, Alan. I assumed you have a perfectly okay marriage. I mean, you don't chase women or anything."

"Only you. She thinks sex is domination, unless she wants it. But she never does, and she gets mad when I try to talk about it."

"It's part of the whole thing! When you feel tender about someone, you want to do it with him. And with you," she smiled, "she's missing a lot."

"She's insecure. She always thought nobody liked her, even her own family. She flunked out of college, went to Europe, came back and met me. I encouraged her to finish college. Now she's a teacher but she's not satisfied with her job and feels tied down by the kids. All in all, she's not a happy person."

"How can you put up with it?"

"Sometimes I've wished I had a lover, but I can't leave my children just because everything isn't peachy for me."

"I can't imagine leaving Paul, because of Daniel. He should have his mother and father."

"And how do you find time for an affair? But here we are."

"You're more passionate than me. I'm more controlled."

"You're the one who stopped on the way to campus and kissed me wildly!"

She blushed. "Tell me what your day is like."

After he did she smiled. "Now when I think of you, I'll know what you're doing."

He was pleased to know she thought of him so often. "Want to see my house? It's nearby."

"Isn't Susan there?"

"She'll be at work by now."

"I'm afraid of being alone with you."

"We won't make love. I'll just show you around."

But his heart pounded with hope.

Up the stairs and into the house. Did the neighbors see

them? To hell with the neighbors.

"We're painting the living room so the piano's under plastic."

"Sometime I want you to play for me."

"Here's where Claire and Philip sleep."

"Lots of toys, even more than Daniel."

He doubted that. She and Paul probably bought Daniel all that money could buy. "Here's where I sleep."

"Alone? Oh, Alan! She really is mean to you."

"And here's where she sleeps." And this is the end of the tour and here we are alone and now what. She said she doesn't want to but... He put his hands on her shoulders.

"Alan, no, not here."

"Olive, let's just kiss."

She entered his arms and pressed against him. Time stopped.

"We can't do this here."

Time passed. He said thickly, "We'd better leave now or we won't be able to."

She straightened her dress and said matter of factly, "Now I have to be careful not to act like I know anything about your house."

He had blood drawn on Friday. When Olive called from home he told her he'd taken the AIDS test, but she wasn't particularly interested.

"I told my mother last night that we've fallen in love," he said.

"You did? Why?"

"You and I are too crazy to think straight. I wanted advice from someone who can."

"What did she say?"

"She said, 'Oh, Alan, I'm sorry!'" He laughed.

"Why?"

"Because she doesn't know what to do either."

"I don't think anyone knows what to do."

She and Paul were dining out for their sixth wedding

anniversary that weekend. Alan was ferrying kids to parties. She told him to reserve lunchtime on Monday; she'd bring a picnic.

ANOTHER LETTER

I awoke happy (kissed the wife, kissed the kids, kissed the dog on her shiny black nose). I have a date with you!

> your eyes are like commas aslant
> which give my heart pause when they punctuate mine,
> your cheeks are parentheses,
> your mouth a round period,
> the point of your tongue
> is the end of the phrase
> on my lips.

It's like addiction. After a shot of you there is calm. A small dose like the sight of you at your desk is good for an hour. A few words are worth two. Lunch and an embrace get me through the whole evening. When you're not around, my craving builds like a restless junkie's. I'm high on Lo.

I want you. I want you in any combination or arrangement. I'll take Daniel, I'll take all the kids, I'll take you in the afternoons or mornings or at lunchtime, I'll take you once a year skiing.

How annoying to want to be together more but unable to get away from our families. We haven't faced constraints like these since adolescence. We've grown accustomed to acting as we wish, and now there's something we can't do. We don't know when we'll see each other next or what we'll do when we do.

And you are uncertain about what to do. Well, we swim in the uncertain sea of life, where catastrophe may interrupt every habit, and even the moment and manner of death are unknown. Certainty is impossible. You know, chaos is ordered only by forcing things into severely constrained systems.

Freedom must accept provisional agreement, diversity and dissonance. Certainty is stasis. Must we choose a too definite course, you and I?

Olive, there's no need to rush. Your decision will come by itself. I'll do what you want. But for now do nothing irrevocable, so all the choices remain.

Lo (and behold): Olive!
I love
lo I ve
O
live!

How about a rutty, smutty love affair, and nuts to noble sentiments? Shall I tell you what I'll do to you? I'll spread your secret parts and violate your skin, penetrate you thrice at once and push myself right in; I'll stretch you on the bedstead, wrap your legs around my head, lick your silken labia and fuck you till you're dead!

CHAPTER 4

"Thank you for the letter," she said as they drove to a park for the picnic.

"Did you like it?"

"Very much, except for the last part," she tittered. "What's the camera for?"

"Pictures of you away from the office."

"Oh, no!" They strolled up a valley past a couple holding hands, past a couple on the hillside, a couple on a bench, couples everywhere, to a quiet table out of sight in the trees. From a wicker basket came china, silverware and napkins, roast chicken, salad, rolls, cheese, pears and oranges and a warm beer which they passed back and forth.

"I don't want to divorce Paul," she said. "It isn't fair to him. And I couldn't leave Daniel."

"I could be a father to him."

"He should have his own parents. I'm fortunate to have a mother and father who loved us. They had their problems but we always knew they'll do anything for us. I want Daniel to have that feeling."

"Then we can either break off or go on this way."

"This way is hard."

"Well, we'll figure out how to see each other and cope with the lonely days when our schedules don't mesh. I'm just afraid you'll decide it's too much trouble."

"We will need to be patient."

"Yes. Or we'll make some stupid mistake and get caught.

We want it to last."

"When I think about getting caught… I just can't do that to Paul. He'd be terribly hurt."

"We should enjoy this, and no one should get hurt."

"It's the way you wrote, it's like being a teenager again. There are things you want to do but can't."

She talked as if they were going to continue, but the spring light was dappled with shadow like joy mixed with uncertainty about how long it would last.

"Listen, Olive, after we move to the new cubicles we won't be able to talk on the phone. What if I ask Steve to trade places with me? Or Harry with you? We'd be across from each other instead of having a partition between us."

"Will they think we're doing something?"

"I'll tell Steve I'd rather sit in a corner cubicle."

"Don't say anything to Harry. Maybe Steve."

Steve didn't want to trade. Alan asked Harry, who laughed. "Why doesn't she ask me herself?"

"I think she was too shy."

"Sure, I'll trade. Tell her to ask me."

But if he did, she'd know he'd asked against her wishes. "Nah, I'm not her go-between."

"Theodore saw you sleeping at your desk and asked if that's how we operate around here. I told him you came in at five this morning and he seemed okay after that."

"Oh, hell. Thanks. What an impression to make on the new boss."

"Don't worry about it. I think he was impressed. But what's wrong with you?"

"Oh, I just can't sleep these days."

"I talked to my mother again last night," he told Olive.

"What did she say?"

"She sympathizes with our dilemma but she doesn't see how we can carry something like this on for a lifetime. She also said that if we decide to end it, the sooner we do the easier it'll be."

"She did?"

"She also sends you her love."

Olive was embarrassed. "By the way, I can't have lunch, but can you meet me at the Cliff House at four?"

Her car was parked outside. He went in and kissed her proudly as three young men at the next table watched. She responded tepidly and said, "This wine is a present from those guys."

"How nice. How was your afternoon?"

"Alan, I must tell you I've been thinking hard. I think your mother is right. I can't go on with you and also my family. I think I have to stop doing this now."

His gut twisted and his field of vision contracted to her face.

"It isn't fair to Paul. He wouldn't do this to me."

How do you know he wouldn't? How do you know he hasn't? Or isn't? And if he doesn't know, what's the harm? But nothing he could say would matter.

"I think we should end this before something bad happens."

"Olive. Paul is so lucky. He has no idea how lucky. You're a wonderful person."

"You're a wonderful person too, and you deserve to be happy. But I can't be the one for you."

"Oh, Olive. Well, at least it's decided."

"We should have met earlier."

They were silent.

We need two Olives. One for Paul and one for me. "Is Fern anything like you?"

"No, she's very different. Why?"

"Oh, I was... If she were like you... She's free, and I..."

"I don't think you'd get along. She's not like me." She looked at him sympathetically. "How do you feel?"

"Terrible. How about you?"

"I feel it's the right thing. For two weeks I'm torturing

myself what to do. I never felt this way before, but it came at the wrong time."

"Oh, well. Olive, I'll miss you."

"Alan, we're still friends. We can have lunch together and talk about music and books."

"At least, this is the right way. No fight or bad feelings."

"You will always be special to me. And you will find someone else, someone who will love you and make you happy and who will be free."

He tried to kiss her one last time at the car but she drew back. He followed her station wagon to the last possible turnoff at the end of the beach. Then he went home.

WHAT HAPPENED AT HOME

I opened a beer and felt sorry for myself. I put on your CD and played *Beim Schlafengehen,* the one from *The Year of Living Dangerously.* I felt like crying. When Philip cuddled next to me on the couch and said, "You're the best dad I ever had in the whole world," I bawled. He asked why. I told him I'd tell him when he grew up.

He started crying. I went to my bedroom. Claire went to find out why Philip was crying. Susan went too, so I went back. The kids left. Susan asked why everyone was crying. I wondered what to say and then I gave up. "Because I just ended a love affair." She asked, "Did you end it or did she?" I said, "We did."

The phone rang. It was my friend Pedro from Madrid, who said he was in town for a week and how was I. What a surprise. I haven't heard from him in a year. I took the phone to the front porch, closed the door, and told him I had ended a love affair an hour ago. "Jesus Christ," he said, "I called at just the wrong time." "That's okay," I said. "That's life." I asked him to call me at work.

Then there was some confused walking around. I told the kids their mom and I might be separating.

Then I told Susan I would move out. I figured I'd say it

before she could.

Then she got mad.

Then she decided she didn't want me to move out. We talked. She wants to stay together. I said I'd stay if we try counseling. I told her that I need sex and also that I can't be married and have love affairs.

I missed you all night. But that's okay. I'm glad we decided what to do.

Thank you for everything.

PART 2

CHAPTER 5

He and Susan quit trying to sleep at daybreak. "I don't want you to leave. I want to work on improving our relationship. I'll call Kaiser today for a counselor."

Claire and Philip came into the kitchen. "We're going to stay together," said Alan.

"Are you sure?" asked Claire.

"Yes, we're sure."

"Nancy Rice is taking you up to their cabin today," Susan said.

"I thought we were going with you and Daddy on Friday."

"She thought we should have some time together."

"They should," Philip told Claire. "You should," he said to them, and Alan wished he hadn't said anything in front of them.

"I have to go to my classroom before I take the kids to Nancy's," said Susan. "Do you want to say goodbye to them there?"

He went to the office sick with the loss of everything and wrote down what had happened, understanding nothing, hoping only to record enough so he could one day comprehend. Should he give this last letter to Olive? Maybe it was too intimate now. Well, she might as well know. He left it for her. He called his mother, who cried. He made coffee. He copied a contract. He straightened his desk. Olive came and stood before him with brimming eyes. "I did not want this to happen."

"It was bound to. Don't feel bad."

"If it hadn't been for me, it wouldn't."

"Yes, it would have. It was coming to this. I just realized sooner because of you." She twisted her hands. "It's okay, Olive."

She turned and left. He drank more coffee. The phone rang and Pedro asked, "Alan, how are you?"

"I'm fine. Well, that is to say…"

"What's going on?"

"I fell in love and she decided to end it. Then I realized there was no longer any point in living with Susan, it's been so lousy for so long, so I told her."

"Jesus Christ, I'm sorry I called."

"Oh, it's okay. When can we get together?"

He had the jitters and wanted a dose of Olive but feared to displease her; then need overcame scruple and he went to sit down in her office. "You shouldn't feel bad," he told her. "You and I had an extraordinary two weeks, and I'm sure we've done the right thing. As for Susan and me, we aren't going to decide anything for a couple months." She wrung her hands. "Uh, do you want to have lunch?" She accepted, to his surprise.

He met Susan in front of her school at the end of the alley behind his office, kissed the kids goodbye, happy his family was still together for the time being, headed for campus, saw Pedro driving toward him, honked and hit the brakes; expressions of joy and amazement, see you tomorrow, on to campus where he sat through a presentation for a project of his by the firm Olive, Paul and Steve used to work for. Her old boss asked, "How is Olive?" and someone else said, "Isn't Olive wonderful?"

Everything was happening at once: Olive's past was in the room with these people, Pedro was from his, presently he would meet her: The fragile line between his elation and their unknowing normalcy remained unbroken only because he retained just enough sense to suspect that this magical chain of coincidence would embarrass rather than enchant them if he blurted out how wonderful she was.

He stopped at a camera shop and met her in the park. "Here, your pictures."

"Some of me, too? I just wanted the ones of you."

"Oh well, keep them. I have some for myself."

"What will you do with them?"

"I don't know... Look at them now and then."

They walked among bright budding plants in a sweet warm breeze to a bench by Stow Lake as he controlled the urge to take her hand. "I'd like to paint this."

"You paint, too?" She widened her eyes at him.

"Now and then something calls out to be fixed for time-less contemplation."

"What?"

"Well, art stops time, one way or another. A painting is complete all at once. It takes time to perceive, but its harmony is fixed. A book takes time to read, but at the end you see the whole pattern in one instant. Same with music, though it's the most temporal of arts—at a given moment it's only noise—still, you sense the structure and feel, however fleetingly, that there is sense to life. That clarity is the goal. Art's an attempt to order the complexity and patternless network of feelings, to rescue something from the ceaseless rush; it springs from a need to enfold and hold all at one time and forever some minute part of this odd experience, this life, this moment of a spring day where you and I share lunch on a park bench."

Her attention urged him on. "We're alive. That's all we know. Life is the basis, the unknowable pulsation outside of which we can't begin to guess. We name things and think by naming we've understood, though our thoughts are as incomplete and ephemeral as the breath we use to express them. The genius of our century is knowing that things can't be put into words."

"I think of all kinds of things, but when I'm with you I forget everything I planned to say."

"Me too. I can concentrate until I see you."

"You just said a lot."

"I wasn't looking at you."

Two women with a baby stroller approached and his heart sank—one had a child at school with his kids. It would not be good if she mentioned this to Susan, especially today of all days. At least for once he and Olive were not in each other's arms. "Hello, Karen."

"Hello," she said and walked on. He regarded the springtime explosion and imagined the place in fall when the greens had darkened and browned. "Everything changes, and yet everything remains the same. Usually we're so busy we don't notice, but when we do, it seems the whole world is magically connected. Even coincidence seems natural, as if there were laws we hadn't suspected and can't fathom."

"I don't know what you mean."

"That woman there, I know her. Yesterday my Spanish friend Pedro called. When we worked together, we skied at the same place you and I skied. I happened to write to him after we met the first time and I mentioned you by name. Why should he appear just now? And as I was driving up this morning, who's coming the other way? Pedro. Out of three billion people, he's on Seventeenth Street at that precise instant."

"Maybe God is putting these things together for you."

"Do these coincidences come from outside or do we imagine them? The feeling you and I had was both—we felt an inner attraction and the outside reciprocated."

"There's chemistry between some people like molecules."

"I think it's biological. We're alive. Life wants to go on living, so it adapts to the changing world. Since nothing could change if everything lived forever, the units of life make room for better adapted ones by dying—you, me, these plants thrusting upward, greening each spring, dying each fall—we all pass away, but first we reproduce ourselves. That's why we feel this tremendous urge to have sex, exchange body fluids, mix our genes, pass life on. You don't can't get closer to life than in sex.

"And love, love is the feeling of participation. The more we live, the more we love. Or maybe the more we love the more we live. It may be an evolutionary adaptation. Our off-spring need years of care before they can live on their own, so we love them. We develop social structures to increase their chance of survival. Marriage. We love our spouse and abhor adultery which weakens marriage and threatens our children."

She sighed. "We will always be dear friends."

"Did anyone notice that Olive spells love?"

She smiled and shook her head. He touched her hand, raised it to his lips and held it there. She continued smiling and as moments passed an undefined hope rose in his breast: Yesterday she couldn't go on; today she let him kiss her hand. But it would be best not to hope.

"I don't feel like cooking," Susan announced, "and the kids aren't here. Let's go out for dinner. She drove to Slocum Stew's, of all places. "Kaiser said their psychiatric service is only for crises and asked if this was one. I said, well, my husband told me last night he's leaving me and they said oh dear, that's a crisis all right and took me for tomorrow." He laughed. "I think we should both see a counselor. We need some help if we're going to stay together."

"I agree."

"Alan, what if you got some disease? How long have you been having affairs? What if you get AIDS and give it to me? What if you already have?"

"I'm sure I haven't."

"How can you know? You can't tell by how a person looks. I want you to have the AIDS test."

"I have."

"You have? What were the results?"

"Actually, I won't have them until next Friday?"

"When did you take it? Why?" Her voice rose and he glanced around embarrassed. My love life is being played out in restaurants. "Good lord, what have you been doing?"

"About four years ago I had sex with somebody a couple times. When I donated blood after that, they tested for AIDS and I was negative."

"So why did you take it now? What have you been doing since then?"

"Nothing. It was the only other time." Why now, indeed? He continued rapidly. "That test was six months afterwards, and the chance is extremely small that it shows up later, so the chance I have it is almost zero, but I thought I'd make absolutely sure. No one's ever been positive four years after exposure."

"Do you mean to say that all this time you've been having sex with me you might have had AIDS?"

"Susan, I don't have it. Anyway, transmission through heterosexual sex is rare, and we've had sex so seldom—"

"You god damned bookkeeper!" she shouted. "You and your god damned statistics. How do you know you didn't get it from this person?"

"She's married and monogamous and has been for years."

"How do you know? What about her husband? What about his partners?"

"I don't think he screws around."

"I didn't think you did either."

"Well, listen, in a week we'll know for sure. If you want, we won't have sex until then."

"Sex! All you ever think about is sex! You're perverted, Alan! You're sick! No normal person is as screwed up about sex as you are!"

"Susan, it's only part of a healthy relationship, but you know, we have it so seldom I probably do think about it a lot. Lord knows I've tried not to complain too much."

"Oh, I'm sick of this. You won't be satisfied unless you're screwing some floozy twelve hours a day. You have a permanent hardon. You're moving out because we don't have sex. You're sick!"

"How are you?" Olive asked.

"Susan's bitter and hurt. We might have a chance if she can wait out her anger, but I'm not sure she'll have the patience."

"I still think it's my fault."

"It's not. Anyway, she might actually be happier if we separated—at least she wouldn't always be anxious that I'd leave. Well, maybe this weekend away will help, though today I'm not very hopeful. But I'll give it my best."

"I hope you have a good weekend."

"How are you?" Pedro asked.

"I don't know any more. Here are some pictures of her. Right now she's at my office but I've lost her, and now I'll probably lose Susan. Though actually there isn't much left to lose. Susan's never believed in me, always tested, wanted proof that I'd stay no matter what, always was afraid I'd leave for someone else and withheld sex so I'd show that I'd stay despite even that, and all these years I've tried to be reassuring but I finally gave up and found some affection elsewhere. So now her worst fear has come true. I sympathize with her, but I'm tired. I'm tired of everything."

Pedro sympathized with him and then vanished from his life again.

He went home apprehensive, but Susan was in a good mood. "I went to the counselor today. She's a nice Chinese woman named Dr. Kronquist."

"Kronquist?" he laughed. Chinese, he sighed.

"Yes," she laughed, "and she said I have to decide if I want to stay with you, and if I do then somehow I have to accept what you did. I said I was so hurt I didn't know if I could. She asked if I like you and I realized that I do... I don't want us to break up."

"Susan, I'm glad. Neither do I." Not now anyway, not until I'm less crazy with sorrow and can think straight.

"And until you get the results of that test, I want you to use these."

"You want to make love?"

"If that's what you want, I'll do it."

"Let's also try to be kind and simple."

"It'll be hard."

"It should be easy. If it's hard," he quoted Olive, "it's because it's not simple and sweet enough."

"Sometimes I'm going to feel resentful and angry."

"I'm sorry it can't be undone..."

"Is it over, Alan? That's what I'm worried about."

"Yes, it's over." Oh Olive, why? "Oh Susan, you're all I have. I love you."

"Oh Alan, I want to believe you."

He rang his piano teacher's doorbell.

"How are you?" Sofia asked.

"Ah, I fell in love with a woman at work. She broke up with me yesterday, and I stupidly told Susan and now she's deciding if she wants to stay married. I can't think, sleep or eat, and you probably noticed I can't play, either."

"Well, it's okay. A man your age meets an attractive girl, a little romance, a little fling—it's nothing serious."

"We weren't playing around, Sofia. She's a good person, not a... It wasn't just fall into bed, have fun..."

"Of course not. You take things seriously."

"And she's serious, too. And fun. And loved me... loves me... but decided not to break up her family. It's best for her, maybe for me too."

"Alan, I hate to tell you this, but if a woman is really mad about a man she'll do anything, including leave her husband and children."

Sofia had Anna Karenina in mind, no doubt. "If she wasn't so honest, if she'd only been out for fun I wouldn't have loved her and wouldn't care, but she's decent, ethical, musical..."

"Alan, don't take it too seriously. Keep your sense of humor. We're most godlike when we laugh." He smiled—he always used to say that. "You'll go crazy otherwise."

"I already have," he laughed.

Susan made love to him without pleasure, which dampened his ardor, and finally the condom's reproach defeated him. "But you haven't come," she said.

"Well then, we're even."

"But I want you to be happy."

"I'm happy we're trying. It'll get better."

Next morning after breakfast she unbuckled his belt. "Let's do it."

"Are you sure?"

"I want to make sure you're satisfied."

"It's not going to work if that's the only reason."

"No, god damn it, we're going to!"

"Susan, no, we'll try some other time."

Suddenly she pleaded, "Alan, it's not always going to be good, especially at the beginning, but we've got to try."

He undressed and put on a condom but soon the initial excitement waned. She clasped him and jerked back and forth. "What's wrong?"

"Maybe it's the condom."

"Don't I turn you on?"

"It's been so long, you know. We need to get used to each other again. Let's forget it for now."

That evening at the Rices' cabin they tried again. "Alan, I feel terrible. I'm failing."

"I'm enjoying it—this is the most sex I've ever had. And I like sleeping with you again."

During the night when he ached for Olive he reached for Susan. She nestled against him and he slept soundly for the first time in three weeks. In the morning she made love without a condom, he came, and she was delighted.

They roved with the children through a glade of tender grass and fresh green leaves. "Frank, you're interested in rites of passage," Alan said. "Here's a delightful story about the christening of a friend of mine." He told how Olive and her sisters had chosen their names.

"The native Americans took names that corresponded to their spiritual attributes," Frank said. "Does she resemble a plant?"

Her nipples are olives, the skin of her breasts downy

leaves, her self-possession a trunk branching into the foliage of charm, she is sweetness rooted in an alien soil… "I don't think so," he laughed. Susan's breathing had altered. "Do you, Susan?" Get her to talk, put her off the scent.

"I don't know her that well. It was funny at the dinner for the Chinese from that veterinary place when she said she liked wine so much—you should've seen the face of the man across from me. I don't think Chinese women drink much."

"No." She's not a very traditional Chinese woman.

"But her husband is such a stick in the mud. I don't understand how she could have wound up with him."

"People end up in unpredictable combinations."

"Yes," she drawled and glanced at him sideways.

In bed she asked, "Was it somebody at your office?"

"No. Anyway, I think rule number one of love affairs is not to do it at the office."

"Oh, good. I'm so relieved. I was worried…"

"That it was Olive?"

"Yes."

"No."

"Oh, good. I couldn't believe she'd jeopardize her health, with a young baby… But I'd be least worried about her—she would surely insist on using a condom."

"She's a very good friend."

"I'm glad. Is it anyone at the kids' school?"

"No."

"Good. I'd be so embarrassed. Please don't do it with anyone at school."

Susan was attentive and gay, curbed her usual sarcasm about the Rices and overlooked things that ordinarily irritated her. Alan tried to be affectionate, held her to fill the pit in his gut, wondered if you can love two people at once, if X plus Y must necessarily exclude Z, if happiness can be calculated and relationships algebraically formulated, why he was asking at thirty-nine the same stupid questions he had at nineteen. Confucius of the Southern Calculator indeed.

Passion did not equal hope and had nothing to do with it, that was sure. He was passionate about Olive but not hopeful, hopeful about Susan without passion. Things might work out. He had to tell Olive things were okay and he could now love her without desperation. But it didn't matter. If it didn't work for her it was no solution—one-sided love was no love at all.

CHAPTER 6

How was your weekend?" Olive asked.
"I'm more hopeful. Susan's trying hard. We're sleeping together and having lots of sex."
"That's nice."

The building was evacuated for a bomb threat. He passed through the crowd to his car and drove off. A couple blocks away he saw her in the mirror and pulled over. She stopped. He walked back and asked, "Where are you going?"
"To campus. What about you?"
"To Burlingame to see my tax man."
"I wish I could come with you."
"You do?"
"Yes."
"Me too..."
"Oh well, I should go to my meeting, anyway."

A letter from his mother arrived at the office. She wrote that regardless of what happened with his dear new woman it might be time to leave Susan, who had never supported him and always torn him down, even in front of the kids, and was getting worse as she got older. The kids would adjust and one day understand.

What might have been clouded his vision of what might be. What was better for Claire and Philip, stay or leave? If he left, he would not have a new home with Olive for them.

Later, think about it later. For now, endure. Susan and I may never attain the bliss Olive and I briefly had, but the kids will be better off if we can achieve some sort of reasonable contentment.

What a shame his mother would never know Olive. She would have liked her. He wanted to show Olive the letter, elicit her sympathy and compassion, but the bounds she'd imposed prevented him; he must help free her of her passion for him. He went for coffee and smiled at his dear new woman. She smiled back and his heart jumped. "Do you want to read a letter from my mother?" She smiled curiously and took it.

The next morning she walked into his office, said, "This is my sketchbook," and left. He was flabbergasted.

There were very competent renderings of buildings, trees and seashores, a Chinese baby in charcoal, a watercolor of a pond and the calendar illustration she'd copied it from. He copied a few and put them in the drawer with her pictures.

He returned the book. "These are great."

"If I have more time I'd like to take a class."

"You should make Paul babysit so you can."

"Oh, yes, maybe… Here's the cabin we rent at Tahoe with Steve and Sharon. This is me as a baby."

"This pond reminds me of Stow Lake in the park last week. Can I keep the calendar page to copy in oils?" She nodded. "Thank you for sharing with me." He watched carefully, hoping to discover a clue why she had.

But she said only, "You're welcome."

There was another bomb threat. He joined the group that Olive was in outside and joked around for a while, then moved on. Somebody asked, "Are you still interested in sailing? My boyfriend wants to sell his boat and I thought of you."

Susan said, "I've told you before I don't like sailing."

"Do you mind if I look at it?"

"Go ahead."

Olive gave him a photo album of China, said, "I marked my favorite pictures," and left. Was she now wooing him? He looked distractedly at vistas of valleys and mountains and reflections of evening sun, lush and romantic like the music she liked, scenes that hammer you on the head and announce: I am Beauty. But he wasn't quibbling. When he returned the book she seemed disappointed to get it back so soon.

He found out where the boat was docked and said he might bring his wife to see it.

Another bomb threat. It was beginning to be boring, but as Harry pointed out, you can die of boredom.

Who knows what goes on behind familiar faces? Somebody want another afternoon off? Anybody been fired recently? Someone disappointed in love?

Probably no bomb. But if there was: A terrific concussion, a shock powerful beyond hearing, things fall, cries and wails as the air fills with dust, you jump up, peer down the corridor into dense smoke and ask what the hell? Or you're on the floor with blackening pain in your ribs, wet hand glistening red before your eyes, walls in tilting fragments, lights out: Are you damaged, is your jaw still there? An animal moan somewhere: Your lover was over there, she was your lover, where is she now?

Some people stayed inside this time, but he went out. Walking calmed him down.

He asked her to lunch. "Where can we go?" she asked.

"China Creek Harbor is out of the way."

"I'll meet you at your car at eleven-thirty."

Why the secrecy still?

They bought sandwiches and sat on a bench overlooking sailboat riggings clanging in the wind. "I'm thinking of buying a boat."

"Do you sail too?"

"I never have, but it's a good thing to do around here, don't you think? It's closer than skiing."

"I read your mother's letter. I didn't know how Susan treats you. You have a hard time."

"Yes… Well, nothing's perfect, like we were saying."

"Your mother also thinks she's a hard person."

"Yes… Of course, my mother's taking my side."

"You said you're getting along better now."

"She's making an effort to be more cheerful. She is a decent person, after all—it's just that she takes her frustrations out on me."

"You are such a gentle person. You deserve a good wife."

"Well, thank you," he said with longing. "I think she realized I actually might leave, so she's trying hard."

"I'm happy for you," she said in a tone of regret.

He bit his tongue. "I'm so distracted I've been driving carelessly since our ski trip. I hope I don't have an accident."

"If you die in a car wreck I would cry so much!"

He glanced at her in surprise. When she told him to drop her off first before he parked at the office, he surprise deepened.

Harry held a wake for their offices. The bomber called as they gathered for champagne so they toasted the bomber and toasted departmental reorganization, drank to their canceled contracts, old offices and new cubicles. Alan silently tossed in his disintegrating marriage, his mother's counsel, Fern's divorce, Olive whom he'd loved and lost but maybe not lost after all, whose animation seemed to be carefully directed away from him.

"Are you going to the horse race with Harry?" she asked Steve.

"I wouldn't miss it for the world."

"He's driving me over," said Alan.

"Why did you invite John Taylor?" she asked Harry.

"Yeah, why?" said Mike. "The only good thing Theodore's done is assign him to another group of suckers." John Taylor had been out of his element during a brief stint as their director.

"Don't be so hard on the guy. It'll loosen him up. Maybe

he'll become more human."

"More likely people will mistake him for the rear end of a horse and place a bet on him."

Alan telephoned Sofia and carefully enunciated, "I'm going to miss my lesson tonight."

"Is something wrong?"

"I'm too drunk. We're having an office party."

"Alan, don't feel bad."

"Everything's fine. In fact, it's simply wonderful."

"Okay, next week. Keep your sense of humor."

People drifted away until only two or three were left. He stepped into the coffee nook and mouthed, "Come here."

Olive quizzed him with her eyebrows. He grasped her wrist, pulled her toward him and kissed her on the lips. With a brief, firm answering pressure she smiled and then went out. Elation! He hurried to get his jacket and accompany her downstairs. "Good night," she smiled. "Have fun at the horse race."

He met Susan at Dr. Kronquist's the next day. Susan said Alan was acting very strange these days. He was going to a horse race, which he'd never done before, he suddenly wanted to buy a boat, he'd had an affair and told her he was going to move out. Why had he told her?

To save her the trouble of kicking him out.

He never showed that he loved her.

She pushed him away when he tried.

He was so physical she thought he was always leading up to sex.

It didn't always mean that he wanted sex.

Dr. Kronquist said sex often became a weapon—one person withheld it to gain control.

Alan agreed but didn't say so.

Susan said she felt deeply hurt and betrayed.

Alan said he was sorry, he hadn't meant to hurt her.

"Then why did you tell me?"

"I was miserable."

"It was pretty obvious, what had happened."

"But if I hadn't told you, we wouldn't be here now. And we need help if we're going to stay together."

"Do you want to stay together?"

"Yes, I do."

"We get along so well," she pleaded.

"We do, except sex, and for a while now almost everything else."

"I thought we were… I'm surprised to hear you say that."

"Susan, think about last New Year's."

"We had that really bad fight, but afterwards things were okay. Weren't they?"

"I sort of gave up then."

Dr. Kronquist said they had to feel free to discuss anything that bothered them.

"Would you do me a favor?" Alan asked. "I do want to know what you feel, but would you try to be polite about it? I've always thought difficult things can be put politely."

"And I've always said," she explained, "that it's better to go ahead and fight and get it over with. But I don't mean to be rude!"

"Sometimes it sounds like it. Honey, I can't read your mind; I can only go on what you say…"

Dr. Kronquist said she was sorry but their hour was up. Next time they would talk about ways to communicate.

On their way out Susan asked, "When do you get the results?"

"This afternoon at two."

"I want to know right away. Can you leave a message?"

"Negative," said the nurse. He called Olive and told her but she wasn't very interested. He called Susan and left a message.

On the ride to the races Alan found Steve to be pleasant, laconic and seemingly with no interests aside from his job. As far as Alan was concerned, interesting things took place outside of work, though these days that had turned upside down. He drew Steve out about his friendship with Olive:

Steve and Sharon often dined with her and Paul, they spent weekends together at Tahoe, he knew her family, they were old friends. You would be surprised to know how close a friend I am too, Alan thought.

The races were fun although he didn't understand Harry's explanations and couldn't tell one horse from another. He lost money, drank beer with Mike and enjoyed the parade of people, the gathering attention as a race began, the sudden crescendo when the horses ran, the roaring climax and release of tension at the finish followed by a murmuring of delight and regret, and then peace again. He lost more money and drank more beer. The buzz and pulsation of events became one with his vast secret. What if he announced, "Olive and I are in love," or more accurately, "I'm in love with Olive."– surprise, disbelief, amusement? He was drunk.

They stopped on the way back to look at the sailboat. The gate to the pier was locked so he and Steve eyed the fence's extension over the water for a minute and then Alan abruptly launched himself to grab its edge and swing around, realized in mid-arc that he wasn't going to make it, and let go. The water was shockingly cold. He paddled around the fence, pulled himself out and stared stupidly at a severe gash on his palm. He opened the gate for Steve, who was fighting to keep a straight face. "Hold my wallet, will you?" he asked and reeled onward.

The boat wasn't the sleek, gleaming beauty he'd envisioned. He shook with shivering and squeezed his bleeding, aching hand. "I must have looked funny, falling in."

Steve started to laugh. "You sure did. I've never seen anything like it. You just leaped out into the bay."

Alan started to laugh. "I sort of misjudged my abilities." They roared with laughter.

CHAPTER 7

I t's like talking in a damned phone booth!" Mike shouted. "My cubicle is a god damned waiting room!" The other project managers grumbled assent and Alan saw at once that it was going to cramp conversations. When Olive arrived, invisible but perfectly audible through the partition at his side, he walked around to say hello. She smiled radiantly and laughed uproariously as Steve described his plunge. Emboldened, he went to another room and phoned. "Hi. Do you want to have lunch?"

"I'll meet you at Slocum Stew's."

He parked in the garage next door and went in to find her as he had at the Cliff House, but this time she had no admirers, and this time she said, "Alan, I did a lot of thinking this weekend. I cannot deny it any more. I am in love with you."

He grinned idiotically, his face flushed, a corona of joy arced in the air.

"I love you. And I love Paul, and I love Daniel. It's like a pie—one slice for you and one for them, one for my parents and sisters. When I'm with Paul I will love him, and when I'm with you I will love you. Your slice is not as big, but when I'm with you I will be a hundred percent."

Life isn't that simple, he thought vaguely, feelings will spill from one slice to another, sooner or later the simile will collapse and she'll reject it and maybe me along with it; but if it reassures her now I'm happy, who cares. "Olive, what happened?"

"Tell you the truth, I was jealous when you said things were improving with Susan. I was wanting you faithful to me even though I have Paul and don't want you in between."

"It's complicated, isn't it?"

"It's simple. I love you. I never told you, did I?"

"This is the first time." The cafe blurred though the gods surely saw the brilliance of their smiles. They glided to the garage and kissed wildly in his car. Two angels walked by and smiled. "They're hot," said one. Hard and damp was more like it.

On their way down the stairs that evening they chatted about tomorrow's meeting with the Chinese. As soon as they were out of earshot he chanted, "I love you. I love you. I love you," and she smiled, "I love you," from the depths of her eyes.

"Good night, my darling."

"Good night, my dear."

He sang a wordless song all the way home, where Susan met him at the door with a kiss. My god, she'll smell Olive! "I need a shower at once."

"May I join you?"

"Of course." Hurry, get there first, wash off the scent! She came in and kissed him, slippery bodies pressed together, knelt and sucked him taut, stood and turned so he could enter, gasped, "I've never been so excited in my life." My heart will burst, this is not possible, let these two worlds become one, Olive's firm adoration and Susan's sloppy charity; no, something is false, I'm untrue to something, someone, Olive, Susan, myself? I'm mixing pastry without a recipe, I'm only an ingredient, not the cook, will the mixture right itself? But the dough is in the oven, the pie is baking, my goose is cooking, I can only watch in wonder.

Olive chatted in Mandarin while he listened happily and enjoyed the respect that the Chinese visitors gave this woman he loved and who loved him. Did they sense the current between them?

"They want you to say if the temperature and humidity

controls will work. I hope you don't mind, I'm telling them all you can do is look for big mistakes."

"Go ahead, tell them anything you want. You know how things work."

Finally she said, "I think there's no use talking any more about your role. Now they have some questions." Their concerns emerged from her full red lips. Were the heating and cooling coils correctly located, what was the proper pumping arrangement, how could they maintain air pressure differentials between the rooms and corridors? "I hope I'm translating okay. I don't understand what you're talking about."

"We've covered more in two hours with you than a day with their interpreter."

"They still think you made a mistake about the heating coil but they're afraid to change unless you agree."

"Well, tell them I never did know everything about these systems and I'm starting to forget what I did. Tell them to move it. They can always move it back if it doesn't work."

She spoke, but he had the impression she omitted his admission of fallibility. "They invite us to lunch," she said. "They want us to suggest a Chinese restaurant."

"Fancy that."

"Do you think their building will work?"

"Probably not, but Art and I figure they will learn from it, try another, and eventually they'll succeed. We're watching the third world stumble into the industrial age."

"I don't know if I want to work so hard. But I tell you this, I would like to visit China with you."

"We should insist on you coming if I go again."

"Yes…" she drawled. One of the veterinarians spoke to her at length. "He's offering to arrange a trip to central China for me," she smiled.

"Tell him to reserve rooms with large beds because I'll be along." She giggled.

After lunch they drove the Chinese to their hotel and returned to work. He parked in the alley. "Kiss me."

"Not here!" But she leaned for a quick kiss.

"Susan teaches behind that window."

"There, with the painted glass? I always think there's something bad about that window and I cross the street."

"How do our lives intersect so much?"

"It's fate, we're fated somehow…"

It was fun to pretend belief in a constellation of chance and it was a convenient way of expressing their sense of conjunction, but he could sooner believe he'd win the lottery than that external forces directed their steps. But if she felt that irresistible stars enmeshed their fates, let him swaddle her in their binding ties. "We're fated to love, Olive."

She smiled and mouthed, I love you too.

She wanted to go to the symphony with him so they picked a program and he bought tickets. He sat on the bench at China Creek Harbor wondering what kept her, was she having second thoughts, had she decided to break off again; surely she'd at least come and tell him… She finally arrived and apologized. "We need a place to meet not far from the office but not on the way to campus so people don't see us."

Ah, she's as deep into this as I am. "It's strange to sit so close in the office but not see you."

"You can hear me sighing."

"It's hard acting like we don't know each other. You're so cool sometimes that it scares me."

"I have to be."

"We must have time alone, and the weekends are unbearably long. What if we schedule regular Monday and Thursday lunches?"

"Okay."

"Olive, I don't want to be demanding."

"It's okay. I miss you, too."

He laughed: The boat riggings rang harmony in the joyful wind, the pale sky embraced the deep blue bay, the world spun through a galaxy of novas, and here at the center of glory two lovers checked their calendars. Then it was back to the office and overheard phone calls and sighs and encounters by the copier with businesslike smiles.

He told Susan, "Olive and I are going to the symphony in a couple weeks."

She gave him a piercing look. "You are?"

"She's interested in chorale music. We'll be seeing *Carmina Burana.*"

"Hmm."

Good old Philip interrupted to complain about a classmate who had stepped on his foot.

Friday it felt good to concentrate on work without her distracting presence when surprise! Olive arrived like the springtime sky to pick up leftover moving boxes for her sister. She gaily showed Daniel off, laughing and petting and chiding. Daniel gave Alan a dirty look and hid behind her skirt. "Oh, Daniel, this is Alan! He's a friend."

"Yes, I'm a friend, Daniel." He carried the boxes downstairs. "Thanks for coming in. You're a sweetheart."

She smiled over Daniel's head.

He took Claire and Philip to see the sailboat. The woodwork gleamed with new oil and the small interior was freshly painted and the kids liked its name, *Malta,* which reminded them of milkshakes, so they told Susan she should see it and she said she would go next weekend. Then back to work Monday, back to Olive. He sat beside her in exquisite torture at lunch with the other PMs—such sweet pain to feel her laughter vibrate in his belly, glimpse her profile, smell her perfume... To yearn for more and know she also yearned, and yet act normally.

He bought a copy of her CD, and Strauss's *Four Last Songs,* and a Shostakovich quartet Sofia had recommended, which was unearthly, weird, from beyond his ken. He translated the Strauss lyrics for her. When he returned her own CD she said, "I wanted you to keep it."

"Well, now we both have a copy. Here, listen to the rest of the *Last Songs*. They're all wonderful. And here's a quartet which, as my piano teacher says, will take you to the moon."

"I have to take the boxes to Fern's house so I can help her pack tonight. Do you want to come?"

When he arrived she kissed him and excused herself. He poked around, found the bedroom where Fern had found Gerald, Olive found him, they embraced, she took off her shoes and they lay down, he lay on her, she wrapped her legs around him. O the aching desire, the sweet reach outward: Now? Here? Let's make love, he said. No, not here, she sighed as they rolled entwined. Why not here, after all, now? There's no one else. I love, you love, senses aroused, no one else, nowhere else.

But no: If Gerald comes in, he'd tell Paul; he'd say: Look you all say I'm so terrible but look, Fern's own sister is no better. Okay, said Alan, not here, not now. But when? When Fern moves into her place in Marin. Yes. Then.

I must iron my dress, she said. Okay, he said, not releasing her, nor did she resist, clothed bodies enlaced on the collapsing marital bed, platform of sororal love, bed of Fern and Gerald and his lovers. They rolled fully clothed, erect, wet, mouths open.

"I need to iron my dress," she said, and went into the dressing room.

"May I come in?"

"No, no, no," she said. He looked at books on the shelf and checked his pants to see if the wetness had spread. They embraced carefully so as not to wrinkle her dress. "We've shown how restrained we are," he said. "We're so mature." They talked softly of this and that, Fern's past and present and future and their own, until it was time to go.

"We need milk," said Susan.

"I'll get it." From the store he called Fern's house.

Olive drawled, "Hello, what are you doing?"

"I am in love with you."

"I drank two glasses of wine, so I feel good. Fern is impressed with your translation. She thinks you must be very talented."

"What about you?"

"Me too."

She handed him an envelope and went back to her desk. Inside was a poem with English penciled above Chinese characters.

Whole family all asleep! Dark night, wine, Strauss, I drunk in the middle of love.

I have no way refuse, deny my feelings; my love for him.

Strange enough (it) is, that close and intimate tender love! Like the music touch my heart deeply. Like music touch my heart deeply.

Now my heart perfectly peaceful, satisfied; his deep love (affection).

Wishing this love can survive, last, can exceed (overcome) customary (social) rules.

Sweet forever!

He was still. He smelled it, considered eating it, reread it. What it must have cost, this avowal, this enduring piece of evidence (O she trusted him!), to write and laboriously translate it, nervous about her feeble art and English (O she trusted him!)! He walked around to kiss her. "Thank you, Olive."

"You're welcome. After I left Fern's last night I found a place we can meet at South Park."

They met there for lunch. "Mike had his interview this morning," said Alan.

"We should not be subject to this. They should treat us different because we already work here for so long."

"Look at it as a way for Theodore to know us better."

"But our reference letters show him important people think we do a good job."

"Things could be worse—John Taylor could be on the panel."

"Oh, let's not talk about it."

"Right. Save it for public talk, the office. Use our time alone for ourselves."

"I don't know how or when, but I insist to go to China with you."

"Yes! What will I say? 'See you in three months, Susan'?"

"I don't have to tell Paul I'm going with you. He won't want to come, anyway. Oh, Alan, can you imagine?"

"We'll do it. Listen, can you loan me ten bucks?"

"I'll pay." He accepted happily. What's hers is mine and mine is hers.

His job interview began with the question, "Can you tell us what you understand the position and its duties to be?"

"A project manager meets with the client to discuss the project scope, budget, his role, and the client's role. He helps select the architect, negotiates the professional services contract, and arranges the initial meetings." He smiled. "How much detail do you want? We could discuss programming, schematics, design development, construction documents, reviews, bid, protests, award, administration and claims."

He described his best and worst projects, the benefit his background as an engineer and project manager brought the university, and his enthusiasm for the job. Then they all laughed about interviewing people they already knew so well and he went back to hang around until Olive left. "Have a good weekend, darling. I'll miss you."

"I'll miss you, too. I'll be alone home with Daniel tomorrow."

"Maybe I should come see you."

"Why don't you come for lunch?"

He drove across the sparkling bay into the hills overlooking it to a door she opened in shorts and dark brown legs with Daniel wrapped around one of them. He hugged her. She was so short in sneakers!

"My men," she smiled.

They sat on the deck feeding Daniel orange slices. "Are you and Paul going to have more children?"

"No, no, one is enough! But I think I'm lucky I have two sisters, maybe Daniel should have one."

"I wish we could have one together."

"Ssh, the lady who lives in that house is a gossip."

"Can she hear us?"

"I'll say you're an old friend. You watch Daniel now. I'm going to cook."

Daniel napped while they ate. "Are you worried Paul will come home?" he asked.

"No, I drove him to work so he doesn't have a car."

"You clever devil! Say, I hear it's the status thing on campus for white guys to have Chinese girlfriends."

"Is that what you're doing?"

He laughed and grabbed her. When they broke she asked, "What are you doing this weekend?"

"Susan's coming to see the boat tomorrow and Sunday she takes the kids to her family's place in Mendocino. I might go to a recital Sofia's giving. What about you?"

"Tomorrow we help Fern move and Sunday Paul goes to the car races. Do you want to have a picnic?"

"It's one of those chances we've been talking about!"

"It's fate, isn't it?"

It was an incomprehensible blend of reality and unreality. He sat at her table savoring her lunch, dancing to the music of her voice, eyes full of her—it was real, yes, she was really here now but the rest of their time belonged to strangers and this warm breeze wafted through a foreign house; she was making him part of a part of her life, making it his, theirs, but only from noon until two; then he'd return to his life, whatever that meant, maybe life was only this rapturous present where the past was as absent as the future and neither mattered.

"Shall we wash the dishes?"

"Put them in the dishwasher. I will run it later."

With vertigo he saw it was the same as the one Susan had chosen for themselves. Reality erupted, the bounds of time melted and for a moment he wasn't sure where he was, how he got there, whether it was Olive or Susan behind him. He steadied himself at the sink. "Nice dishwasher."

"Paul says it's the best one."

She tidied up, led him to the living room, and put on the *Four Last Songs*. They necked on the couch and his eyes filled with tears during *Beim Schlafengehen,* her favorite:

> And the unguarded soul
> Will soar in free flight
> To live deep and thousandfold
> In the magic realm of night.

"Do you want to make love?"

"With Daniel here…? No…"

Daniel fussed in the pause before *Im Abendrot.* She stopped the music and left him gazing out at the faraway sky, cheek cooling in the breeze which replaced her cheek.

"He won't stay down much longer."

"Do you remember I told you my dream before the ski trip? We were leaning back, kissing, with a feeling of new love…"

"Yes?"

"You were leaning over me on a couch like this…"

She kissed him thoroughly.

> Alone, two larks are rising
> Dreaming, in the fragrance.
> O! Still peace!
> Is this, perhaps, death?

Is this, perhaps, life?

"Now I will always think of this when I hear the music," she murmured.

At the door she balanced Daniel on her thigh with one arm and embraced Alan with the other. "See you Sunday."

A short, wet sail in a strong wind terrified Susan but she said okay, if you want it buy it. He went back the next morning and learned how to raise the sails, run the outboard and the bilge pump, where things were from bow to stern. At eleven he called Olive. "It's me. Is Paul there?"

AN ORDINARY EXPLOSION 69

"He left at seven. Where are you?"

"The harbor. I'll finish up and come right over."

"No hurry."

Yes there was, he'd wasted four hours they could have had together. He told the guy he had to leave but they could finish next weekend when they sailed to the City.

Olive had him follow her to a grocery store and leave his car there, since she didn't know when Paul would return. She drove to a park and spread a blanket on the grass while he opened the hamper and poured wine. They lay and necked and broke occasionally to monitor Daniel, who toddled around exploring. "You and Paul don't spend much time together."

"He's tired when he comes home. I cook while he reads his car magazines and sometimes he reads at the table, then he goes to bed. I'm the opposite, I stay up late with my glass of wine and read."

"So you really only see him on weekends."

"Oh, he goes out while I stay with Daniel or I go out with Fern and he stays. Tell you the truth, lately I see more of you than him."

Good, good. "Susan never wanted us to do anything apart. I think she was afraid I'd meet someone else."

"And now you have."

Daniel bent as if to snatch a ball from a little girl and Olive raced to him. "I worry he will bother other people."

"They have kids; they won't mind."

"Some people mind very much. If Daniel hits her they'll think he's a brat."

"You're a good mother."

"You're a good father, too. Who is this man, Daniel?"

"Dada."

"No," she laughed, "it's not Dada."

"It's a good thing he can't talk."

"Yes, he would tell Paul, 'I spent the day with Dada.' Daniel, this is Uncle Alan."

Alan laughed. "What will we do when he does start talking?"

"I don't know, but we don't need to worry about it now. Do you see a bathroom?"

He read Daniel a story and assured him that his mother, whom they both loved very much, would be back soon. Quite the happy family: Caucasian father, Chinese mother, son a blend, it's perfect, we'll pass. But how many husbands and wives still act like lovers?

Daniel fussed until she returned and rocked him to sleep. Then they nestled in vinous contentment. "Tell me about your loves," he said.

"In Taipei I had a big crush on a boy who got on the school bus after me, but I never met him. I was too afraid. The nuns taught us well-behaved girls don't fool with boys."

"Hah! You've changed."

"We used to go by the school for diplomats and watch the American boys. We thought they must be very happy, so big and their light skin and hair, big round eyes, from another world like gods."

"Now you're married to one and in love with another."

"I never dreamed," she laughed. "Then the Indonesian. I don't think about him."

"I try to accept things, even the bad—especially the bad— and discover why I did them, or at least understand enough to avoid repeating them."

"I studied hard to keep my mind off it. Anyway, I had to work extra because of my language."

"It paid off. You're very successful now."

"But my English is so poor I'm ashamed to talk."

"Your English is fine. You express complicated ideas and you always get people to do what you want."

"Paul makes fun."

"Well, he shouldn't. We all have faults; what counts is how hard we try to be decent and honest."

"In college I realized I have to be serious. I worked, I didn't date, until my last year when I met Billy Wong."

"Your next love?"

"It wasn't really love. He was fun to be with, he made me

laugh, and when I went to bed with him it was very good. Before him I didn't know it could be."

"It wasn't with your husband?"

"It was awful. He always finish very fast and didn't care about my pleasure. Billy Wong was kind and he cared."

"You didn't marry him, though."

She laughed. "No, I was matured a little."

"And then Paul, and then me. So I'm only the fifth man you've loved and the fourth you've made love to?"

"Yes. You must be much more experienced than me."

"Oh, I've had sex with several women and a few men, but I was in love only two or three times and never anything like this."

"You had sex with men?"

"A couple times."

"Oh Alan, I can't believe it! Paul would never consider doing that. Why? Were you in love with them?"

"No, partly out of curiosity, partly because I was always horny and it was there."

"You're so open, so willing to try everything! Someday I want you to tell me what you did." She shuddered with glee.

"Sure, but now you're telling me about you."

"Paul doesn't have much sympathy. After Daniel's born I felt no love for this strange new baby, and there must be something wrong with me, a mother who doesn't love her child. Paul was kind the first week but then impatient, told me snap out of it, get out of my bad mood. I hated him—I was so unhappy and lonely, and he's so inconsiderate. When you invited me to the symphony, it was the first time I went out. I was so happy."

"Do you remember taking my arm as we walked to your car? I was asking myself if I dared kiss you."

"Like this?"

"Mm hm…"

Daniel stirred. "After all these years I forgot my feelings about Paul and I was happy to be eighty percent happy. Now I'm comparing him with you and thinking about his bad qualities. It makes me worry because there's Daniel."

"Well then, think about the eighty percent. Don't dwell on the rest."

"You're such a sweet, caring man. I tell you, Paul is the meat and potatoes, but you're the appetizer and dessert."

The shadows lengthened, Daniel woke, it was time to go. "Lunch tomorrow?" she asked. "Noon?"

"Susan and I have a counseling session until twelve, so I'll be a few minutes late."

He got home before Susan and the kids arrived tired and grumpy. Susan was coming down with a cold. He put them to bed and listened to Strauss.

In the morning Susan's eyes were streaming. "I feel terrible, but we have our session and I have to teach."

"Call me at ten. If you're too sick, I'll go alone."

She was still in bed when she called.

"Why don't you stay home this afternoon too?"

"I can't."

"Susan, I'm afraid you'll get really sick if you don't take care of yourself."

"That's all very good, but I have to do what I have to do."

Olive was just four feet away and he felt inhibited. He switched to French. "Susan, I don't know what to say… I love you."

"I wish I could believe that."

"Look, doesn't going to counseling show I'm trying?"

"Oh, I guess. I'm sorry. Go, or you'll be late."

Friday Olive, Saturday Susan, Sunday Olive, today I'm nursing a marriage and an affair. He sat wearily on a bench in South Park and closed his eyes. Hands covered them. "Guess who?" He pulled the hands to his mouth and kissed them.

"Alan, I hope you won't be disappointed. Saturday's our symphony, but Paul's starting his new job Monday so he wants us to go to Tahoe this weekend. Is it okay with you?"

"Of course. Our families come first."

"I feel bad about this, but he said he'll stay home if you can't go some other time."

He was tickled by their asking his permission for a weekend together. "Don't be silly. Susan and I will use our tickets, and you and I will use the ones Susan and I have in two weeks."

"Thank you," she said tenderly. "Alan, I want a weekend to ski with you next winter."

"Do you think we'll do any skiing?"

"We might not leave the room in two days," she laughed. "We should start to save our money every week."

"If we each save ten dollars, by January it'll be six hundred. Is that enough?"

"We can stay in a nice hotel I know, with big beds."

"We'll have to go outside now and then so we come back sunburned."

She laughed. "You keep the money for us."

"I have a headache and a terrible cough," said Susan.

"Oh, you poor thing. Did you go to work?"

"I had to. I can't just call in at the last minute."

"Did you tell them you'd be out tomorrow?"

"Alan, I have to work. I need to pay the tuition."

"We have enough, don't we?"

"I had saved enough but you spent it on a sailboat."

"Susan, the sailboat's coming out of our other money."

"Where do you expect me to get it?"

"Well, I assumed we'd use the mutual fund. You know I wouldn't spend the tuition money."

"Oh, forget it."

He waited until dinner to say, "Listen, Susan, Olive wondered if we could swap symphony tickets. Paul wants to go away for the weekend."

"And she'd rather go with him than you?"

"Well, naturally," he said as naturally as he could.

"What if I'm too sick to go?"

"It's five days off. You'll be better by then, don't you think?"

"All right. Go ahead."

"I'm worried about you. You'll get pneumonia if you don't take it easier."

"Oh, don't worry about me."

He put Olive's ten dollars and ten of his into a billfold at the bottom of his drawer.

They met at a park near campus and walked into the trees for a sandwich. Alan pointed out two men kissing, the hasty encounter of strangers rushing through love's irreducible mechanics. "This is a gay pickup place."

"Good, nobody we know will come here." Then, hesitantly, "I didn't understand the poem you gave me."

"'Had we but world enough, and time, this coyness, lady, were no crime.' He's exhorting her to love before they grow too old."

"Is that how you think about me?"

"No," he cheerfully dissembled. "It's about love and the passage of time, two things you make me feel."

"I think sometimes you know so much and me so little."

"Olive, you have a spark, a love of life, that is very uncommon."

"You don't have much money, do you?"

"Hm? We're comfortable, but we have to be careful. We don't make as much as you and Paul and we have two kids."

"We don't worry about cost. Paul says when you buy you should buy the best. But it scares me more than anything to be old and poor, and now I have a child. I think I must start a saving program."

"Ah, the grasshopper becomes an ant."

She didn't understand so he acquainted her with Aesop, and then she reacquainted him with the fable of her lips. A man walked by on the needle-covered path and smiled. It was sad that their audience must be composed of strangers.

Susan was in bed with a fever and cough.

"You'll never get better if you keep working."

"I can't afford to stay home."

"We can't afford to have you sick."

"I have to earn back the kids' tuition."

"Susan, we have plenty of money in the bank."

"No, we don't. You spent it on the sailboat."

"Susan, please, you've got to see a doctor."

"We'll see."

At lunch with an architect he pressed his calf against Olive's shin under the table, she pressed back–hoo, hoo, footsie!– and the humdrum scintillated with danger. She was talking about the new Corvettes. "Olive, both of your cars are gold. Do you and Paul like gold?"

"No, they're bronze."

No, we don't drive pretend gold cars, you dumb cluck, can't you tell the difference? No, we don't like gold? Leave Paul out of it, he's none of your business?

"I didn't go to work today," said Susan.

"Praise the Lord. Did you see a doctor?"

"No."

"For crying out loud, Susan, you are very ill."

"They just tell you to take it easy."

"And they give you antibiotics."

"I feel too rotten to sit around a waiting room for hours."

"You won't wait long. Please, please go tomorrow. It's probably pneumonia by now."

"We'll see."

He waited a couple blocks from the office. Olive picked him up and asked, "So where are we going?"

"Glen Park? We can stop at a deli."

"I had an idea."

"Yes?"

"Do you want to go to Fern's place?"

His gut turned over and spun. Here it is finally. Wait a minute, does she mean what I think, uh, and what about the deli? He could barely ask, "Really?"

"Yes," she drawled.

"Yes. I do."

Halfway across the bridge he said, "To think of my wife sick with pneumonia and me going to make love to another woman."

"Don't do this if you're not comfortable. Do you want to do this?"

"Oh, I do! It's ironic, that's all…"

They arrived at a nondescript apartment complex whose only charm was a view of a tidal flat. They sat on Fern's bed and kissed. Then Olive removed her dress and took a towel from her bag and smoothed it on the bed. He undressed and sated his hands with her body's smooth solid curves, ran his hand down her back under her panties as he had in the dark night of the ski trip, removed them and unclasped her bra. Large erect nipples with small areolas on small breasts, smooth brown unblemished skin, a light cesarian scar on her full belly between a large navel and salient mons with a small patch of wiry black hair above a naked vagina. He put his lips on hers and tongue to tongue advanced between her open knees.

"Good lord, I love you."

"Oh, Alan."

This time he came too. They lay gasping happily.

She folded the towel and returned it to her bag. He brushed their hair off the bed.

"Is this Fern?" He pointed to a picture.

"Yes, and that's her friend Bob from work. We have the same taste in men—Caucasians."

"You're both good looking, but you're the beautiful one."

"I want to spend a whole day with you. We can drive to Calistoga for lunch."

"We should do it on a Friday before you start working them again."

"I wish it's you who's coming to Tahoe this weekend. I'll miss you."

"I'll miss you too, coy mistress no longer."

And then to the office to pass the afternoon in a golden, or bronze, haze.

CHAPTER 8

The doctor says I have pneumonia. Are you still going sailing tomorrow?"

"If I don't we won't get the boat for two weeks."

"I'm supposed to stay and take care of the kids with pneumonia?"

"I am sorry, but I'm afraid to sail it over alone."

"What about the concert? Are you going by yourself?"

"Of course not. I'll sell the tickets at the door."

"Will you give Olive back her money?"

"Well, no... They're our tickets now."

"You and Olive are still going to the last concert?"

"Well, yes..."

"Okay. Give me my money back, then."

The low gray sky and fog roaring into the bay scared him and when he realized they were the only boat out he wondered about their judgment. "Don't worry," said the guy, "these boats never sink." But as the bow slammed each wave in a gust of cold spray and they heeled over so far the gunwale was submerged, he gripped the tiller in numb terror.

Susan wanted to know why he was two hours late. "I'm sorry," he said. "There's not much you can do to speed up a sailboat." He showered and left to sell the tickets, gave her twenty, put twenty in the billfold in the drawer, and went to bed.

He and Olive walked out the long pier to see the boat.

"Fern and I rode bikes at Tahoe and I talked about you."

"Did you tell her we're making love?"

"I can't, she'd be shocked."

"Shock me."

They undressed on their knees in the low cabin. He was hard before his clothes were off and too excited to run his hands from silken bra to skin and down beneath her panties before taking her on the mattress in the cramped, stuffy bow.

That afternoon he laughed to hear her telling Steve that she'd just done her first full day's work in two months, what with the reorganization, interviews and move. She lied so well he almost felt he wasn't there.

He left the house Friday morning at the usual time but instead of driving to a seminar in Sacramento as he'd told Susan went to Fern's. The BMW was out front and the apartment door was cracked. A towel was on the bed and soon the floor was strewn with clothing. This time he took the time to enjoy her bra and panties before removing them.

Three hours later he suggested, "Let's go out."

"Calistoga's a long drive, and it's already eleven."

"How about Sonoma?"

They dressed lazily. "For a long time I try to figure out what I want to do about you. Maybe we should spend one day making love and then end everything. Maybe pretend it didn't happen. Or go skiing for a weekend? Go to China? I didn't know what to do."

"Do you now?"

"I only know I can't end this, I want you too bad. But I don't know what will happen."

Her uncertainty made him nervous. "All we can do is enjoy our time together."

"I'm spending the night here and tomorrow we're going to eat out breakfast in Sausalito."

"I'm sailing with Steve. Should we meet you?"

"Mm, I don't know. I think I should just be with Fern. I need to think. Last night I was giving Daniel his bath and

he's splashing and making happy noises. I was singing and
Paul's watching television on the bed. He told me be quieter,
we're making too much noise. I got very mad, I'm taking care
of Daniel and he's not doing anything. I was so angry I slept
on the couch. This morning he ask what I'm doing. I told him
how I feel and he apologized, but sometimes I think you're
so good to Susan, why can't Paul be good to me like that?"

"Oh, Olive, I'm sorry. You do have to tell him how you
feel—he won't change otherwise."

"Sometimes I don't think he can." A bit of sadness as
they drove among green vineyards. "Sometimes I wonder if
I drink too much wine. I always joke but maybe other people
think I'm alcoholic."

"Don't draw attention to it and it won't occur to them."

"Do you and Susan go to winery concerts? We come here
with Steve and Sharon, bring a picnic and drink wine. We
should do that, all of us."

"How naughty!"

"We'll have to behave ourselves."

He pointed out a house near town. "Friends of Susan's
family live there."

"You know people everywhere!"

"Yeah, everywhere spies." He imagined meeting Vinnie
as they walked around the square: Oh hello, Vinnie, this is
Olive Lo, who works with me. How very nice to meet you,
Vinnie would say as she gently studied Olive, and how is Susan? Susan's fine. Everything's fine. Simply spectacular. Olive
and I are here for a seminar. Vinnie's eyebrows would rise minutely. We're studying adultery. And she'd tell her husband:
The oddest thing happened today—I met Alan Donner in the
square with the most striking woman…

They drank a bottle of wine with lunch, laughed at stories
he invented about other patrons, she paid, and they left in a
fine fuzzy state. "I had a lot to drink," she said. "You drive."

"I think I'm dreaming. Am I really here with a beautiful
woman in her luxury car on a spring day in a carefree world?"
His elation was disturbed, however, by a jagged insinuation

in the back of his mind that they would inevitably separate. The day would end, the world would reassert itself, they were children playing at happiness, pretending this was life... But just now it was a splendid facsimile, a warm afternoon of love under the trees at a winery, an embrace before some tourists, laughter as they bought a bottle for later, a stroll arm in arm and a smooth cruise back along the highway. "Where shall we lunch Monday?"

"Alan, I don't know if I want to have lunch Monday."

Sudden discomfort, the flush of wine an abrupt ache behind his eyeballs, heat, the note in her voice. "Why?"

"This, I'm, we're getting too close. I need some time to get my balance."

"Are you all right?"

"Yes, I just feel a little strange... I think it's better we don't see each other so much."

The scenery slipped around in sliding panes of shadow. "Olive, if that's what you want..."

"I don't know... It's nothing serious. How do you like driving the BMW?"

"It's fun. It's tight, like you."

"Paul says it's a safe car. The TV commercial says you don't brake, you drive a BMW out of a bad situation."

"Well, it does beat a Toyota."

When they returned to Fern's she called Paul's mother to check on Daniel and they made love a fourth time, gently, until it was time for him to leave. He showered off her scent and drove home manufacturing memories in case he was asked: Sacramento was hot, the seminar was dull, I'm tired, we must have fucked for a full five hours, whoops, cancel that, the traffic was bad...

Susan asked if he wanted a shower before dinner. Sure do, he said, and took another. Steve called to confirm sailing the next day and said they'd all received job offers and he'd left a message for Olive since she hadn't been at work either. Hee hee. But glee was tempered by uneasiness about her noncommittal mood so he went out and called her at Fern's. "Olive, I love you so much."

"Me too. Listen, I do want to have lunch with you Monday. I don't know what came over me."

O thank god! The world was right again.

When he rang the doorbell in the morning Steve was on the phone and waved Alan to an extension. "So what was the point in wasting our time with all that? I'm disgusted."

Ah, magic. Olive was on the line. "They made us run around like crazy people." Her throaty voice increased by four degrees the warmth still pervading his groin.

"Well," said Steve, "now we can get back to normal and do our work."

Fat chance, Alan thought, work will never be normal again.

They went to the boat, crouched in the cabin where he and Olive had undressed, stood on the deck two feet above the spot where they had lain, hanked on the jib, raised the main, cast off and motored into the bay.

"I thought you didn't know how to sail."

"I don't," Alan laughed. "I memorized the book last night."

The wind hit, *Malta* heeled over, and they charged through the spray. Steve shouted, "This is great! The city's all around us and we're totally alone!"

Elemental peril amid the social: wrestle the tiller braced almost standing against the lee side and smile: if I lose control we pitch from sensibility into the freezing chop: there was no time to think: he was exhilarated.

Bliss was it in that dawn to be alive... He waited on the bench in South Park humming lazily.

"Why hello, Alan," came a cheerful voice. "What are you doing here?"

"Good lord! Marian!" Kids in the same classes, played together, had sleepovers. "What a surprise!" Bliss, indeed. What if Olive had had her hands over his eyes?

"What are you doing, having a picnic?"

"I'm meeting a friend for lunch. What about you?"

"That's my office, there. I'm going to put money in the parking meter."

"Don't let me make you late!" He walked quickly away. When Olive's car appeared he waved her over, hopped in and said, "Let's get out of here. Susan's best friend's office is right there."

"Did she see me?"

"No. Damn. Now we can't meet here."

"You know people everywhere."

"You'd think you could keep from seeing them in a city this big."

"Well, do you want to come to Japantown? I have to buy something."

As she wrote a check for hand lotion he was surprised to see that she was embarrassed. "It's expensive, but we have to work hard to stay beautiful for you guys."

"You know, now that we're making love. I'm much calmer. I can work again."

"I'm glad," she smiled. "By the way, that other music is too strange but I want to keep the *Four Last Songs* with your translation."

Susan told Dr. Kronquist, "It's so uncharacteristic of him to spend my tuition money on his own pleasure and sail all day while I have pneumonia and two kids to care for."

Be honest, never tell a lie, but not necessarily the whole truth. "I felt bad, but it was either get it then or wait two weeks for the guy to return from vacation."

"It seems like he's trying to get away from me."

"We've often talked about doing new things; I decided it was time to start."

"Is it related to your affair?"

"No, except that made me realize we should try to enjoy ourselves more."

"It is over, isn't it?"

Okay, now lie. "Yes."

"I always said he shouldn't tell me if it happened. You could have spared me all this anguish."

"I am sorry, but if I hadn't said anything, we might not be here trying to improve things."

"It sounds," said Dr. Kronquist, "like it's difficult for both of you to express your feelings. We'll talk about that next time."

She took his arm on the way out. "Alan, I hope this works. I want us to stay together."

"Susan, I do, too." They were different people and he loved them differently: Olive with a blade's keen sunlit edge, Susan with friendly familial warmth.

"I'm selling my summer opera tickets."

"Why?"

"Well, I have been spending a lot, and I'd rather have the boat."

"You're acting like an ass."

"And it's that much more time you're saddled with the kids while I'm out enjoying myself."

"But the opera is so important to you."

"I'm trying to make some sacrifices, too."

She didn't fall over with gratitude.

He and Olive lunched at Slocum Stew's. Daniel was with Paul's parents because he was sick and she couldn't take him to her parents. Soon they were going on vacation and Heather would take him, but she would have to reciprocate by staying home with Heather's son. And Fern was on a business trip. Would he like to meet her there Saturday before the symphony?

What time?

Let's see, symphony at eight, dinner at six-thirty, drive from Marin, what about five?

"Dare I leave that early?" he wondered.

"Paul won't care when I leave."

"Lucky you."

The world shrank to clasped hands and an open gaze of desire, conversation stuttered, silences lengthened, presently they called for the bill and sped to the harbor and undressed on their knees and crawled head first into the bow and spread a towel.

They returned to work sweaty and relaxed, where mundane comments glimmered with secret meaning and it was bittersweet to sniff the lingering scent of sex yet sit side by side like strangers.

Susan said she'd drop Philip at a birthday party, visit her sister with Claire and be home around six. Alan said fine, don't rush. Perfect, he'd be gone before she was back. He sailed with Steve under an incoming storm, returned swaying and salty to the empty house, showered, put on a suit, and as he was choosing a tie Susan came in.

Oh damn and drat. "How's Beth?"

"She's fine. Why are you all dressed up?"

"I'm going to the symphony. Did you forget?"

"But it's only four-thirty."

"Well, we're going to dinner first, you know, and I figured that since you were going to be at Beth's we might as well meet early."

"Hmm," she said and left the room.

Well, I'd better not say any more, act as if nothing's irregular and I don't even imagine anyone could think anything's odd, maybe she thinks it is but would like us to pretend it's not or maybe she's not wondering about Olive at all but thinking I spend too much time away, well, I can't guess, she should say what's on her mind, she can't expect me to respond to what she doesn't say. I'm tired of gently drawing her out to express all that's wrong with me and sitting there mute and stupefied and repentant until she finally grows tender and accepting and sends me on my way with an understanding kiss. He knotted his tie, kissed her goodbye and left.

Olive was already there. "I brought some chicken and the wine from Sonoma. Are you hungry?"

"I'm hungry for you."

An hour later he murmured that they should leave, but as

darkness fell and the drizzle turned to rain they began again.

Much later they watched traffic flow by in the rain. "We forgot to cancel our reservations at the restaurant."

She laughed. "Now we can never use our names there again!"

She followed him to the City. They parked near Olive Street and walked under his umbrella to the symphony. "I'm dizzy," she said.

"Me too. Sailing and wine and sex."

"I don't know why I am. Tell me about the music."

"They're playing only one piece, Bruckner's *Fifth*."

"What's a fifth?"

Hmm. Well, let's start at the beginning, and he tried to prepare her for music less straightforward than Puccini.

Afterwards she said, "You'll probably think I'm very simple if I tell you what I thought."

"I want to know everything you think."

"Music speaks to me direct."

"It's pure emotion."

"I tried to listen for relations between the parts, tell you the truth just hear the parts, but maybe I'm too tired, my mind wandered off to daydreams about beautiful places."

"They say the best beginning response is unfocussed receptivity. You learn to differentiate later."

"Sometimes I would suddenly come back and be aware."

"Maybe you were falling asleep."

"Maybe. I feel very tired."

"Me too. Everything is rocking back and forth."

"Maybe we're hungry. Let's eat. Paul told me to spend money on you because you bought the ticket."

She was so lethargic over supper that he grew worried she was giving up, all the paradoxes were too much. He tried to coach her. "I'm no longer trying to figure things out. I'm just accepting it all."

"I just feel tired."

The room was rocking like a boat. He suppressed the unresolved questions about their marriages, the insoluble moral dilemma, his misgivings about her endurance, the fact that she was paying the bill again. They kissed goodbye in the rain.

CHAPTER 9

Do you have any dirty magazines?" Susan asked. Surprised, he reached under the bed. "Don't you have any with men? I don't like these with just women."

"No, I don't."

"Why don't you get some?"

The next night she looked at what he had bought and said, "Ugh. Why are the people so unattractive? And how could anyone want to do this? She looks like she's in pain."

"I think she's faking an orgasm." He kept his hardon hidden as she silently flipped the pages, and when she threw the magazine aside and directed him aboard, he moved as sedately as he could so she wouldn't know how aroused he was.

"I've been thinking," Olive said. "As long as Paul doesn't become impossible to live with, I will continue like this. But tell you the truth, if we're discovered I might deny everything, ignore you completely."

"I accept. I'm glad you're telling me, since you won't be talking to me if we're discovered."

"You're so understanding!"

"Listen, why don't we meet Sunday for a movie?"

"It's too bad we can't talk when we know our plans."

"Suppose I call your answering machine at work tomorrow and tell you what I'm doing. Then you can tell me if you're free."

"What a wonderful idea!"

He was going out with Susan that evening, he told the machine, maybe he'd be free tomorrow, check at noon.

"Do you feel like that place in South Park?" asked Susan. "How nice!"

"And then a movie. Alan, we must go out more often. I've been jealous of your other friends—you and I need to have some fun, too."

They did have fun. He was happy because she was happy, he loved her and she loved him, the food was good, the evening was warm and the streets were crowded with happy people. He called Olive's machine from the theater lobby to tell her how good he felt and where they'd dined.

In the morning he called his own machine from a grocery store. Olive had been to the movies with Fern, she wished she'd been with him, she couldn't get away Sunday.

"Why didn't we think of that sooner?"

"We're pretty slow, aren't we?"

"Do you want to come water the plants at my parents' house?"

She undressed to bra and panties in her old bedroom and found a towel, but in a while she said the bed held too many memories. Funny girl, he thought. They disengaged and re-coupled on the floor.

After he showered she said, "You should learn Chinese."

"Tell me how to say 'I love you.'"

"Wuo ai ni."

"Mei Li, wuo ai ni."

She laughed. "Wrong accent. Like this."

Back at the office she came to his desk with ten dollars for the ski trip and a list of Chinese characters. "These are me and my sisters—Mei Wa, Mei Li, Mei Ju. Mei Wa means beautiful country. My father was happy after his escape from China. Mei Ju means beautiful pearl and we always think she's a beautiful little pearl. My name is hard to say the exact meaning, something like beautiful beauty."

"Olive means nipples, dark and firm and round."

"Sh! Lo means gong, the music instrument."

"Lo Mei Li, even your name is musical."

"It's unusual even in China."

"Everything about you is unusual, Beautiful Beauteous Gong. Wuo ai ni."

"Sh! Someone will hear you!"

"But who would understand?"

Harry said, "I must be getting old. Nancy's already talking about what we're going to do when the kids go to college."

"Well, Harry, we've outlived our biological usefulness. We've reproduced, our kids are almost old enough to take care of themselves, in a few more years they'll reproduce and as far as the human race is concerned, we can die."

"We're finished?" he laughed. "There's nothing left now but croak?"

"Think about it. Young people are slim and attractive, they fall in love with other slim and attractive young people, they mate, start a family, raise the kids, establish a career. They have it made, they've survived, procreated, succeeded, life is easy. Then what? They get lazy, love is a memory, and their waists thicken. Look at all the fat middle-aged people."

"We're done? Washed up?"

"You and I know it—we've had vasectomies. The world doesn't need more homo sapiens the way it did when we were hunter-gatherers; now we're copy machine operators who don't die off as fast as we used to. So the vasectomy evolved."

"The Donner theory of biological usefulness!"

"We've done our duty and the rest is gravy."

"Well, not me, not yet. This contractor here's claiming extra work and I can't quit till I straighten him out."

They went to Fern's and made love. His pager beeped, they uncoupled, and he called Theodore, who wanted to know if he'd issued a report. Yes, he said, guess what I'm doing with whom, he didn't say, and reentered.

They ate lunch late and watched the fog roll in over the hills. "Sex with Paul isn't very good, not like with you."

"I'm glad you think so about me, but I'm sorry for you."

She shrugged. "We don't do it very often."

"How often is often?"

"Since the ski trip we only did it twice."

"The poor guy… If I were in his shoes, I wouldn't let you out of bed."

"Me too. Sex with you is better than Billy Wong."

"You say the nicest things."

Susan couldn't make up her mind whether to ride horses with a friend or go to a circus with Alan and the kids. He'd been encouraging her to ride. Sunday morning she asked, "Are you sure it's okay?"

"Go, you'll have fun."

"Okay. I don't like the circus anyway."

"Great. I'll see if Olive and Daniel want to come."

"You'll what?"

"She mentioned that Paul was going to some car races and I said we had a ticket but you might not go and if you didn't I might give her a call."

"Oh." She left abruptly.

Olive smiled when they met at the auditorium. "Hello Claire, hello Philip. Do you remember Daniel?"

"Hello, Daniel," said Claire. "Do you remember me? We met at a man's house who went to China."

"Hello, Daniel," said Philip and headed inside.

Philip spent his allowance on a bundle of twinkling fibers, they found seats, and a noisy constellation of children waved sparklers in the blaring dark. Daniel squirmed along their feet to Claire's lap, Philip pointed him to the action below, Olive bent across Alan to watch, her scent expanded in his nostrils. Philip's light broke so Alan went to exchange it. When he returned, Olive and Daniel were gone. "Where are the others?"

"They went outside."

"I'm going to the bathroom. I'll be back in a minute."

He found them in the lobby playing hide and seek. He joined, Daniel ran up a flight of stairs, they followed, turned a corner and embraced dizzily, holding the handrail to keep their balance. "I should get back," he said and rushed away.

When she returned she said, "Daniel's tired and cranky, but it's so noisy he can't sleep."

"Let me hold him." He slipped a hand under her thigh. She removed it and whispered, "What if someone sees us?"

Who would see more than a family of five? But two of the kids are Caucasian—well then, she's my second wife. In the roaring circus tent was a family, well, not really, but whatever we are, it's sweet to be together, her son asleep in my lap.

When they left she kissed the children goodbye. He kissed Daniel and pecked her cheek and murmured, "I love you."

"Yes," she drawled in the husky low syllables that throbbed in his gut. "Goodbye Claire, goodbye Philip."

"Are you okay?" he asked Susan. "You seem unhappy."

"I'm not sure I can stop resenting what you did."

"What, what I did?"

"Your affair. Is it really over?"

"Yes. It has been for a couple of months." It was two months to the day since he'd sat crying on the couch.

"Olive, I feel like an ass lying to Susan, and I'm afraid you'll think less of me because I'm a liar."

"Alan, there's nothing else to do. If you tell the truth, you and Susan will break up. I'm lying to Paul. If you go in the water, you're going to get wet."

"You're right. I just don't like lying."

"I don't either. To be totally honorable, we break off with each other or break off with them. Tell you the truth, I'm sorry for you. This is not fair. I'm not willing to give you a hundred percent, but you would for me."

"Oh, sweetheart, I'm happy with the way it is."

"Well, it's not a perfect situation."

"No, we're both dishonorable liars." They laughed and he felt better. O love. O vile lie.

He put his hand on Susan's thigh while they watched a skinflick she'd sent him to rent. She pushed it away.

"Do you recognize this music?" he asked.

"No."

"Isn't it beautiful?"

They watched in silence until she finally lay back to let him climb on and afterwards asked, "Did you enjoy that?"

"Yes, did you?"

"It was okay."

Olive took him to her parents' house again, to the bedroom floor, her above and him arched up to complete the circle, both ends joined at mouth and groin. The doorbell rang. They stopped breathing. She peeked out the window. They began again and he crawled atop with the dumb full beast outstretched to take her from behind.

She watered the plants and they drove back to the office. "I feel tired and empty."

"Well, you've missed a lot of work, you're worried about childcare, and to top things off you just had quite a workout. Me too, I'm tired." And melancholic—the joy of their fusions was always tempered by the knowledge of imminent separation. As much as he tried to savor each sensation and fix each tryst in his memory to obliterate her absence, time arrived and receded like the landscape visible only a few more moments in the mirror before it vanished. "Susan's feeling very insecure and I have to reassure her constantly."

"Maybe she senses your affair isn't over."

"Maybe. I always have to watch what I say. But I shouldn't complain to you."

"I don't mind. Fern tells me her troubles."

"Well, I don't want to waste our time on things we can't change."

"It's all right. We must share our problems, too."

Susan was in a terrible mood. He finally closed the bedroom door and insisted she tell him why.

"It seems that whenever I leave you alone, you're doing something with Olive."

"Is it her, or are you jealous of women in general?"

"I sense that her marriage with Paul has some problems. She seems like she'd be a good match for you, and you're obviously attracted to her. I'm afraid something will happen between you and you'll leave me."

"Susan, I'll stop seeing her. You're more important."

"Oh, you don't have to do that."

"I will. I want you to be sure I care about you."

"I want a monogamous relationship, but I don't think you do."

"I do. I am monogamous. You know, all those years it hurt to be suspected of having affairs. I wasn't even considering it."

"That's not true. You made a pass at that party just after we were married. And you always look at women."

"That's true, I did. I'm still embarrassed. And I do look. But I don't want more than one at a time."

"I've always been abandoned by the men I love. My father abandoned me. John Duncan left me in college and now you're going to leave me. I don't want to be alone. I'm afraid of being alone." She began to cry.

"Oh, Susan."

She pushed his arm away. "You said you were only going to stay two months, and two months are up."

"I meant we should try for two months and then see if we want to continue. I do. Do you?"

"I still think you're going to leave."

"Well, look, suppose I did. You wouldn't be alone. You have a network of good friends."

"Monica told me I'm remarkably strong to cope with all this. I am damned strong. Anybody else would've had a breakdown."

"That's right, you are strong."

"I keep repeating to myself that I'm a wonderful person and you're lucky to have me."

"I know that. You are a wonderful person, and I am lucky to have you."

Olive called from home, where she was babysitting her nephew. He told her that Susan was afraid she would take him away from her. "We can't talk about each other in our homes," she said. "We can't be together outside work if Susan knows. We really must be careful because if we have to stop seeing each other at work too, we will have no place left. I was sorry yesterday we only had time to make love. There's not time for talking and spiritual closeness."

He tried to say that they would lead a strobe-lit life, a life in time-lapse photography, devote one session to making love, another to discussing books, the next their families—but he was at his desk with people all around so could only mumble.

"I don't understand."

"I'll explain to your machine." He called it from a private office and she later replied that they needed to be patient.

She came to work Friday to catch up. "I'll be happy when my parents return and take Daniel again."

"I'll miss watering their flowers."

She laughed. They sat eating sandwiches in her car in a campus parking lot. "Alan, I am sure now I do not want to leave Paul. This is my decision."

He hadn't known she was still considering it. "Okay."

"To be safe, we must see each other less. The more we are passionate, the more dangerous it is to be together. But it's okay for me to have lunch with you. I have lunch with the other PMs."

"Sure, friends have lunch together." As he leaned for a kiss, three people they know strolled around a corner and said hello.

"Sorry. I keep forgetting we're friends."

"You better remember."

Susan called that afternoon to ask if he could have a beer. He met her at a nearby bar and they drank and chatted about the French boy who was coming that weekend. She went to pick up the kids and he hurried back to Olive. "I'm terrible. I'm so bad to Susan."

"Why?"

"I leave her and run straight to you." He looked around and kissed her. "I'm crazy for you, Olive."

"Oh, I feel so sorry for you."

He kissed her, drove home and called but she'd gone, so he talked to her machine. "If we're so prudent that we never see each other, there'll be nothing left. We have to take opportunities like just now being alone in the office."

He moved the phone to the piano and called again. "The only way I can think of to show how much I care for you is write a book for you. In the meantime, listen to this. Robert Schumann wrote it for a woman he loved. It's called *Aveu,* avowal. He avows his love." He played exuberantly, longingly.

She left a message. "Hi, it's me. I love the piano part! You are so talented! I like the poems you read to me but I don't understand all the words. The music talks without words. Thank you. You are so sweet."

He heard it the next morning, pleased to have pleased her, flattered by her admiration—she was hooked, she wouldn't leave, she loved him. "I don't think Paul appreciates you, and sometimes I get mad at you for sacrificing yourself when you could have me, but you're trying to factor in the happiness of others. We'll continue as we are, it's fine, we're as happy as we can be in this imperfect world."

She replied, "Alan, I must tell you that I can not, will not, leave Paul. He does take it for granted and doesn't pay enough attention, but I have not been fair to him, haven't told him my dissatisfactions and ask him to change. Your care shows he could be better and we seem to be a perfect match sexually, but he hasn't done something so wrong he deserves a wife to run away from him. In his eyes and my parents and my sisters, probably also your mother, I'm the faulty one, not Paul. I'm the one who fall in love with another man, I'm the one wronging him. They wouldn't be proud.

"If we're discovered at work there will be a terrific scandal. You and I wouldn't feel very comfortable. You may not have thought about it. We might even be forced to look for other jobs."

She sighed. "The timing is wrong, our marriages happened before. If I walk out, I would be too guilty to be happy. Maybe you think my love isn't deep enough, but I have to exhaust one marriage before I can start another. Maybe in five or ten years… And maybe then you will feel differently. That's the chance I have to take. I got to do it this way now."

She called again later. "Hi, it's me. I haven't heard from you all day. Is everything okay?"

He replied Sunday. "I heard your messages last night from a pay phone when I picked up Claude, but I didn't have enough change to answer. I don't expect you to leave Paul and I have no right to be jealous. We have so much already! You're fun to be with, talk with, joke with, and kissing you is like eating candy. Making love to you is like rolling in whipped cream and shaved almonds with my mouth open and never getting full. I'm too greedy for you. I have to remember you can't eat only candy." He was lying on Philip's bed and thought he heard Claire coming so he hung up. Nobody came so he called again. "Listen, my love, you seem nervous. Being in love and married causes tremendously conflicting feelings. Do you want to cool off?" He thought she might relax if she thought that she could. "Shall we be normal friendly colleagues for a while?"

Late that night she responded. "Hi, it's me. You're so nice and understanding. I do feel guilty that we do it so often. I want it too, just like a kid, and want to when the opportunity rises. Even if we're husband and wife it wouldn't be boring. But I don't think it will last long if we do it this risky and regular. Is this what you… Now I'm losing… I'm not making sense any more. I just love you very much. I love to kiss you. I love to… love love love with you. Good night."

CHAPTER 10

Claude was the son of Alan's friend Jacques. Jacques was in Libya and couldn't get back to Paris until July and his ex-wife was god knew where, so the Donners had agreed to take Claude for a month. He'd been there less than a week before they regretted it.

"He bullies Philip," Susan told Dr. Kronquist, "and he's obnoxious to Claire. They both try to avoid him."

"He's an only child," Alan said. "He never learned how to get along with siblings. And he's fourteen and alone in a foreign country. He's insecure."

"He can't stand being wrong and argues ferociously about everything. When our kids play games with him he even argues about the rules. And he's French. Their school system values competition over cooperation, you know."

"I'll suggest that he let them win sometimes."

"They don't care about winning—they're upset because he cheats."

"I know, but I'm not sure he'd understand an appeal to his sense of ethics."

"Good luck with Claude," said Dr. Kronquist. "What about yourselves?"

"When I hug Alan he's always thrusting his pelvis against me. He can't be affectionate without being sexual."

"What? I'm trying to give you a full hug, not just an upper-body one. Anyway, sex, affection and love shade into each other." Olive and I know this continuum in our bones!

Stop thinking about Olive.

"Can you show affection without being sexual, Alan?"

"I guess not." Susan smiled as if she'd won a point.

"I can live with you on a spiritual level," Olive said, "but I know you think sex is an important part."

"Yes, but we can cool it down if you want."

"I want to. My feelings are all in turmoil."

"Okay. I figured out why people having affairs get caught: They can't keep it to themselves. They're either so happy they need to share it or too guilty to bear it alone."

"Which are you?"

"Happy."

She bumped his shoulder. He stoically walked along but when she bumped again he grinned and bumped back, hair-trigger penis stiffening at once, pulled her into a recess, embraced, broke, walked, and they ducked into another. By the time they reached her car they were panting. "We're just great, aren't we."

"Yes," she drawled.

"One lunch with no sex. Congratulations."

The concept was fine—not letting her nerves break things off—but when he returned from campus the next day and she wasn't there, initial curiosity about her whereabouts suddenly gave way to panic: Where was she? What was she doing? Was she having fun? Was she with another man? He couldn't breathe, he couldn't see… She walked in and handed him an envelope. Inside was a greeting card with a single Chinese character. "It means 'love,'" she whispered.

The agonized constriction in his chest evaporated in a smile. "How was lunch?"

"I had lunch with Stephanie."

"Oh yeah, I forgot."

Then he heard her say on the phone, "I'll go to a room where I can shut the door and call you back." His chest constricted again. What, or who, was she concealing. But the card? How many proofs did he need, how frequently? From some objective viewpoint he must appear insane.

After a sleepless night he told her machine, "Sometimes I'm afraid my intensity will put you off. Relationships can be political—if one person's crazy about another, the other has the power to manipulate him."

She listened to her messages when she arrived and said through the partition, "We're too old for that."

This sensible assertion was a relief but he still wondered. He mentioned the phone call and she laughed. "I have a small project Stephanie needs fast, so we're building it without a permit. We don't want publicity."

"Oh, of course you don't!"

"I bought two tickets to a piano recital. It would be fun to go with you."

"I'd love to, but let me think about it. I'm not sure how Susan would react." The remains of his anguish melted.

She left a message that night. "Hi, it's me. They're asleep and I'm drinking my fourth glass of wine. Protect yourself, do the right thing for yourself. Decide what you want to do. At work you just hop and jump and try to do your job. After a few drinks you're on the moon or Mars, want to be free, totally forget about morals. Is that maybe the true, genuine feeling, with no binding or rules?

"Paul and I argued, a little silly domestic thing, but I was very mad. I start to feel, I'm not blaming you but I can't get rid of my anger, can't you just comfort me? But no budge, he's out of the house with Daniel to the park saying I should be in control. If you and I are husband and wife, would you still be caring and sensitive after fifteen years? Or would you tell me behave yourself and don't be a rotten kid.

"Life is imperfect, so be happy with what we have, right? It's very sweet, very special to me. I love you tenderness and careness. Well, didn't see you much this week, but we have many years yet together. I love you."

He replied in the morning. "I wish I could help, but don't

worry, things will get better. As for me, I'm not going to break off. I'm trapped in love with you."

"Hi, it's me," she said that evening. "Don't take any chances with Susan about the piano recital. Don't push our luck. We should go slow now. There's a Chinese saying: When it's a big hot flame, it dies quickly; if it's slow it will last a long time.

"I had a good day with my mother at Stanford Shopping Center. I like that place, I love attractive things and pretty people. I'm looking forward to Monday and the chance to see, talk and touch each other. Life is so odd."

He called her at home Saturday morning. "Is Paul there?" She hesitated. "I'm sorry, you have the wrong number."

Oops. He called her machine. "I'm sorry, my dear. Susan's out for the morning. Tell me when to call."

She called his. "Hi, it's me. I hope I didn't hurt your feelings. Paul was sitting next to me at the table and I didn't know what to do. Now he's gone to work."

He called but there was no answer so he called her machine. "Congratulations, you thought fast. Call me at home if you hear this before noon."

When the phone rang, he raced Claire to answer.

"Hi, it's me."

"Aah, contact at last!"

CONVERSATIONS BY MACHINE

We will develop the habit of uninterrupted speech. Will we stop listening when we're together, restless and impatient to speak? And as we spend more time on the machine, we'll spend less in person. Finally the affair will be mechanical, disembodied, only a ghost.

(She was amused.)

Claude hopped around the boat showing off, stepping on the sails, tangling the lines and bossing Claire and Philip until Alan lost his patience and began pointing out his mistakes. He fell silent and then Alan was ashamed. Poor Claude was an awkward teenager, too old for children but not yet an adult, shy with the girl his age they'd brought along, or maybe simply not fluent enough to follow the quick conversation. To make him feel better, Alan gave him the helm. He steered gravely.

"Hi, it's me. I finished *Love in the Time of Cholera*. I like it as something to share, talk about, also because I'm sharing four thousand years of culture, the world beyond us two small people. Bye."

He heard the message from a pay phone at the harbor while the kids were in the bathroom.

"Hi, it's me. I'm puzzled and frightened. I'm very critical of Paul lately. Is it because I'm comparing him with you, or is it I'm fed up with his insensitivity? I shouldn't give you just his wrong side. He is honest, principled, knows what should or shouldn't be done, never cheats or lies. I trust him. He wants to do well with our family. He tells me he loves me, I'm everything to him. He doesn't criticize me, he's generous with me, allows me time with my parents and money to spend on them, lets me go to parties and shows by myself. I get freedom and respect.

"The scary part is I don't feel much toward him lately, or is it my guilty feelings are causing me to invent bad feelings about him to justify my actions to myself? Before, I was never too critical. I can brainwash myself to overlook his bad side and like people. Now the risk is my bad feelings will snowball and overwhelm the good ones. But how can I dislike him for the ten percent? What am I doing? I'm setting myself up to not like him.

"You don't dislike Susan even though you love me. You are more of a doer. You would jump to me or stay with her. Am I a typical woman? I don't have guts but at the same time I complain.

"Lately I'm telling you a lot of my complaints. If you want to be serious about us, you have to take the happy and the troubled side of me. Don't worry. When you see me Monday, tomorrow, I'll be fine. Bye."

THE BASIC QUANDARY (STILL)

is to comprehend where we fall between total commitment (divorce and remarriage) and total disengagement. The position obviously can't be defined, as it shifts daily, one of us ascending, one descending, both confused, one upset at home, one at work…

The trick is to assimilate the idea of life as multifaceted beyond comprehension and accept the incongruities in our situation as we accept them elsewhere.

(She told him: Sometimes I don't know what you mean.)

She returned the book. "I'm proud of myself. I didn't think at first I could read it."

"Good literature's always easy."

"Maybe for you! Alan, I'm embarrassed to ask you something. Will you correct a letter I'm writing?"

"Why would you be embarrassed?"

"Sometimes I ask Paul but he gets impatient. He says I should take English classes."

"How are you and he doing?"

"Oh, it'll be okay, I'll get over it. But I don't want to talk about it. Let's talk about the book. I like the part where Fermina Daza knows her husband is seeing another woman because she can smell her."

"Yes! That's why I always shower before I go home."

"I love your smell. After the ski trip, I didn't wash my nightgown for two weeks because it smelled like you. I slept in it every night to remember."

"And what about the old couple who only saw each other once a year?"

"It's not enough." He kissed her but got a cool reply. "Let's go back. I'm busy."

Just before quitting he asked, "Done with the letter yet?"

She grumbled something, then said, "I have my period. Maybe that's why I'm so sensitive. Don't worry about it."

But he worried—she was edgy, wouldn't talk about Paul, wasn't sharing her feelings.

Susan said Frank Rice was going to meet him at the opera house with an extra ticket to *Gotterdammerung*. She served him dinner and sent him off. Brunnhilde sent Siegfried off. Was Olive sending him off, too? At intermission he told her machine that he was concerned about her unhappiness with Paul. "Tell me if I can do anything. Can I help get your mind off it? Let's try new things in different settings, expand our horizons." Then he watched Siegfried lose his life trying new things in different settings.

He couldn't sleep afterwards. At three AM he checked his machine and found a cheerful message saying how happy she was. "It must be my period. I'm human like everyone else, with my moods and crankiness. If you don't know that about me, we'll only have a superficial relationship."

In the morning she said hello to Harry and handed Alan an envelope with her ski money.

"I went to the opera last night."

"You did?" she said with surprise.

"I like opera. It's fairy stories for grownups."

"It's like sex, games for grownups," said Harry.

"Yes…" She laughed her throaty laugh.

WHAT'S THE PLOT?

A good romance has conflict and crisis, obstacles overcome, clever people and compelling circumstances, foreign settings and gripping action. Where's the interest in the lifelong love of a man and woman? How can I write our story? I want an ode to Olive, to love itself, to bliss, Brunnhilde's pure rapture, the divine burning core distilled and refined of anxiety and uncertainty, untainted with the day to day deceptions of life.

Suppose a guy who deceives his family and is only honest with his lover falls in love yet again with someone else. Will he hide the second from the first and both from his wife in a daisy chain of truth and lies, love upon love? How many can there be? What happens if they're all on the rag at the same time? Hoo boy, where's the bliss then?

Olive gave him her machine's code number so he could listen to messages people left for her. "How sweet. Why?"

"I don't know. Do you want to go shopping with me? I saw some white jeans last week with my mother. I want something to wear when I sail on your boat."

"White clothes get dirty."

"I don't care about that, but I'm not sure if they look good." She modeled them and he smiled, so she bought them. They sampled perfume, anointed her ears, daubed his wrists; he nibbled her neck and licked her ears. She laughed. "You better take a shower."

"Tell you the truth," she told him that evening while Susan was teaching and Paul was in the park with Daniel, "it felt perfectly natural to go back to work, no deception because we didn't make love. You can't do it all the time anyway, even in the books and movies."

"With you I could." He lay on his bed. Claire and Philip played in the living room and Claude listened to music.

"Wouldn't it be nice to just say, 'Paul, I'm going to spend tonight with Alan.'"

"It'd be wonderful! That's how it should be."

"But I never could. Only in a movie."

"Speaking of movies, tomorrow's your last Friday off. Do you want to celebrate with lunch and a movie?"

His heart jumped happily as he walked to her. They embraced and walked hand in hand an indecisive block or two. Why did they always have such a hard time picking a place to meet or eat? He was afraid she'd be dismayed by his suggestions. Anywhere was fine with him—formica, tattered linoleum, vinyl walls—what mattered was what took place, but she cared about ambience—glassware and tablecloths, lacquered teak tables with chrome legs, clean expensive places with potted plants. Why was it hard for her? He didn't know; sometime he'd have to ask. She picked a staid gay restaurant and asked the waiter to recommend some wine. They gazed at each other and the world began to shrink.

What did they talk about? Nothing in particular.

They must have said something. Oh yes, many things, some that seemed important and some inconsequential.

What did they eat? Something with pasta and spinach. After two glasses of wine they saw only each other.

When it was time for the movie they took his car. Why not hers? Because they remembered that a senior staff seminar was taking place just two blocks from the theater and they thought his car was less recognizable than hers. What did they decide to do if they met someone on the street? They decided it was a risk they couldn't avoid.

She left him alone in the theater for a minute. He went to the bathroom and dashed across the street for peppermints. When he returned, she offered some peppermints she'd just bought across the street. They laughed. They sat in the last row and held hands. When the lights went down they began kissing. The movie had something to do with a janitor in a milk plant but they weren't watching; their eyes were closed and they were tasting each other's wine and peppermint. After a while they whispered, shall we go? Where? The boat? She hesitated, considering the time and when to pick up Daniel. He hesitated, somewhat curious about the movie.

Let's go to the boat. She nodded. They walked silently to the car. He drove, heart beating, stomach in throat, nothing to say. She was quiet, waiting, wishing for the ride to end, nothing to say. A stretch of time when nothing happened, a state of anticipation. Did they say anything at all? Alan said, "This is such a strong desire, isn't it?" Olive said, "Yes."

They parked. They walked, they opened the gate, they walked out the long pier. They patiently did what they needed to get from the theater to the boat, from decision to action.

How long was the pier? Like the ride from the theater, it passed. How was the weather that afternoon? Warm with sharp glistening light. What did they do at the boat? They unlocked it and went below and took off their clothes except bra and panties and lay in the bow. Did they do anything new this time? Yes, they faced the other way so their heads were closer to fresh air. Why? It was hot and stuffy. Was that an improvement? Yes. Anything else? They made love. What's new about that? It's always new.

They made love wildly, their hearts raced, they were intoxicated. The whole world was there in the bow, or rather, nothing outside the bow existed, nothing else mattered.

What did they do next? They kissed and relaxed, they checked the time, they dressed, they were happy.

It was late afternoon. He drove her back to her car. When he reached the office at a quarter of five someone asked why he'd bothered to come in. What did he do in reply? He smiled and shook his head.

Happy messages the rest of the day.

Alan, at six, how happy he was.

Olive, at seven, from her bathroom phone, quickly agreeing.

Olive, at nine, with Daniel in the background, "Mmmm, I'm going to say everything now. I hear your voice and I just felt soooo sexy! I'm crazy right now, I had such a good time! I'm so happy. I love you a lot. And just put everything aside—try to enjoy it.

"Fern and I went to a restaurant together. We had lots of wine and we're very happy, and we came home and Paul's going to see that car racing movie, and Fern's out on the deck smoking, so I finally have a chance to say hi and, mmm, just miss you a lot and… I don't know, what can we say… It's so much longing and… I mean wanting to and I can't deny it and it felt so good, and it's just wonderful, but reality is reality and I'm not going to think about it right now, I'm just going to enjoy it. Everything's fine, I'm very happy. I wish you're here so I can hug you. Bye."

SUNDAY MORNING

I can't quite recover the simplicity of an idea I had upon awakening, more a feeling of acceptance and an absence of the usual aching yearning for you in bed next to me. It included an absolute certainty that you are there for me.

BACK TO REALITY

"But reality is reality and I'm not going to think about it right now." What did you mean? What reality? It's all real. Everything we do with each other is as real as what we do with our families.

(She answered: I often wonder what it would be like to live with you, but the reality is that we do have families, so we can't live together. I'd like to do many things with you but can't because of reality.)

SUNDAY AFTERNOON

We took the kids to a street fair. People swarmed slowly back and forth and spilled into alleys. At one corner we paused to watch a juggler at the still center of a dense concentration of watchers. I scanned the faces in the crowd, comparing them with yours, finding not one that approached yours in beauty, but would have felt no surprise to see yours appear.

Claude and I spoke French, a foreign language in a foreign crowd. The place felt as alien to me as it must have to him. I was at the same time a part of the buzzing community and apart in my hidden passion.

OLIVE

O veil. O veiled love. L'amour voilé.
Our love lies hidden.

CHAPTER 11

You got a haircut."
"Susan doesn't like it."
"I like short hair." They were looking for shoes. "I hate to shop. I like to go, buy what I want and leave. If I'm rich I'll hire someone to shop for me."
"I'm the same."
"We're not the same, because I don't care how much it costs. By the way, how much ski money do we have?"
"A hundred eighty dollars."
"That's not much." She did a sudden about-face. "We have to go! I used to work with that guy at B&M!" A bit amused, he followed.
Back at the office he smiled when she told Steve she'd seen old so-and-so downtown but hadn't had time to say hello. "By the way, I have the Fratelli Winery music schedule. Do you and Sharon want to come?"
"Sure. I'll speak to her tonight."
She turned to Alan. "Would you and Susan like to come?"
"Where?" As if he didn't know.
"We go to the winery for a concert, bring a picnic and drink lots of wine."
"I'd love to. Let me ask Susan."
When Susan left to teach and Paul had taken Daniel to the park, Olive called and he told her Susan had accepted.
"Good. You know, it's really fun to go to work these days."
"It's very comfortable."

"We're so comfortable we better be careful."

On the Fourth of July the Donners and Claude met the Rices for a bike ride around Angel Island, just over the water from Fern's where Olive was at a barbecue. "Do you think Frank really works when Nancy takes the kids to their cabin?" Susan asked later.

"Why? Do you think he sees another woman?"

"Marian told me he made a pass at her at a party."

"But he and Nancy seem to like each other."

"Well, there are different ways for people to get along. What matters is to find something that works."

Hey diddle diddle, the cat and the fiddle! Was she willing to let the spoon run away with the cow?

He asked his mother, "Do you think what Olive and I are doing is immoral?"

"No. Immorality is hurting other people."

He repeated that to Olive and told her what Susan had said.

"Well, that's easy to say if it applies to someone else, but different thing if it's you."

"Yes, but saying it was the first step."

"Maybe. By the way, I'll bring a picnic tomorrow."

What a life. He met Susan at Dr. Kronquist's, talked with her, kissed her goodbye and met Olive ten minutes later.

"Put this on your list of ironies," Olive said. "At the sex counseling session with Paul, he told me his regret is I'm not passionate enough."

She drove to the Marin headlands, changed into her new white pants and they carried the hamper to a log on the beach. *Hadrian's Memoirs* is difficult. Can you explain what he means?"

"'The lover who leaves reason in control does not follow his god to the end.' Love is so exceedingly rare, Olive, we're fools if we don't take it as far as we can."

"Why do I love you so much?"

"Why indeed? Tell me."

"You're tender and gentle, interested in music and ideas. Why do you love me?"

There is no reason, there's only love. It has no reason, no cause, no effect; its existence is its explanation. I suppose it could be anyone but it happens to be you. I can list your qualities and the hues of my love, but not why it happened. Pick a reason, any reason. "Because you live life so exuberantly."

They returned to the car and drank the last of the wine, kissed and kissed more madly, he unbuttoned her fly and put in his hand, she rubbed his crotch, their senses rose in buzzing motion. "Do you want to make love?"

"No."

They kissed in a blue-green landscape of desire.

"Well?"

"Yes?"

"What do you want to do?"

"Will you suck me?"

She leaned over the gear shift. He didn't want to gag her but was too excited to keep from thrusting.

"Shall I get a towel?" She went to the trunk, draped it over his lap and recommenced, contorted in the passenger's seat. Blue sea filled his empty eyes. Then she crawled up, fastened her mouth to his, and continued with her hand as he slipped his own into the tight crevice of her buttocks, inserted a finger and rubbed to her rhythm until he arched.

"My god," he said when he could talk without gasping.

"This is great, you in your shirt and tie and erection. I'll think of it at our staff meetings."

"No one ever did that for me before."

"Do you mean in a car, or that?"

"I mean with so much gusto. Do you want me to do it for you?"

"No thanks, it was just fun pleasing you and watching you. Poor Paul. He doesn't know what he's missing."

The office was relaxed when they returned. It was Friday afternoon and somebody suggested going home. Alan chuckled. "Some people disappear for hours at lunch and then want to leave early."

Olive said in a low forceful voice, "I should throw a rock over this partition."

THE BEST OF ALL POSSIBLE WORLDS?

She'd like to do away with rules but fears perdition. Within the limits of our relationship she is utterly free—she can let loose her propriety knowing circumstances will return it since her transgression is bounded by the infrequency of our meetings.

THE HUNT (FALSEHOODS OF LOVE)

I am tracking her. I don her mood. From the range of moods I can myself feel, I select the one she feels. (She calls me sensitive, but I'm only paying attention.) I match her breathing during sex. I echo her concerns. Freedom from rules is not an issue for me, but I treat it seriously, without dishonesty, since it is one aspect of the whole thing.

To agree when she talks of fate is false, but I tell her I agree. To be agreeable. To reinforce the impression that we think alike, to foster her sense of destiny so she won't even consider struggling. And it does name what is ineffable, and maybe it points toward meaning, but I cannot accept a premise which posits external agency. Maybe she too is jesting... No, she believes in God, God Who Has Ordained This, Who Protects Us From Discovery. I'm a fraud. There is nothing but the random coincidence of our thoughts and feelings, the bare facts of our passion. Reasons yes, but Reason no.

THE TEMPORALITY OF BLISS

I will write a book to preserve this, to fix changeless and eternal this rapture. (As one might seek to bottle summer's attar against a winter night? No, not for recollection, but forever.) Futile and foolish hope. If we know anything, it's that everything changes. Nothing can be fixed. And not only that: Love is love of a living creature, and creatures change.

ALIENS

Olive is Chinese. She is foreign, exotic, glamorous, intriguing. She is the Other, the lover, the person not yourself, another self with whom you join, you who sense your own self so strongly that you must accept on faith alone that the world and its people and creatures and plants have selves themselves apart from you.

One of love's joys is surprise at our lover's unanticipated actions, the subterranean surprise of being sought by another, another's secret tongue warmly licking an unknown place, the once known and again known yet always astonishing intimacy, the welcome lovely child, the familiar of dreams, the shock of everyday charged with uncanny valence.

PREDETERMINISM

Certainly there is a biological urge toward reproduction, a physiological predisposition to certain activities, a mechanical engorgement of body cavities, a swelling of organs which feeds sensation back to the cortex, and so forth. Certainly the urge toward closeness and union I feel at the sight of my beloved is based ultimately on the property of certain molecules to replicate themselves. All this is chemical: The excitement of my senses and erection of my body at a mere fingertip touch of the small slick area between her legs, the confusing impulsion to thrust as between the tips of my thumb and index I roll her nipple, as into the palm of my hand fits the smooth and cool curve of her breast.

"Hi, it's me. I'm shopping in Chinatown. Would you like to do that with me some time? Paul doesn't like the mess, he says it's too dirty. I really enjoyed it yesterday. I like the beautiful scenery and the silence. I liked our picnic. It was fun. Bye."

"Hi, it's me. I'm at Union Square having my hair cut. We had a nice dinner last night with Steve and Sharon. We talked about you. I pretended I don't know a lot about you. They don't understand why you bought a boat, since Susan doesn't like water or boating. I didn't say a word! I compared it to Paul's Triumph, everyone needs a hobby. They understood—maybe Alan bought the boat to get away from Susan. We all laughed.

"Steve said you know something about every subject. I said, huh? I said to Steve if you think Alan is smart, he must be, because Paul says Steve is smart, and I think Paul is smart. The mathematics of it.

"They're looking forward to the winery concert. I don't want to overanticipate, because that way it may be a letdown. I want to tone it down, not let my hopes get too high.

"I reread your mother's letter, which may have been a mistake. I started to puzzle again. It gives you a different taste in your mouth. The letter implies that Susan is terrible. Why did you put up with it for so long? You deserve more—a person like me for a long-term wife. That's what you need."

He answered, "Susan's out for a while. If you hear this before noon, give me a call," and waited watching sunlight on the olive tree outside his window.

"Hi, it's me."

"Olive, my dear!"

"Chinatown reminds me and Fern of our childhood. Sometimes the sights and smells are disgusting and we joke about the peasant people there, but if Paul criticizes, we think he's making fun of us, so we have to say it's perfectly okay. Isn't that silly?"

"It's okay to poke fun at yourselves but not for anyone else, huh?"

"If Paul goes to China, he'll want to stay in the best hotels."

"You don't meet anyone that way. You might as well stay home and watch a documentary."

Susan told him a friend was having another affair. "She says her husband's a good man, but boring. Her home life isn't exciting enough."

"Suppose she could say, 'John, I'm going to spend tonight with so and so.' Would that kill the excitement?"

"Why are you asking the question?"

"I was just wondering."

"I don't think it would work very well."

Lunchtime on *Malta,* love in the hot bow in a stench of gasoline, they didn't care, it didn't matter. No time to talk, back to the office.

They talked that evening. "This is working out well. Love in the day and talk at night."

"What will we do when the days are short and Paul doesn't take Daniel to the park?"

Alone in the office all morning, back and forth between desks, touching, caressing hands, thighs, faces. Susan came in with Claude so they could take him for Mexican food before he left. Olive said hello. Oh, hello! Susan tried to be outgoing. "Have you read *The Joy Luck Club?*"

"I don't have much time to read."

"Oh, you must. I'll make Alan bring it to you."

Mexican food didn't please Claude. They sighed, Susan took him home, and Alan walked over to meet Olive at Five Lakes, the restaurant she went to on the rare occasions when she didn't eat with him or the other PMs. "Well, how was it seeing Susan?"

"I had to pretend I don't know anything."

"I felt odd, but you looked completely relaxed."

"Ha! It wasn't as easy as all that!"

They necked in her car behind the restaurant. "I'm afraid I can't read *Hadrian's Memoirs.* I need something easy now."

"I'll bring you *Joy Luck Club.*"

"Fern told me she didn't think it was an accurate view of

Chinese life. I want so, so bad to go there with you. And I want to go skiing with you next winter."

She called that evening and said Paul still hadn't come home. Poor sap, thought Alan, squandering time he could have been with her. But so much the better for me.

He awoke at four in a familiar despair that was becoming tedious—doubt about her commitment, fear that she wouldn't continue. What caused it? The way she put things sometimes: I want to go skiing with you next winter, as if it was in question... He probed for reassurance at lunch. "My feelings are very mixed these days. I'm happy and worried—happy we're together but worried it won't last."

"I'm mixed too, happy and guilty. I'll tell you something maybe I shouldn't. When I saw Susan I thought: I look up to you, you're older than me, respected at work, accomplished, successful, musical, deep, profound. I respect you and admire you."

"And you're smart, successful, sexy, glamorous, small and vulnerable, kind and caring."

She smiled. "But that's not what I want to say. What I saw is Susan doesn't respect you. She's older than you, maybe she treats you like a little brother. Force her to respect you. Don't slap her around, but assert yourself. Paul had some friends with problems and the woman left, he asserted himself, and now they're happily married. She says, 'He stopped being such a wimp.'"

Do you think I act like a wimp? "I'll invite you over to give her Olive lessons. 'Watch us, Susan, this is how a wife should act.'"

She laughed, and that was that. But when they talked that evening she continued, "I'll tell you why there are mixed feelings—this is based on a faulty foundation. The house might look good, but its structure is flawed."

"You're right," he said without enthusiasm.

"You're willing to change everything but I'm not. It's the same beginning problem."

He was sorry he'd said anything. "Oh well, I'm willing

to live with it the way it is if you are."

"We can't change anything. Let's talk about something else."

"Claire's so fed up with Claude she went to work with Susan tonight, and Philip's lonely and hurt."

"You should hang up and pay attention to him."

"I should, but then I wouldn't be with you."

"We'll be together another time."

He joined Philip. Later he called his mother. "I was wondering why you don't read about affairs that last a lifetime. Do you suppose it's because they're boring? Tolstoy said all happy families are the same. Maybe happy relationships like this don't interest writers."

"I don't think they're boring, but they probably don't usually last long, though it's not impossible. I wish you both luck."

Olive told his machine, "Hi, it's me. Try to be less worried. I love you."

"Really I'm perfectly fine," he lied in response. "We have to talk about something so I tell you whatever I'm feeling at the moment, and just then I was worried. Don't you start worrying now."

Another sleepless night. She was right, his mother was right, the fundamental flaw, how could it last, the problem was insoluble, one person he lived with but didn't love, another he loved but couldn't live with, two situations, two people, need to meld the two, need them to become one, need someone who will reconcile circumstance and passion, what if I did meet someone who would live with me? What would you have me do? Leave you and go with her, marry her and continue with you? With or without her knowledge? Or would you want me to dump her and stay with Susan so we could continue our after all relatively stable arrangement? Would these questions torment you as they do me? Should I tell you? Would you be amused? Is honesty sometimes as brutal as malice? Is reserve necessary? To what extent can I reveal my insecurity? What are the rules? I'm all alone without a guide and I'm losing control.

In the light of day, in her presence, the questions vanished like shadows from a dark corner. It was a quiet day. Just before five she came for help with a letter and leaned close as he read it, arm around her waist, her hand on his cheek. He removed his arm to make a correction, she straightened up, and Susan walked around the partition and said, "Hello."

He almost gasped. "Hello, Susan!"

Olive stepped back. "Uh, he's helping me with my writing."

"Oh, excuse me. Do you want me to come back?"

"No, no, we're almost done. What are you doing here?"

"I thought I'd see if you want a drink."

"Sounds good. Just let me finish this. Do you want to come, Olive? What about Steve? Want to invite him?"

"I don't know. I'll go ask him."

"I will," said Susan and walked away.

They rolled their eyes. "Please come," he whispered.

"I don't think I want to..."

"If Steve comes?"

"Maybe."

"There, that's done," he said aloud. "Look okay?"

"Yes, fine, thanks."

Susan returned. "Steve says he's busy and can't come."

"That's too bad." His heart was racing. "Maybe if I go ask. Be back in a minute." He and Olive walked away. "You sure you can't come, Steve?"

"No, I have to meet Sharon. Some other time."

Olive picked up her purse and jacket.

"You're coming?"

"Yes."

"Thanks."

They sat with heads close to hear in the noise, so close that each breath inhaled Olive's perfume; they talked about children, work, Claude, books—Susan said he always gave her books nobody could read, like one called *Hadrian's Memoirs*—he bent to adjust his socks and rubbed Olive's calf. She didn't move. When they said goodbye he walked with Susan to her car, and as soon as she was out of sight headed back to meet Olive by her car and pull her for a kiss.

"Don't! You're much more daring than me!"

"Kiss me goodbye and I'll let you go."

She wouldn't. "That was really scary!"

"Well, nothing happened." He wanted to reassure and soothe her, calm her fear, make everything go away, but could only squeeze her hand and race home to make up for the time he'd spent with her.

"I knew at once what was going on when I saw you together," Susan said. His heart stopped. "I could see she was embarrassed. I even thought about leaving for a few minutes without her seeing me, to give you a chance to finish."

Thank you heaven! We might have been kissing when she came back.

"She's such a nice person! Now that I know her, I'm so embarrassed I was jealous. It would be like you being jealous of Jorge."

What if she is having an affair with Jorge? That'd be irony!

"Maybe we should ask her if she wants to take our extra opera ticket. Do you want to?"

"Oh, maybe. Do you want burritos for dinner? I'll go get some."

He called from a pay phone. "I win, I'm leaving the first message. Don't worry about anything, it's better than you can imagine!"

"Hi, it's me. Amazing, isn't it. Still beyond comprehension. Ninety percent could be disaster, ten percent we were super lucky. Absolutely at the instant we were concentrating on work and not goofing around.

"Mixed feelings. One. The drinks were fun, a success, everything natural, even from my judgment it was excellent, told Paul about it."

"Two. It was scary. What a close call, could be scream, could be shouting, could be everybody come around look at it. It's beyond imagining."

"Three. It makes you think what are we doing, risking our lives like this? Isn't it crazy?

"Four. Also my feelings about Susan. I like her. She's very sweet. I can see she could be not very sweet with you, but on the other hand she's a nice person.

"It's just crazy, I can't even analyze it. I went to China-town, had my wonton soup, then came home, played with Daniel, didn't want to think about it.

"I don't know if she thinks everything's okay, as normal as she acted, or could it be she acted, too? She seems like a straightforward person but maybe she was embarrassed about me knowing about you guys not getting along and wanting to act super friendly.

"You can't be so risky. What we're doing is way beyond safe. It's so easy to run into and get caught by other people.

"All this goes back to the fundamental structure. We set up something totally crazy. If you don't want to break away from your own family and do it in public, in bright open, then you go into the secret things. What do you do when things are discovered? Is it disaster? For you it might be different, for me at this point it is a disaster. So you want to minimize the chance of discovery. To be safe you have to be discreet, act very normally. That goes back to before we went skiing. It needs to be thought about.

"I've been through a lot of screwed up things when you don't have them set up right. Eventually they will fail. That's not a very pleasant thought. Anyway, if worse comes to worse we can still be friendly loving, not physically but emotionally close, and that's fine.

"All right, enough for tonight. I should go to bed. I took some cough medicine so I'll be drowsy soon. Bye."

"Susan thinks you're the cat's meow. There's nothing to worry about. She was jealous, but now that she's getting to know you she likes you, which means we're safe.

"I agree we have a contradiction between the absolutes of all and nothing, but we're learning, we've gone through some phases. My earlier hope that you'd leave Paul is resolved; now the problem is your guilt and fear of discovery. We'll figure out how you can relax."

"Hi, it's me. Can't get control of all my feelings. But I won't analyze or decide until I'm capable. I'm just reacting. As for Susan, she likes me, it's hard to hurt her. Think of Paul. What if Paul likes you and we do this, aren't you uneasy?

"We shouldn't do that at the office. Other than that, it's okay. I can't conclude anything. We should cool off. Don't feel bad, don't worry. No decision now. Bye."

Alan took Claude to the airport, checked the baggage, and then they had two hours to kill. "Excuse me, I need to make a call." Claude watched curiously as he listened, deposited more quarters and listened some more. "Messages from work," he explained. He wanted to reply, but not with Claude standing there. "Let's go sit down. You know, I'm sorry we didn't do more with you. We should have told you we'd be working and the kids were in a summer program."

Claude blushed. "I'm used to being alone."

"Well, we feel bad about it."

"I had a good time."

It hadn't seemed like it, but maybe he'd forget the loneliness and retain a few good memories, and at least he could brag about his month in San Francisco.

"Excuse me, I have to go to the bathroom." He went to a phone. "I understand about liking Susan and not wanting to hurt her. I feel the same about Paul." Not true. "We don't want to hurt anyone." True. "So we must keep them from finding out." Very true. "You're right about work. No more kissing and hugging—it's fun but it's stupid. Better to do less and last longer." False and true. "Let's only take the God-sent opportunities like Fern or your parents leaving town." If God arranges their trips, then God approves our trysts. "Or *Malta,* the boat's safe. We like that, and we should do it." True, true, true. "Why not? But when it's risky we'll just enjoy everything else—the books, the music. What do you think?" I think it sucks. "I love you so much I'll do anything for you. I'll take whatever you want to give and I won't ask for more." Mostly true, but that last was false.

He bought a pack of cigarettes, smoked one and kept two and handed the pack to Claude. "Give this to Jacques, will you?"

"Hi, it's me. I heard your airport message. You must be happy Claude is going? We should be on the conservative side. Makes me happy to know you love me, and I do love you. If we cut the things which make me feel guilty and make us get caught, it would be nice. Once a year... Or whenever... I don't know. When I think about Susan it doesn't relax me. Not to repeat everything, it's mutual understanding. What is in my life? What do I like? I enjoy exchanging thoughts, discussing culture, music, books. Let's have lunch Monday, something non-fattening. Bye."

Claude walked happily through the boarding gate. Alan smoked and waited until the plane was aloft. "Hi. I feel bad because I don't think Claude had a very good time. What I'd like to do for lunch is go to *Malta* and make love, but that's up to you. I love you."

On the way home he smoked the last cigarette and then chewed gum so Susan wouldn't smell it.

POSITION STATEMENT

I saw myself in a mirror, wholesome grownup in jeans and tweed jacket, and wondered how someone who looks so ordinary can harbor these feelings and act like this. Was that reflection, that image I've come to associate with upright, correct social responsibility, was that me? Is it I who am so mixed up in this business?

Sometimes I'm sorry I got you into it. Of course you're a consenting adult, but are you aware of all I've said with the aim of getting you more bound up? I hate coercion, but I'm selfish and want you to want me.

I was sad sending Claude to his father, who is dear to me and whom I rarely see, and when I heard your message I felt like crying. I can't quite say why. I felt the way I did at the Cliff House, though not as empty, because now I know you love me as much as I love you.

Later I listened to the recording of Horowitz in Moscow. The writer of the liner notes said that as a tear rolled down the cheek of a Russian, the same tear rolled down his. For some reason that did it, and as my head fell back and my mouth opened in a sob I saw your face with some sort of painful premonition.

So much of life is static, drab routine. To be aware of time's dynamic—to feel movement, change, activity—we travel, ski, sail, read, love. Emotion, blissful or anguished, reveals the succession of instants, but when it reaches a certain strength it overwhelms our sense of temporality, durations become arbitrary blocks arranged in space, there is no longer pro-cess—only the present extending through space, and a vague recollection that once we knew what it meant for time to pass.

Is this life? A drab immensity with no intensity at all, punctuated by vortices of joy or pain?

CHAPTER 12

"Why do you go to work so early these days?" Susan asked. Today I'm worried sick. "I'm writing a book. I go down early to type it on the computer."

"Are you sure it's not something else? You seem so nervous these days."

"I'm sorry. I guess I'm thinking about the book."

Well, maybe he could pull all this blather together some day and call it a book. He typed what he'd written and called it a position statement. Statement of worry, position of weakness. Now, give it to Olive or not? Better not. If she thinks I'm weak, it'll increase her fear. How scared is she?

He probed when they met at Five Lakes. "It's the same damn thing, isn't it? We have such a hard time knowing where we are."

"It's like a glass of water on a slide. At top and bottom things are balanced but not in between."

"Sometimes I wonder if I could do anything to get you even more mixed up with me."

"What do you mean?"

"Maybe if I said or did something differently."

"How could you influence me? Give me flowers?"

"Oh, you know, sometimes I try to express my thoughts in a way to shape your response. Or when we talk about what might happen if we're discovered, I don't mention the terrible things I've imagined in case they haven't occurred to you."

She considered. "It wouldn't make any difference. I like

you for what you are, not what you say. I think what happened Friday is this. Before, my focus was a closeup on your face like a zoom lens; now I step back and see the larger picture, and it's the same picture. I also think you have a stronger need for sex."

"Yours is strong too, you know. What if we scheduled regular lovemaking and lunches—if we knew we have time for both talk and love, we wouldn't act as crazy."

"For me it depends on the feelings at the time. A schedule wouldn't work."

"Oh well, I need to reduce my hopes so we're on the same level again."

"It's hard when one of us is on a different level." She was very matter of fact. "Would we have gotten together if we met before Paul?"

"Yes. Maybe. Probably not. I wouldn't have left Susan with a baby even though I knew my sex life wasn't likely to improve. I felt the way you do now."

She nodded. "Bad timing. I don't think sex with Paul will ever be great, either. But do you realize how many bad feelings there will be to divorce and remarry? I'd always feel guilty about Paul and know it's because of you. This way we keep it pure and simple."

Good. We keep it. That affirmation was what he sought. In the parking lot she hesitated when he bent to kiss her, but then responded. Another affirmation.

There will be no thirteenth chapter in this book. Friday was the thirteenth. I'll write thirteen out of the numbers and that day out of what happened. I have become superstitious. I read the horoscope, play the lottery, seek to rearrange the world by renumbering it. How have I sunk into such hebetude?

Susan wouldn't say why she was upset when he went to bed early. He didn't understand her and didn't know where he stood with Olive. He was too confused to sleep and risked her picking up an extension to call from his bedroom. "I've erased two messages. I can't get things to come out right. I know things are okay, but I can't quite grasp it. I'm going to cover my head with the pillows and sleep."

"Hi, it's me. When we both don't have things to say and we're all stuck, does that mean something? Could it be we're holding back feelings, is it I want to be less involved? I don't know. There is a gap. There's not much choice for you besides coming down to my level, and that's why I feel unfair. Of course, it's your choice. I wish this whole thing can bring you happiness rather than agony. But this is all I can offer at this point, so let's leave it.

"I just hope thoroughly you're not compromising too much, not being taken advantage by your wife, by your lover. After all, this should be a mutually happy thing. I want you to be calm and happy like I am. So I hope it's not me setting up rules and demanding this and that.

"Oh gosh, I don't think we ever can get this clear. Let's just leave it for a few days and settle it and don't talk about it and then when we're all calm and clear and you have enough sleep, then think about it, okay?

"Actually, I'm putting my mind on work. It's really a happy thing knowing you're next to me and care so much about me. And Daniel is so cute. I'm a very happy mother. That's my life. Chores, busy, totally enjoying being Daniel's mother. And I'm happy to have you.

"That's the basic idea. Tell me everything, I do want to help each other and work things out. You have to be able to trust me, rely on me all the way, right? Bye, dear."

He felt better the next day because of how her message ended and because it was a rare hot day and because she accepted his and Steve's invitation to a quick sail at lunchtime, and mostly because whenever he was with her nothing could be better.

She poked around the cabin with pretended delight.

"You should see us on a windy day," said Steve, "boat tipped over and spray flying. It's exhilarating!"

"I hope you know what you're doing."

"Alan's a great sailor."

She laughed at Alan. "Can I trust you?"

"You can trust me, Olive!" he laughed back.

But at home his unease returned. He shouldn't compromise, she said. Why? Did she feel she was taking advantage of him? Was she? And if so, and he didn't compromise, where would it leave him? Without her. He had no choices.

He went to bed early again sick with uncertainty, crawled under the covers sick with everything, and was disturbed by malformed dreams: She is lying, she's had many lovers, she isn't a faithful wife, all her talk of caring is a phony trick... And awoke even more tired, and remorseful too—it was Philip's birthday, poor Philip, so mute and unhappy with a dad who no longer paid attention.

She took him shopping and he chose something for her to give as a gift. "You have good taste," she said. "I should put on the card: From Olive and Paul and Alan. Now let's pick a book to read together I know something about, a good history of architecture."

"Do you still want to meet Monday? You said once that you'd need to be close after seeing me with my wife at the winery concert."

"Yes, but it's true my feelings have changed."

"Now I'm the one who's going to need reassurance. After all, there's nothing to keep either of us from walking away if it becomes too difficult."

"It depends on your feelings. No matter what happens, I will always have special feelings about you."

That was not reassuring. He tried to ignore a sense of impending change.

ANGUISH

She is more distant. She didn't give me the ski money this week—did she forget or has she reconsidered? Friday the

Thirteenth. She's decided to be more discreet. If she knows the depth of my fear will she draw back more? Have I descended from a lover to a fling? How can I protect myself? Shall I pretend she's a fling? Should I try to find another girlfriend? Should I pretend that I could to give myself the illusion of freedom? I am not free. I am obsessed. I can't even think of anything else without feeling I'm betraying her.

"Maybe I'm sick. I feel insecure, and I'm afraid you'll get fed up if I tell you—you said you get tired of hearing Fern complain. I guess I'm worried that you expect me to be perfect. I wish you could tuck me into bed where I could hear you doing homey things around the house. Well, I'll get better. Most of the time I'm happy and self-confident. I must be sick. I love you, my dear."

"Hi, it's me. One important thing: Be one hundred percent honest, show true feelings, good side and bad side. Otherwise it's superficial, you get that everywhere. Sorry I don't have much time with you this week. I'll always be there and always care for you, and what you told me is not silly at all. It's different from Fern's situation. You're not that weak at this point.

"When we meet Susan in the office, there is a sort of shook up in me. I care a lot, but I began to see the whole picture, the reality side, and now it's a little different in me. We have to act more related to the reality. Sunday concert will be hard because we're going to be very nice to the spouse. It might not be easy to take, but that's what we have to do. Hope you feel better. We can have lunch Monday. Bye."

The motor cut out as he and Claire returned from a sail Saturday. As they drifted slowly into the breakwater he pushed the bow away with his feet and ran back to the cockpit to steer. The boat bumped the rocks. To his vast relief, two men in an inflatable tossed a line and towed them in. Claire helped secure the boat and fold the sails as he grumbled about the trouble and expense of an overhaul and in passing checked the gas tank. "Shit."

"What's wrong, Daddy?"

"The tank's empty." She waited while he made a call from the dock. "I found out why *Malta* stank of gasoline the last time. I hadn't screwed down the vent cap and it all leaked out. See you tomorrow."

He couldn't wait for tomorrow and called her house that evening. Paul answered.

"Hi, it's Alan."

"Hello."

"Is there anything Susan and I should bring?"

"I have no idea. Olive has totally organized the whole thing. She is out to dinner with her sister. I will give her the message in the morning."

His staid complacency was irritating. "Thanks."

"Goodbye."

Sharon wailed, "We'll never make it by five! That lady will kill us."

"No, she won't," said Alan. "She won't mind."

"Sharon and Paul have a thing going," Steve said. "She pretends she's crazy about him and they kiss and go on."

"Oh, Paul is so handsome! Have you met him, Susan?"

"One time at the symphony. Oh, and at a dinner Art Laguna gave. I didn't see him long enough to get an impression."

"We're going to be late, we're going to be late!"

Late to Sonoma, town of love! Will she hang on her husband as she hangs on me? I'd touch her, hold her, kiss her—will he? Will she play it utterly straight or give me a glance, a wink, a hidden hand under the table? Good thing Sharon's agitation covers mine.

Sharon rushed into Paul's arms, Olive kissed Steve and Alan, Susan kissed no one. Olive reached into the wicker basket. "I'm going to take my aspirin, better now than the morning after. Anybody want some?" Chinese noodles, chicken, salad, "I toasted the croutons myself," china, silverware, glasses, napkins.

"This conductor's a Mozart specialist," Alan told Paul.

Paul grunted and turned to Steve. "Do you remember when we went water skiing with Fern?"

"That was a terrible day!" Sharon laughed. "The boat broke down, the car broke down, we all had hangovers, and we waited hours in the hot sun while they got it fixed."

Alan joined the laughter; Susan was politely amused.

"Nice sunglasses, Olive," said Steve.

"When I told the man I'll take these he said, 'Don't you want to try them in the light outside?' I said, 'Oh, no, I just want them to look good on me!'"

Alan laughed at everything, Susan didn't laugh. The laughter of cheerful affluence was all around in the warm evening, sleek blond wives seeking diversion, stately plump men, patrons of the arts, descendants of Mozart's own audience, complacently anticipating a guided tour through modalities of passion, foreboding and fear to a final affirmation of self-knowledge.

Olive served the salad as the music began. The croutons crunched audibly in the silence, Sharon tittered, Olive giggled and glanced at her, giggled harder, tried to stop, choked and avoided Alan's smile as he winked and took another mouthful and crunched. She convulsed. Paul gave her a reproving look. She ducked her head. Alan rested his elbows on the table and gazed up at the tall oaks with a straight face until the croutons were moist enough to swallow unchewed. The mauve sky mellowed into dark.

She laughed uproariously the moment the music ended. Pressure relief. Paul was phlegmatic. Sharon sent him for wine. When he returned Steve was saying, "Alan took us sailing at lunch last week."

Olive laughed, "It was the hottest day of the year."

"Would you like to go sometime?" Alan asked Paul.

"That would be nice."

"How about next weekend? What about you two?"

"Sure," said Steve. "I'll always go sailing."

"I'll come if you go on Sunday," said Sharon. "Will you,

Susan?"

"No, I can't sail. I get seasick."

"So Alan abandons you?"

"Oh, it's okay. I don't like sailing anyway."

"This coffee was a good idea."

"You're ingenious, Alan."

"It's perfect," said Paul. "You can bring it every year."

Alan turned to face the stage after intermission. It was simpler than avoiding her eyes and worrying that someone might find his indifference overly scrupulous.

Finally, walking behind the others on the dark path back to the parking lot, he was able to touch the nape of her neck. She didn't break stride.

Paul and Sharon staged a passionate farewell, Olive kissed everyone, Alan inhaled as much of her as he could and there was nothing left but the ride back.

At home he asked Susan if she'd enjoyed herself. "Yes," she said politely and silently went to bed.

"The reality thing to do now is back off," Olive said.

"I know. It's just that I wasn't prepared."

"I'm sorry for you. But I must say I'm glad it was me who came back first."

"So am I—I'd rather be the one in pain than you."

"Still passionate when the other cools off."

"Well, there's bound to be some pain with the joy."

"Don't worry." She patted him on the shoulder like a mother comforting her son, and the gesture made him start crying.

"How did it get to this point? How could this have happened? I don't understand anything any more."

She hugged him. "Can I do anything to help?"

Make love to me. Reassure me. "No, the main thing is knowing you're not going to leave."

"Well, we have a long life ahead of us."

That afternoon he dropped a note over the partition. "Today is our four month anniversary." She dropped back a drawing of a cake with candles that said HAPPY!! and Lunch

Friday? and he finally began to relax.

The next day they drove downtown to meet with one of their architects. Coming out of the garage they passed a couple walking hip to hip, arms entwined, engrossed in themselves. She laughed. "I wonder if they're married to each other!"

"Just what I was thinking!"

She squeezed his hand. "I forgot to give you my money last week." Things were normal again.

"Pick a birthday card for a friend of mine."

Into a shop for a look. "You like my choice, er tai?"

She laughed. "Second wife! Where did you learn that?"

"Oh, I'm an old China hand."

He left the meeting when his part was done, and when he got back to his desk a message on his computer said, "Re: mood: I'm glad you're feeling better. I wish you and your lover much happiness."

He called her machine that evening. "Everyone's outside watering the plants so I can tell you how enchanting you were today…"

"Hi, it's me. I'm really happy to hear you're so cheerful. And also hope you and I are in the same wavelength now. Ah, we just have to constantly adjusting our different levels. Whatever degree we're in, if we don't expect more than the other person, we can be truly happy. It's so happy to have you. It's very nice that someone in the world cares about me so dearly, like a second wife." Laughter. "Tomorrow busy with another budgeting thing, be alert, try to concentrate. Thursday I'm quite booked too, so the next time to be with you is Friday. And we can do anything—you think about it. I'm not going to tell you what I'm thinking. I miss you. Bye, dear."

He remained serene though they saw each other little and a repair to the voice mail system disabled communication and even when she canceled Friday's lunch to eat with a client. She called afterwards to ask if he wanted to meet her at *Malta* with some wine. He left a message for Susan saying he was going to have a drink with some of the project managers and drove to the harbor. They opened the boat and leaned against each other.

"I'm so happy with you, Olive. This must be as close to paradise as we can get, except that for us time continues to pass and in paradise it doesn't exist. You know, when Goethe was old somebody asked if he'd had a happy life, and he answered that if he added it all up, it came to an hour or so. I've already done better thanks to you. I'll die happy, having loved and been loved so thoroughly, having had a few moments like this, so complete nothing could be added. I wonder if we're near death in moments of intense love. We're so keenly aware of the ephemeral skin around us that we must be closer to whatever is outside. Is paradise there? Well, I don't want it–it could only be less than this."

She said little, smiled, and that was enough. She shared his joy. In return he listened to her concerns about work, Daniel, Paul. He sought to understand, clarify, amplify. She told him he was sensitive and gentle but that she'd never imagined how deep he was. She asked if he'd smoked marijuana. "Fern and I do now and then. Sometimes we rent a porno film. We have fun!"

"Do you do it with Paul?"

"He won't smoke it. He's not adventurous like you, just drinks a beer or watches TV in the other room."

"He's a very controlled person. Drugs make him lose control so he doesn't like them."

"You know, he's a little nervous about sailing with you. Actually, he's afraid of it, thinks it's dangerous."

"Really? No more than sports cars."

"Why are you taking him?"

"It's a way of being close to you." He sighed. "It's not you, but through him I'm near you. Also, I'm curious. He is your husband, you know."

"I know!"

"Claire and Philip saw a boy drown Tuesday."

"Oh, no! What happened?"

"He dove off the raft at Lake Temescal and never came up. Philip said all the kids were crying. Eventually the guards found his body and a helicopter took him away."

"Did he die?"

"They told the kids it wasn't certain, but I think they were trying to make them feel better. Claire said it was like a bad dream."

"I would die if that happened to Daniel!"

"It's scary to think how close death is all the time."

"We are really, really lucky. You try your best and still this can happen."

"Oh, Olive, we must appreciate our happiness—its memory is little comfort when it passes."

By now she was in his lap and they were kissing between thoughts. "Are you working on your book?"

"I'm jotting down thoughts, taking notes, but I don't know what it's about. Us, and happiness, but then what?"

"You need a plot."

"Some books convey the marvel of life without one."

"Think about *Love of Cholera*. He has little things to show how people really are, but there's also a story, how Florentino waits all his life."

"What's our story?"

"That we have normal lives and this is adding something special, making it so much fun, so alive, so happy."

"Do you want to make love?"

"What time is it?"

"Five-thirty."

"Fern will be waiting for me."

He waited.

"I have my period."

"I don't mind if you don't mind."

They undressed and lay in the bow.

"Oh, my god, Olive."

"Alan, Alan, Alan, Alan, Alan."

Time stopped again in the small cramped boat floating in white light on the fringe of a bay.

After she climaxed he was tired. They cuddled and purred, she stroked him, excited him. "I've had mine. You have yours. Do whatever you want."

He entered again briefly, then lay alongside, penis rising from its underbrush like a dousing rod, the solid fleshy stalk blind-eyed, full in his hand and fuller, its purple head swelled, the eye opened and spurted a thick blob on her belly, then thin long threads like a fishing line cast to the silver fish in the spring in the brush on her mound...

"What time is it?"

"Seven."

"My God. Fern will be worried."

"Call and tell her you're late."

"No. I'll just go and say traffic was bad."

"Wouldn't she feel better if you called?"

"I don't want to think about it. I don't like to make her worry, but I won't think about it."

"Are you sure?"

"Stop talking about it."

She put the bloody towel in her bag and they dressed and walked back along the pier. "It's like adding salt. Paul is the meat and potatoes, and you're the seasoning. I'll think about you sailing."

"Did you have a good time with your friends?" asked Susan.

"Very much," he said on his way to the shower.

CHAPTER 14

Vacuuming made him think of Olive. Household chores conjured visions of the part of her life he didn't share, domesticity, which if shared would mean sharing all. He once asked how she and Paul allocated the housework and she said, slightly embarrassed, that they had a weekly cleaning woman and the laundry ironed his clothes. Extravagant, yes, but a pleasant counterpoint to Susan's thrift.

When Susan left for groceries he turned off the vacuum cleaner. "Hi. Did you have fun with Fern? Was she upset you were late? I'm so happy today I can hardly stand it. As you say, we are lucky we have each other for seasoning. You're beautiful and intelligent, a good mother and good wife and good lover and I love you and I love you.

"Philip's concerned about our safety tomorrow sailing because of the drowning. I've had to reassure him about the life preservers, radio, motor, spare sails and oars, poor kid. Well, my dear, I should get back to my housecleaning. Bye."

"Hi, it's me. Fern was worried. We went to dinner, talked, drank a bottle of wine, went to bed. I felt like calling you but there's no privacy. Yesterday was lovely, but still, it's against my... No, I don't regret it. It felt great and I loved it." She laughed. "There's such intensive feelings, but on the other hand, it's I feel oh, I couldn't do that to Paul. But don't worry, I feel fine. I'm going to stay home with Daniel tomorrow. We'll think about you guys. Be careful with Philip. Bye."

Sharon threw her arms around Paul, Steve asked to see his new car, and Alan and Philip waited while with slow, complacent pride he removed the canvas cover and suffered their admiration of an old MG.

For his sake Alan reviewed the safety and man overboard procedures. As soon as they were underway Paul looked at Sharon from under his brow and told her about his own sailing experiences. Once the mast collapsed and another time they struck something and lost the rudder.

"You're scaring me," she said.

"This is not the safest sport."

"Don't worry, Sharon," said Steve. "Alan knows what he's doing."

"But you never know what you might hit," said Paul.

"It sounds like you've had some unusually bad luck," said Alan.

"I hope you left it at home," said Sharon.

Paul smiled significantly and seemed pleased to have worried her. Wouldn't it be handy if he fell overboard and drowned before they could pick him up. Suppose Sharon and Steve were looking away and someone gave him a little push... Alan smiled. They all smiled back.

"How's your new job?" Steve asked.

"I have the authority to make decisions, not like at the university. I would never work there. Olive tells me how much time you waste when the deans change their mind. I have to laugh. You're not responsible for anything, and nobody cares if you make a mistake. Screw up once in the development business and you're out."

"Yes," Steve laughed. "It's frustrating sometimes."

Alan said nothing. If Paul needed to denigrate their work, his own wife's work, who cared. A job was only a job, and he pitied anyone whose self-esteem depended on his position. Olive had told him people thought Paul was arrogant, whereas he was actually shy; and he'd heard her on the phone reassuring him about his performance. Maybe his insecurity began with the full mouth of bad teeth he kept covered. He tried a little frivolity to liven things up, but Sharon glanced to Paul for direction, and his ponderous replies established that he was superior to wit.

"We are going on our fall camping trip with my parents and Fern in two weeks," Paul said to her.

"Where are you going?"

"We are going to a park in the redwoods. I had to make the reservations myself."

"You must be looking forward to it."

"It's a lot of work this year. Gerald always did the planning, but of course he's not coming this time." He sounded mildly resentful.

No one said anything. Paul didn't explain who Gerald was, and Alan suspected he'd be discomfited by needing to reveal such undignified family business but wasn't malicious enough to ask. He was determined to be pleasant even if it included pretending to be unaware of a snub.

Philip asked what caused the tides, why the bridges charge tolls, why the fog was over there and not here. Alan told him.

"You are very patient," Paul said.

"Well, of course. They're honest questions."

They reached Sausalito and sailed along the waterfront looking for a place to tie up.

"Keep going," said Paul. "I used to live around here and I think there's a dock somewhere."

"Hi, it's me. Isn't it funny? When you think about it, isn't this crazy? You went out with my husband on the boat where we—" She laughed. "This is a top secret. If people find out, they probably will kill us. Daniel and I are having a good time on the deck, playing in the pool."

Her husband found nowhere to tie up until they reached a decrepit pier across from a park with a bathroom, which was good, because her lover's son urgently needed to pee. They went ashore into a maze of rotting warehouses, welding shops and motorcycle garages with tough-looking men who silently watched. Philip raced to the bathroom but the door was locked. Alan went to the park office for a key, and the caretaker asked, "Where are you tied up?"

"Over there."

"If I were you, I'd get out of there right away."

He told the others, so they returned more directly by clambering under a fence and skirting a dirty marsh. "Strange place," he said. "I never thought Sausalito could be so sinister. I feel safer on the boat."

Steve distributed sandwiches and Paul handed out candy. "Almond Rocka," Philip read. "This is delicious."

"Roca," said Alan.

"I say Rocka. Thank you for the Rocka, Paul."

"He has good manners. He is a nice boy."

"So is Daniel. You have a nice son."

Paul's expression showed that he didn't need to be told.

"Can we sail under the Golden Gate Bridge, Dad?"

"The wind's against us and the tide's coming in, but we'll try."

"Hi, it's me. Daniel is taking a nap. I'm relaxed, reading my book, making myself a little lunch. I just wanted to say it's very nice to know that besides your life, there's someone who really cares. It's a happy and sweet feeling. That's all, see you tomorrow. Bye."

"We're not going to make it to the bridge, Philip."

"Why not?"

"We just can't make way against the current, sweetheart."

"I really, really want to go under the bridge."

"I know, but we have to get home for dinner."

"Can I have another piece of Almond Rocka?"

"Why don't you save one for Claire?"

"There are three left. Do you want one, Paul? Sharon? Do you, Steve?"

Paul said, "That was a big success, wasn't it?"

They tacked to the cityfront and flew back with the wind

and current. At the cars Paul submitted to Sharon's goodbye kiss and told Steve they really must get together soon, he'd have Olive arrange it.

Alan said, "I'll have to take her sailing now."

Paul turned to uncover his car and didn't reply.

She returned Alan's towel when they met at *Malta* the next day and apologized for the stains that remained after she'd laundered it.

"Forget it. Listen, I have the solution. Paul and Susan should be killed in the same boating accident."

"I'm not shocked," she laughed. "I know you're sweet."

"I actually watched over him more carefully than he could ever have imagined; you never would have believed it was accidental."

"I was thinking the same thing," she laughed. "When the police came I would say yes officer, it was probably my lover who pushed him off."

"You know, I see now that Paul may be boring, but he is decent, honest and solid." It was the best he could find to say.

"Are you sad?"

"Well, I always want more of you than I have."

"You can't eat chocolate all the time. I'm stubborn, and I know this is the right way. I only feel bad because you'll be frustrated there isn't enough sex."

"Well, you may be stubborn, but you do have a wild streak, and sometimes you'll tire of hamburger—"

"—and will want to eat chocolate!"

I lose my senses over the curve of your chin, the oval below your lip, that small detail of your olive face, such a tiny fraction of your body, your soul, your self—merely your sweet chin excites me beyond control.

The curve of your cheek, the slant of your eye, the white when you open it wide… The submarine fish in your mouth that plays with my tongue…

I fade in and out, always intoxicated…

She showed him a note she'd written to Paul:

First of all, this is a friendly letter.

I don't want to start an argument, nor to give you any pressure. Also, I do feel very close and sweet towards you lately and I want to keep feeling this way. But I do think I should let you know something is bothering me; rather than keeping inside and accumulate the anger.

The story is: I would like a little more attention from you. I know your job takes 80% out of you. I support you all the way for working hard. Daniel takes 10% and misc. chores another 5%, so all you have left is 5% for resting. I would like to share the 5% with your magazine.

I was unhappy about yesterday. You came back after a whole day trip and Daniel and I were excited to see you home, you only talked to me few sentences then you were lost in the magazine. I feel you didn't even give me a courteous attention. It is ok to be tired, but I felt sad that to you reading magazine is more soothing than chatting with me.

My feeling is reinforced this morning by talking to Steve. He said a lot of things about the trip and keeping on saying, "Oh, I am sure Paul told you this." I felt sad.

Maybe I am right. Maybe I am all wrong. Maybe I demand too much. Too critical? But if this is how I feel more than once. I should let you work it out with me.

"Should I give it to him?"
"Sure, you have to talk."
"Thank you."
"I love you, you know, and I want the best for you."
She suddenly kissed him. "I don't know why I love you so much. If it doesn't last, it'll be a tragedy."

"I'm opening a package from Jacques," he told her machine. "He thanks us for being kind to Claude, describes life in Libya, blah, blah, blah, now what's this? A jar. Good grief, it's animal parts. Ah, I see, confit de cuisses de canard. Well,

well, duck thighs in grease. And some espadrilles, French sandals, I'll show them to you sometime."

"You were saying you have a bad side I haven't seen. What could it be? You know, once you have a baby you realize bad moods are selfish, it's not fair to the baby, then you see it's not fair to anyone and before you know it you're not the egoist you were. You've changed since high school, my dear, and anyway, I like you as you are. No matter what you do, I'll keep loving you."

"Hi, it's me. You are a sweetie. Bye."

LETTER TO JACQUES

Habibi,

Thanks for the espadrilles and cuisses de canard.

I'm madly in love with a Chinese woman at work, thirty-six, married, eighteen-month son, who madly loves me back. Mei Li is beautiful, good mother, bilingual, likes architecture, music, history, travel, wine, sex—in short, an ordinary person. We've decided not to dismantle our families for a new one together. Actually, I would do it, but she wants her son to have his nuclear family and feels she'd be an ass to divorce her husband only because he's an insensitive boor. Maybe she'll change her mind, but for now that's how it is.

Something that might amuse you: We have long conversations via the marvel of our office answering machines, a droll electronic dimension which complements the physical. I leave a message. She replies and says her husband is out until two. I can't call then but tell her that Susan leaves at three. She goes shopping and reaches me at three-fifteen from the store. Oscillations of an imperfectly elastic system approaching equilibrium.

What of Susan? She knows something happened last spring, believes (I hope) it's over, works with me on our own relationship. An imperfect system approaching what?

Habibi, I no longer know what to expect, nor even what's happening. My reason is escaping. Sometimes I feel the only thing between me and chaos is the act of writing to try and convey this wonder. My life is composed of unconsidered moments: Ecstasy is pure and untempered, but anxiety is unmitigated by reflection. The possibility for pain is boundless. I am without defenses. Everything seems possible.

But I have never lived so profoundly. Is this a mid-life crisis? Am I an adventurer? I'm not seeking sensation for its own sake. I cannot control myself. Is this something that happens to others too? I don't know.

Life continues. We try to feel a bit of it as it goes by. At this moment I am happy. The kids are fine. They're happy, they grow older. We grow older. When Mei Li and I go skiing this winter I'll bring the Sauternes you gave me last year. Have a good summer. Hello to Claude.

They stole kisses all day. "How did Paul react to your note?"

"He was defensive."

"Well, you've planted the seed. Myself, I have mixed feelings," he smiled. "Though it's the right thing to do, I'm not sure how well I want you to get along."

"He told me he thinks the only reason you took him sailing was so you can take me. Sixth sense? I told him maybe instead of Taiwan I should go to Hawaii with him and Daniel. He said yes, we must spend more time together."

"Couples do have to."

"But we're always doing separate things."

"Sure, but you risk falling in love with someone else." She smiled. "Susan told me I should never have an affair—I'm too frank to keep it secret." She giggled.

He counted the ski money. What would he tell Susan when the time came? Who would he be skiing with? He'd need an accomplice she couldn't compare notes with.

"Hi, it's me. Paul came home late, tired, didn't go to the park. No time to talk. Tomorrow after my diet clinic, want to

meet at Five Lakes? It's not far away and also we'll behave! Also
I'd like you to tell me about Alexander the Great's period."

"How much do you weigh today?" he asked.
"One hundred two and a half. Why?"
"I'm writing something for you."
"Paul told me how much he loves me, and he said, 'Daniel
will only be with us twenty years; you and I will be around
long after.'"
"He's wiser than I thought."
"No marriage is perfect. Even between you and me there
might be something that won't work out."
"I can't imagine what."
"Maybe I want a more luxurious life than you."
"I still think we'd be happier with each other."
"Come with me to buy flowers for Susan. You give me
advice about my marriage, I'll help yours." They laughed.
"What do you want to know about Alexander the Great?"
"Theodore told me he's his favorite person, so he must
be a great man."
He gave her a thirty-minute synopsis of Greek history
and they kissed goodbye.

"Hi, it's me. Enjoy so much spending close time with you,
not necessarily rocking the boat time, but civilized talking. I'm
not saying the other part's not… But you know what I mean.
You're my only source I can ask stupid questions. I don't know,
there's a certain spot in my life you fill. Is that telling you no,
you don't fill everything?" She laughed. "We'll never find out
unless we live together, but at this point I assume there will
be some gap, definitely certain areas not going to be perfect.
But, the knowledge you have, the culture you share with me,
I guess we share the spiritual part."
He answered, "I love having someone share my excitement about history and culture. I fill a need for you and you
for me; that's why we're having an affair. Of course we'd find
flaws if we lived together. I'm unresponsive when I'm tired,

and after I've taught you all I know maybe you won't think everything's so wonderful. But I have the romantic notion that a passionate, loving marriage can surmount its partners' imperfections. Will we stay together unmarried? I do hope so.

"I'm reading a history of American sexuality." He read her a paragraph. "It isn't totally your history, my dear, because you're a mixture of two cultures. That's another thing we have in common—I'm a mixture too, of small towns and France and the city."

DYNAMIC GEOMETRY

I weigh 152.5 and you 102.5. Our combined mass of 12.75 stone is sometimes joined by a slightly conical cylinder 6.25 inches long, tapering from a basal circumference of 5.5 inches to 5 just below the lower rim (5.5 again) of the bulbous mushroom at its tip. Its volume is more or less $LC^2/4pi$, or 12.43 cubic inches. At times it's as small as 2.25 inches long by 3.5 around, a volume of 0.97 cubic inches. Since the larger bulk is mostly blood, assume the smaller is muscle, which is 80% water, so actual tissue displaces only some 0.20 cubic inches. The ratio of volumes is less than 2%. Although tissue is denser than water, as we know because the drowned boy sank, let us neglect the difference. Now, blood plasma is 92% water, which weighs 0.036 pounds per cubic inch. Continue to neglect the odd percentage. The full cylinder weighs less than half a pound. During coition, our 255 pounds share one half of a pound in a volume of 12 cubic inches and the mushroom's rim rubs back and forth across the side of your cervix. Have you noticed?

> Susan took a bath and Alan checked his messages.
> "Hi, it's me. They've gone to the park."
> He called her at once.
> "Be careful!" she said.
> "I'm talking to my sister."
> "I'm just thinking of you kissing me..."

"I'm thinking of lying on top of you..."

"Do you lie on top of your sister?" she laughed.

"Oh, Olive."

"Don't call me that!"

"Mei Li, wuo ai ni."

"You're naughty! I was thinking about a plot for your novel, but it's hard. The story doesn't have an end yet."

"Some don't. Anthony Powell wrote a very long book about people slowly changing without end."

"Maybe. But your taste in books is on a high level, like mine for movies. Uh oh, here they come. Bye."

"Hi, it's me. It's been a tiring week. I don't mind busy, I just don't like stressed, feeling incompetent or didn't do things right. Also, Paul couldn't sleep, two o'clock he wakes up, worries about work so it snowballs, so I have to do more, take care of Daniel and chores. The last few years he's jumping from job to job and each time he has to establish himself.

"When I was giving Daniel a bath I was in the mood to sing. I love to sing, especially Chinese songs, but most of the people who lived with me said oh please, would you please not to sing. I know I don't carry the tune, but it doesn't matter. When I'm so happy with nobody listening I make big, loud noises, singing all the way I want. Daniel doesn't mind, he thinks I'm happy and dances along. He's my best audience, I guess.

"So, dear, I'm going to clean up the house and put the dishes in the dishwasher and go to bed. I just love your tenderness. That's the beginning of the story."

She took him shopping for wine and flipped to the back of her address book. "Here's my scorecard. I mark stars for how good they are, but when I started I didn't mark less than three, so now I forget which are the bad ones."

"Why? You didn't want to offend them?"

She giggled and kissed him, bumped and nudged him in the aisles, touched at the checkout stand. "Do you play the lottery? Let's buy a ticket. This will be my first time."

"What would you do if you won?"

"First I will take all the project managers and their families to Hawaii for a party, then I will travel. What about you?"

"I'd donate to the kids' school and Amnesty International, quit work, and write a book."

"How nice. You know, if John Taylor saw us here, I would just tell him we are in love."

He was astounded. "You would?"

"I would." She smiled.

Susan and the kids left before Harry and Steve arrived at his house Saturday for sailing. He played some Scarlatti for them. Olive arrived in a flurry and cheerfully poked around the house, making it something they could talk about in front of others. Alan showed them the duck and espadrilles. Another thing. Then away to the harbor, the other bedroom, the one they couldn't talk about. He recited the drill on man overboard and safety, and off they sailed onto the sparkling bay.

Harry opened a bottle of wine. "Karen took the kids to visit her parents so I'm by myself."

Olive said throatily, "And what are you doing all alone in that big house? Are you having visitors?"

"I rented a video called *Best of Oral*," he smirked. "Want to come over and watch it?"

"No, no!" She laughed.

"Watch it and come?"

"Doesn't it just make you more frustrated?"

"No, it actually gets boring after half an hour."

The bay was choppy and spray flew. Alan gave Olive his slicker and pulled on the pants. They exchanged a look. We're clad in a single outfit. Love danced like Scarlatti on the waves. We are at yet another node in the timeless grid of vaporous intimacy.

As they neared a waterfront bar in Tiburon Alan sheeted the sails and motored in, cut the outboard and hopped off. There was just enough breeze to push the boat away from the pier. He grabbed the stern as the bow swung out and desperately wondered what to do next, while carefully avoiding two hundred curious eyes on the bar's deck above. "Drop your sails, asshole!" somebody yelled. Good idea. He calmly said, "Drop the jib, Steve. Now the main." When the main dropped, so did the boom. Olive and Harry sat quietly intoxicated as lines and sails and boom came down around them.

"That wasn't too cool, was it?" He tried to act sober as he stepped back on to secure things and remove a layer of clothing before following them up the pier.

"Where's Olive?"

"In the bathroom."

"Me too." He went inside and kissed her when she came out. She looked around, led him into a corner, and they embraced breathlessly in front of several crowded tables, then happy and dizzy rejoined the others. Harry scanned the women, Olive drooled over a bunch of bare-chested young men, Alan played her confidante, confident that he was hers. Marvelous how their exaltation was invisible.

Another boat arrived so he went down to make room by moving his. When he returned, Steve said, "Olive went to a bakery."

He waited a beat. "I'm going to have a look outside." He ambled with his beer into the street, didn't see a bakery, crossed and looked back, there it was, went in, there she was choosing pastries, her own beer on the case. "Olive." An open-eyed smile. Put his arm around her. She turned and kissed deeply, a firm writhing eel, muscular and responsive, pressed to his length. The countergirl smiled.

"I always come here with my mother to buy bread."

They were playing at life again, life was a game, they were playing at choosing pastry. She giggled, nothing mattered, reality was Olive, her small taut body, scent in his face, salt on her lips cool and firm and open against his.

"Look at us, carrying beer around like this."

"We're naughty, we're bad. I love you."

"Yes," she drawled throatily, two ascending syllables.

They cast off with more aplomb than they'd docked with. Harry took off his shirt, Steve opened more wine and unpacked sandwiches, Olive fell asleep. Alan gestured to the hills tawny and green nearby and crystalline blue in the distance. "Look at us: Sailing through paradise without a care in the world. We're so fortunate to have the time and money for leisure like this. Think about people in Calcutta, Ethiopia—poor, starving, no potable water—we're the blessed of the earth."

"It's the life of Reilly," said Steve.

Harry nodded. "This is a beautiful place. Clean, light, the weather's always good. Friends from the east always want to move here."

"And it could all change at once," Alan went on. "The nuclear holocaust is only fifteen minutes away. Atmospheric ozone is disappearing. AIDS is killing us, the deserts are expanding, the rainforests are vanishing."

They stared at him.

"Our fortunes can change overnight, you know."

"You're weird," said Harry.

"It just occurs to me now and then." How fragile, how incomprehensible his fortune, his precious sleeping Olive. How little it meant in the blue immensity. How important.

"Come back to earth, Alan. I'll loan you *Best of Oral* to get your mind back on the important things."

He laughed. He could scarcely recall pornography's anonymous friction. Sex and love were inseparable from Olive, the fresh memory of her body against his, her thigh now pressing his as if by chance.

The old immigration center on Angel Island came into view. "Olive." She slept. "Olive," he repeated as on their vinous first night. "Olive, there are the buildings from *The Joy Luck Club*."

She woke in blank inertia. "I feel queasy."

"Can't hold your wine?" Harry asked.

She stared at the buildings. They cleared the island and the wind suddenly hit with spray and heavy chop. "Jesus

Christ, that's cold!" Alan yelled.

"You sissy," said Harry. "Look at me, bare-chested."

"It's sobering me up, at least." The lee gunwale was under water. "We should reef the main, but let's have dessert instead."

Olive passed him the sack. "I can't eat anything."

Oh, don't get sick. Let this be a perfect day.

"I have to pee. Don't look." She went below.

Why look? I know what I'd see.

She came out wearing the white pants. "I'm so smart, I brought a change of clothes." She sounded better.

"I have to pee, too," said Harry. He crawled forward to stand on the bow. Alan joined him. "Don't look."

"No," she drawled.

In the city's lee the wind dropped off, blocked by the buildings but gusty when they passed the streets, calm, gusty, calm. They motored to the slip and put things away. Alan hosed off the boat in an alcoholic haze, swaying from fatigue. His foot slid off the pier into the water and his shin struck the edge with a sharp pain.

Harry laughed. "Some sailor you are. Can't even step off a boat!"

It hurt like hell but he was too drunk to tell how much. "I'm making a habit of this, huh, Steve?"

He limped up the pier and went to the bathroom with Harry and Steve, finished hastily and rushed out to Olive, turned her face and kissed her solidly. She turned away and he turned to face the men's room, saw Steve walk out look-ing toward them: time stopped: began again with the thick creep of cold molasses: he continued turning, took two steps away and leaned against the railing and stared toward the boats. She turned her back.

No one said anything.

Jesus Christ, what have I done.

He was afraid to move. Now what? This cannot now be undone. What will I say I was doing? This won't go away, will it. What did he see?

After some time (how much, not much, enough to begin

CHAPTER 15

Hi, it's me. They just headed to the park, won't have much of a chance to talk. I really think he saw something though not the whole thing, but he saw something unusual, because his expression is half smile half puzzled. So I assume he saw most of it to rouse his suspicion. I don't think Steve is the kind of person who will ever bring it up, but he will start to feel curious.

"One thing good is we weren't kissing. I mean I wasn't kissing you too, it's you kissed me. It's one-sided action, not like we fell in love with each other. Actually it's not that unusual, other people at B&M used to like me a lot, just say you were a little bit drunk, you fell in the bay, you came up with that crazy thing.

"Don't ever do risky things like this. I feel okay, don't feel bad about that. I don't know what to do right now, in the office, how do we want to handle this. Think about it. Not to worry until we figure out what to do. Anyway, I care a lot about you, see you, bye."

Susan left and Alan patiently played with Claire and Philip until he could announce bedtime and reply. "Maybe Steve saw me kiss you and maybe he didn't. If he didn't, then nothing has changed and we can stop worrying. If he did, maybe he didn't believe it. I think all he saw was me moving away from you. Maybe he's passing curious about why I was so close, so we'll have to be careful in front of him, business-like, nothing warm, and after a while his curiosity will wane.

I think everything's okay. I'll stop acting so foolishly at work. You're absolutely right, it's not worth the risk—a goofy moment exchanged for complete disaster."

He hung up and tried to play piano but was woozy with booze and sailing and worry, tried to read but couldn't concentrate.

"Olive, my dear, my love, I must feel the way you did when Susan walked in. This shocked the hell out of me. I promise you, I promise us, that I'll stop doing such foolish things. I keep getting greedy. Forgive me. I know what we have to do, but I keep pushing. I'm sorry."

He slept fitfully, played and replayed the scene, turned again from Olive and saw the door open and Steve step forward, imagined stepping out the door, tried to see what Steve could have seen, did see, saw, seesawed between dream and memory until he got carefully out of bed at five and telephoned from the living room. "I have the answer. Honor would compel me to apologize to you and tell Steve I acted unilaterally. So pretend I apologized. Now, should you tell him I did or should I? Or would it draw his attention? Let me know what you think." Then to get her mind on other things and remind her of the wider world and why she liked him, he told the Circe and siren stories. Very appropriate.

"Hi, it's me. Yeah, sometimes you do silly things, like touch me under the table. I don't blame you. It's like if I look at your face after having intimate things with you, I just all concentrate on you and not think about the world any more. There's so much feelings, wanting, desire, and so much restraints, you wish you could be free and you start doing dangerously.

"The whole thing is not so bad. If you and I are passionately kissing, that would be the end. But I know Steve. Even if he saw what he saw, he's such a discreet person he wouldn't say a thing to me, to you, not especially to Paul, might not even to Sharon. Only thing is he'll wonder if there's something going on between us, so we'll have to do even more careful show in front of him. Basically I agree with the scene you come up with. I might talk to him, say you were really drunk and see how he reacts, shows different facial expression. Don't say anything until I find out.

"I think the camping with Paul is a three day trip, we're leaving Friday. The last day I'll see you is Thursday, then you're on vacation two weeks. Monday I have errands if you want to come. Reserve Wednesday lunchtime, I have a plan, I should do it before you go away. Bye, dear."

Later that afternoon: "Hi, it's me. I can't believe I did a nice conversation and accidentally erased it. I guess you can't hear all the good things I said. Basically the feeling about possibly might not be able to do what we're doing makes me very sad... I can't imagine that.

"I was saying besides the love, the careness, we like the history part, music, the thinking. It adds so much meaning to my life. I really am happy and enjoy being with you. The love part makes me feel valuable and special that someone in the world cares about me this much. I'm sure you do too, but I put more restraints on myself. I do get affected by other people's—" Noise in the background. "Anyway, basically that's what I was thinking. Somehow we really have to make sure—" More noise. "Got interrupted by Daniel. I want to keep this going for many, many years. That's why I want to have a steady and very calm situation.

"What other good things did I say? Trying to do it again, being disturbed by Daniel, can't put it very well together now. Anyway, miss you. Bye, dear."

So she wasn't drawing back. It was a transient spike on the curve; though the function was unstable, it wasn't discontinuous. As long as Steve hadn't noticed.

He went to work, waited for Olive to arrive, and walked around.

Steve laughed at him. "You can't stay out of the bay, can you?"

"I sure got drunk."

"You did?"

Olive said, "It was a fun day, but I felt queasy after

drinking so much."

"Poor thing," Steve said. They chatted. He seemed perfectly normal. The only way to know for sure was to ask but that was out of the question. As usual, the only certainty was uncertainty.

Olive gave him ten dollars, her calendar, and a note from Fern. Her calendar showed lunch on *Malta,* busy afternoon, Tuesday meetings, Wednesday morning seminar together and noon to three, "Save this time. I have a plan." Thursday morning staff meeting. At four, "Get together?" Friday, "Camping trip. I'm gone, your last day."

Fern's note asked for help editing a love letter to Bob. Alan felt flattered, vaguely avuncular, and enchanted by her ingenuous candor compared with the ruses of himself and her sister, who told him at lunch, "I don't know if she should keep chasing this guy Bob. He doesn't seem to want anything more than be friends."

"Well, she may get hurt, but it's how she'll learn."

"She told me, this is funny, 'I'm lucky I can go out with anyone I like, but you can't, you have a husband and family.'" They laughed pleasantly. "Why do you like me so much?"

He leaned against the cockpit. "I can share my deepest impressions with you: this seat hard beneath us, this winch in my ribs, the wind cooling my face, the stays clanking, the birds, the blue sky and the bridge, your scent. When we're together everything is completely here now."

"Can't you tell things like this to Susan?"

"She says don't be silly, be practical. Olive, what matters is how much I like you, not why. Why do you ask?"

"I think on a ten scale you love me six, but it moves up because you're not able to see me as much as you want. Suppose you don't eat sugar for ten years and then you get some yogurt—you'll think it's your best ever dessert."

"This is more than that, Olive," he said unhappily.

"In Taiwan I fell in love with a boy on the bus. I always get excited before his stop and when he got on I'm really melting! I even love his hand holding the strap. I loved him more because I couldn't meet him."

Had she forgotten she'd told him this?

"Here in America you go to a bar, meet a girl, trade names, find out there's some interest, go dancing. Before you know it, it's all over, you're in bed. No love."

He didn't want to discuss the role of adversity in his love; he wanted affirmation of hers. "Why do you love me?"

"Sometimes you say or do things that are exactly what I'm thinking. During the ski trip dinner, I thought maybe you'll spend the night and come to my bed. Saturday I was thinking you might come out of the bathroom and kiss me."

"Isn't it amazing?"

"This morning I can't stand it anymore, so I went up close to Steve and talk low, 'Wasn't Alan drunk?' He said, 'No, I think Alan and Susan are different from us, they drink a little and think they're really drunk.' And I said, 'No, but I really think he was… He fell off the dock…' And he said, 'Well, he didn't seem to be.' I gave him chance to react, don't you think? I opened my eyes wide but he didn't say anything. I don't think he saw, but I want to act like he did. This is so fragile it can break in a second. I can't get over when Susan walked in. All that day we're touching, I'm holding your face in my hands. At that very instant I was standing up and you were writing. God's really watching over us."

God or not, they'd had some mighty good luck.

He enjoyed the seminar on diversity in the workplace, the presentation about changing demographics and cross-cultural miscommunication, approved of trying to understand other points of view, agreed that listening was vital, and liked watching Olive. He was delayed meeting her afterwards a few blocks away by police directing traffic around a motorcycle accident and mused on the good fortune that preserved him from death and dismemberment.

"Where are we going?" he asked when he got into her car.

"To Fern's. What did you think of the seminar?"

"I liked it. It was better than most."

"I think it's stupid we can't even make jokes now."

"There's plenty besides race to joke about."

"They're too sensitive. I don't mind if somebody jokes about Chinese."

She was forgetting Paul's jokes about Chinatown. "When you consider the discrimination some people have experienced, I see how they could take a joke as an insult."

"I am foreign but I never felt discrimination. They're being stupid. They're making something out of nothing."

"Do you really think so? Haven't you ever felt you weren't being taken seriously because you're a woman?"

"People have to listen to me. I'm the project manager."

"Sure, you're in a powerful position, well-educated, attractive and well-spoken. But many people never had your opportunities and don't even know how to begin."

"Well, if they can't take a joke, that's their problem, not mine."

She did have a scornful streak that must be reinforced by Paul's arrogance. He'd noticed a disdain for the clerical staff and a cavalier attitude with waiters. He dropped it.

"This is Fern's last business trip for a while. I don't know what we'll do after this."

"There's always *Malta*."

"Yes…"

He wondered what scruples accounted for her laying a towel on the living room carpet this time instead of the bed. He skinned off her bra and panties. Her pink and pearly gray lips parted and protruded like an anemone from her central mound, that tangled private nest, silent, magnetic, which sought his kiss… Her thighs embraced his temples…

"Tell me about your fantasies," she murmured an hour later.

"Ah, there are so many… Right now I'd like to watch a skin flick with you and Fern. You and I would kiss and touch, get really excited, undress, make love. But what would Fern do?"

"She could have Bob!"

They laughed. "I want to hear about your gay experiences."

Rather than waste good foreplay material in their present afterglow, he gave her a PG trailer for an X movie later: A couple horny evenings with friends, looking up a coworker for relief, a night in a motel hitchhiking.

"Did you like it?"

"I never really got turned on. Men's bodies are too familiar, too like my own. It's like masturbation, exciting but lacking the strange mystery of union with an alien. Now if there were a woman there too..."

"You're so adventurous! Paul would never in his life dream of doing that."

"Would you?"

"I don't think so. Maybe. If the situation was just right and the right person."

She kissed him, grew aroused again, made love again entangled in the electrical cords. How funny we are, we always wear our wedding rings.

She smiled. "That was a lifetime first."

"What?"

"Two orgasms in one time."

"You sweetheart."

"I'm hungry. Let's go eat."

He was sorry to shower off the smell of love so soon.

"I was telling Susan how fortunate I feel. When I see the homeless, I think there but for the grace of God go I. The line between our happy existence and theirs is so thin it frightens me. 'Don't you think so?' I asked.

"'No,' she said, 'never, someone will always help.'

"'What if I died, your family died, you were blinded, your investments failed, you lost the house and couldn't get a break,' I asked, 'you never worry about things like that?'"

"'No. I'm educated, I'm white, I have friends. That's nonsense, that grace of God business.' I was very surprised."

Olive shrugged. "I often think I'm lucky. Everything can change so fast."

He took her hand. "I'm so very happy with you in this moment shared out of all the uncertainty of our lives."

"It's four o'clock. I'm not going back."

"Sometimes I worry about being away so much."

"Think of all the talking to Mike or driving to meetings. This is just time we're not wasting there."

As she drove back to his car he laughed. "You and I didn't need that seminar this morning. We already have our own intercultural exchange of body fluids."

"Do you have any dirty magazines?"

"Yes... Why?"

"Where do you keep them?"

"In a drawer under the bed."

"We keep a stack in a closet where Daniel can't reach. I don't know what we'll do when he's older."

"You have porno magazines?"

She kept her eyes on the road. "Yes. I take one to the living room after they're asleep. Sometimes after I'm done I'm so relaxed I fall asleep and put it under the couch and forget. I wonder what our cleaning lady thinks. She's an old Chinese lady, very proper. She never said anything but next day it's back in the closet." She smiled. "Paul buys the magazines. I'm embarrassed to do that, but he's embarrassed to pick out the videos. It doesn't bother me. I just make my choice with these big guys in there. It's funny."

"Oh Olive, how delightful!" He imagined her, composed, matter of fact, briskly making her selection, a wholesome woman with depraved tastes.

"I can give you some of my magazines."

"I'd love it."

"I just give them to Fern after I'm done, anyway. I'll mark the pictures I like."

"Ooh, what fun! I can't wait to see what turns you on! I'll do it to you."

He was too intoxicated with her to go directly home, so he bought some cigarettes and smoked one and walked around to readjust his frame of mind.

Susan met him at the door with a kiss. "You smell like garlic."

"It must be the Chinese food I had for lunch." He took another shower and ate another meal.

"I saw the worst motorcycle accident on the way to work," she said.

"Really? Where?"

"By the park on Dolores Street."

"What time?"

"Just before noon. The motorcycle was on the ground, and they were putting the rider into the ambulance."

"Good grief, motorcycles are dangerous."

"It made me very upset."

"I'll bet." It would have been more upsetting if she'd seen them go by five minutes later.

"I'm sorry we haven't had more fun this week with the kids at camp. It was a chance to do something, but I'm so busy teaching, you know. Away nights, or doing lesson plans."

"That's okay. It doesn't matter."

"It does matter. I don't want you to be out having an affair."

"Don't worry."

"You wouldn't tell me if you were, would you?"

"No," he smiled. "You wouldn't want me to, would you?"

"No."

She left to teach. Olive called, Paul wasn't home yet, they talked, Paul arrived, they hung up. He left a message about love, sex, odor, Proust and his madeleine, humor in literature, Henry Miller on the smell of sex. She called back when Paul took Daniel to the park.

"Susan told me she's afraid I might have an affair."

"You know, I'm not jealous of her, but if you go to Europe together I would be."

"Why, she'd be sharing something you want to?"

"Maybe. I don't know. I'm too tired to think."

"Will you miss me when I'm gone?"

"I don't know. I haven't thought about it much. I'll find out next week."

Paul returned, they hung up. She wasn't jealous of Susan, but he was jealous of Paul, that callous idiot who didn't know what a jewel he possessed.

"Hi, dear, it's me. I was watching a program about China somewhere in Yunnan Province, and it's so pretty with the Chinese music. I really want to go with you. So, somehow you got to, we got to make it work, okay? Bye."

Still nothing peculiar on the Steve front. He must have seen nothing after all.

Olive was sunny during the staff meeting and he had to stop looking at her and remembering how her insides felt so his thoughts wouldn't be on display when everyone stood to go. They rendezvoused later at a music practice room on campus where he finally played his avowal directly to her smiling eyes. As they walked to the garage she said wearily, "I'm so busy, shopping for the camping trip, buying toys for Daniel, other chores, trying to find time for my lover…"

A cloud on the horizon, her weariness, but when they met later at the Cliff House she sat close and talked about his vacation. "Will we miss each other?"

"I know I will," he said.

"Well, don't think about it. Just have a good time and when you come back you'll be all rested."

"I hope I won't find you don't want to continue."

"Who knows? I don't know what I'll think when you're not around for two weeks."

The clouds rolled in and out. "I'll leave messages whenever I can. When Susan joins us next week, though, don't feel bad if you don't hear from me."

"I won't. Don't worry. And if you don't have much money, use our ski money for the phone calls."

"That's for skiing, not phone calls."

"Why are you so gentle?"

Her tenderness surprised him. "Because you give it back. You give me so much."

"No matter what happens, we will always be special friends."

It was more like fog, advancing and retreating. He pulled

her to embrace before they separated. She drew away like she had last spring, but then closed with him for a deep kiss. They drove along the beach again but this time side by side, until he honked and turned off and she waved goodbye.

"Hi, it's me. Not much, just to say hi. And, maybe I'll be the one who misses you like crazy. But anyway, I do want to emphasize again that whatever we went through a lot of worry time, uncertain time, ups and downs, I really felt good about having you in my life, because your tenderness and your caring and your such a love makes me feel so happy, and life is wonderful because of that. Anyway, just wanted to say that. Bye."

Her grammar drove him crazy. Did she mean "feel good" or was "felt good" a revealing slip? He replayed it. Did he detect a note of finality? The messages always raised concerns that only her presence could assuage since her expression clarified her meaning, although his presence probably overwhelmed any doubts she had, and her presence overwhelmed his acuity. Maybe slips on the telephone communicated more truly than speech face to face. The whole damned thing seemed as uncertain as ever.

She called him at the office from home in the morning and asked, "What did you do last evening?"

He hesitated. "Susan and I made love." He was going to say that she was incomparably better, it was more obligation with Susan than pleasure, but while he paused she said, "I read in *Joy Luck Club* when the mother throws her ring in the sea where her son drowned, her hopeless sacrifice to change fate."

"When it's too late. I know. It's like trying to say goodbye. I want to say something meaningful, but there's nothing except that I'll miss you."

"I'll miss you too," she said affectionately.

He put the records from a music appreciation course Susan had taken into a drawer at her desk as a surprise and reminder of him during his absence, and went to lunch.

"Hi, it's me. Actually a silly thing, it didn't set very well when I heard about you and Susan. For some reason, I guess ups and downs, I don't feel too… I don't know… Don't worry about it, I know inside how you feel so it's just a minor thing. So anyway, have a good trip, don't worry about me, I'll be here and I will be happy to see you when you're back. Bye, dear."

He didn't want that to be her last impression, so he called immediately. "Olive, I'm sorry I told you."

"It's okay, forget it."

"I left a surprise in your drawer."

"What is it?

"You have to wait until Monday."

"Say hi to your parents for me."

"Okay."

"No, don't really!"

"I talk about you so much they know you already."

"Oh Alan, I don't know if you should."

Finally they said goodbye the final time.

CHAPTER 16

Olive seldom actually read a book; she rented tapes to listen to in the car. She loaned Alan a history of the Mediterranean for the long drive to San Diego. Dates and names and thoughts of her at some campground in the Sierras blurred together while Claire and Philip sat uninterested in the back of the van. They arrived at his parents, hugged, unpacked, strolled to the beach, ate dinner, chatting about everything except the only thing that mattered. When the kids went to bed he left a message for Olive to hear when she returned from camping and called Susan to say they'd arrived safely.

He bodysurfed to exhaustion and sprawled on a towel, cast off from the present, blind to the future, numbly adrift in chilling wind and clammy salt. His parents, their house, their town, his children—all were familiar but he was alone. He wanted to talk but found nothing to say. He could describe Olive (though her qualities were irrelevant), but even knowing her and him (though he hardly knew himself), how could they comprehend? It was incommunicable.

Describe her family: Son, husband, husband's brother, sister in Lebanon; it would mean nothing to his parents, their son's lover's husband's family. Her parents, her sister's failed marriage, her other sister, nephew, brother-in-law. What did it even mean to him? He was not part of it.

Her friends: One married couple, one bachelor, another couple or two, infrequent visitors from Taipei. She had few friends and there was nothing special about them. Her hobbies? Wine, opera, flowers, books on tape, her weight, shopping, her lover... She was a very ordinary person.

Their love, then? But there was no story, no motion, no change, only a poem of deepening passion whose details meant nothing to anyone else.

It was like falling off a cliff. A person on the ground, his parents, say, might notice two specks moving down against the granite backdrop but wouldn't hear the rushing air or grow accustomed, as he was, to its muted chord. Meanwhile the falling couple had no clue as to their height, and the cliff's face was beginning to look like a landscape seen from an airplane. Maybe their lives had become perpendicular to the earth; maybe they were flying; they might be orbiting. Only time would tell.

"Hi, it's me. We're home. Daniel must be going to his terrible twos, he did a lot of testing. Fern said nice things about you. I'm tired, bye."

He was in Ensenada with his parents and kids. She'd be at work. She would savor these foreign smells and sounds. He bought her a pair of onyx earrings and wondered where to hide them while camping with Susan next week. The kids were buying earrings for her. He bought a teapot.

"Hi, it's me. At lunch the others ask me to go with them but I declined. They joked I must have a date! I did miss you today. Bye, dear."

"Mom says she's happy for us. I think my dad disapproves, but he's tactful enough to say nothing, or maybe he hasn't paid attention. He doesn't pay attention to Mom, and in fact she told me she's wondering if she'd be happier living alone. I told her that you and I have talked about meeting in Coronado and she said she'll babysit for us if we need it. She's on our side, my dear."

"Hi, it's me. We were surprised to see Daniel this weekend not being an angel. Still, it's a nice thing to do, camp—once a year! I'll go to the wine store at lunch for my supplies. Borders & Marshall's party is on Friday, I'll drink for you.

Don't think about me too much. Clear your head. Is this really what you want? It's like clearing your palate, drinking a lot of water. Bye."

Clear my palate? Is it that you only want what's best for me? (All I want is you.) Or would you like me to discover that I want you less than I thought? (It would simplify your life.) Are you trying to wean me? I'm so confused.

"Hi, it's me. I went to the wine store today. Just buying wine makes me happy. It's almost as good as buying fresh flowers, so I still have hope, right? I've had some questions about your projects. It's fun, able to talk about you legitimately. This Sunday Paul's going to the car race. Daniel and I might visit my sister. What has Susan been doing? Have you talk to her? Of course you have. Well, bye."

He hadn't talked to Susan. Hers was not the voice he craved. He called Olive at the office next morning to chat. "So do you miss me after all?" he asked.

"Tell you the truth, with work routine and your desk right there, I probably don't miss you the way you miss me. It was funny talking to your telephone next to me."

"I bet. Well, I really will be out of touch next week."

"Well, we'll live through it. Enjoy yourself." She seemed a bit curt, but then, she was at work, and they had talked for quite a while.

"Hi, it's me. I hope I didn't sound unfriendly this morning, I was in a work attitude. You can think about this: At lunch I went to Five Lakes Restaurant and I sat where we sit and ate the food we eat and read *Joy Luck Club,* and when I got to the part she finds out why her mother left behind her children, I start to cry, just sob with a napkin. These days, anything with babies touches me deeply. So, I left the restaurant with tears in my eyes. Bye."

Good, good, but it would have been better if it was his absence and not babies. "For some reason Dad wants all us kids to know that clinical depression can be treated with drugs. I told him not to worry about me—I'm crazy, not depressed. I'll try calling you at home tomorrow evening."

His sister Berenice arrived, another familiar face that felt somehow insufficient. They walked through a salt marsh and he told her he was in love, but he couldn't convey what it meant. It didn't even seem real to him. He grasped at the wind for words to embody his feelings but they skittered away like birds in the bushes. It would only make sense if she knew Olive. When you come to San Francisco, he said, we'll find some excuse for you to come to my office and you'll meet her. Berenice expressed neither surprise nor shock. She said fine, I'll look forward to it, I wish you my best.

"Hi, it's me. I can't talk to you tonight. Daniel's invited to a party for a neighbor boy, so we're going there. Here comes Paul now. Bye."

Toward the end of the week Philip asked, "When you and Mom get together, are you going to fight?"

My poor dear. "No," was all he found to say.

He needed to hear Olive's voice so he went out for milk and called the office. "Hello, darling. This may be our last chance to talk."

She told him about Daniel's party and asked, "So are you looking forward to Susan?"

"No, I'm worried. The night before we left, she was angry that we were going without her although we'd planned this months ago, and she doesn't like my family anyway. She was so mad she slept in the living room and didn't even say goodbye to me."

"Tell you the truth, I'm not jealous of her camping with you, not like if you're going to Europe."

Love, love, love and then goodbye. And then return with the milk and call Susan.

She was cold at first. Then she said, "I bought something at Victoria's Secret."

He was surprised. "I can't wait!"

"Well, I'm not going to bring it camping. I'm not going to have any of that, camping. Not without a shower nearby."

"Well, see you tomorrow."

They went to the beach. When Claire and Philip left the water Alan swam beyond the waves into the swell where he floated up and down watching the horizon contract and expand and contract, then paddled back to where the swell met the bottom and cast himself onto the rolling liquid slope aware of only cold water and motion and the air breaking above, and then out again and in, swept along the beach as far as the jetty where he crawled numb onto hard sand and walked back and waved to his family, went out again and dove and bobbed in and out of the waves until he was caught and smashed in twisting forces of fluid and sand and surfaced and stood disoriented, senseless, numb, half-blind. He'd lost a contact lens.

When he could move again he staggered to a pay phone and called Olive. "Wait a minute," she said, and to someone in the background, "Shall I get back to you?"

"I miss you. Do you miss me?"

She laughed.

"Can you say yes or no?"

She only laughed.

"Okay, goodbye."

Back home he put in an old spare contact. Things were out of focus, out of kilter, and he couldn't regain his balance.

He checked his machine the next morning while the others said goodbye. "Hi, it's me. I couldn't talk yesterday because John Taylor was at my desk, and Steve, Mike and Harry were there. Then I didn't get home until nine after B&M's party last night. Paul is in the shower. If you're still there, this is for you. Bye."

Aahhh.

Susan hopped in at the airport without looking at him. His heart sank. "How are you?" he asked. He leaned to kiss her but she turned so his lips met her hair.

She shrugged. "I've been alone for a week and it'll take me a while to get used to people again."

Philip climbed into her lap and she held him woodenly.

Claire gave her the teapot and earrings and asked if she could wear silver posts. "No." After a moment she put them on.

"Which route shall we take?" Alan asked.

"I don't care."

They drove in silence for a while. "Shall I open the window?" she asked.

"Sure, if you want."

She didn't move. There was noise in the back seat and she said, "Philip, leave Claire alone."

"She's bothering me."

"I am not!"

Susan asked, "Would you like the window open?"

"I don't care. If you do, go ahead and open it."

"Mom, Philip's pushing me."

"Philip, read a book."

"She won't give me one."

"Claire, why are you doing this to me?"

Alan unrolled the window.

"So you did want the window open!"

"It's getting hot."

She looked up from the map. "I see the mountain beyond the road over there."

Not knowing what she meant, he said, "That's nice."

"Did you say that in a mean way?" Claire asked.

"No."

"He didn't say that in a mean way," Claire told Susan.

"What?" Susan said.

"Never mind," Alan told Claire. Things felt wrong and he didn't know how to right them. Everything was as blurred as his vision.

When they unloaded at a campground that afternoon, he discovered that he'd brought only one tent.

"How could you do that?" Susan shrieked. "You were supposed to bring both!"

"I don't know how I missed it. I'm an idiot."

"What are we supposed to do now? We can't stay here.

You've ruined our vacation!"

"I'm sorry, but look, two of us can sleep in the van and two in the tent."

"We can not. I don't want the kids apart from us."

"We can each sleep with one of the kids."

"We'll have to go home now."

"Oh Susan, you choose the tent or the van, and I'll take the other."

"And where will the kids sleep?""

"Well, one in the van and one in the tent."

"Oh, all right. Go to town and buy some food."

Philip drank a soda on a bench outside the store and he drank a beer and smoked a cigarette until he felt calm enough to return. They avoided each other the rest of the evening.

Susan complained about the heat in Death Valley. She got crankier when the air conditioning at the visitors center didn't work. He tried to enjoy the kids, but they'd missed her for a week and wanted to be with her, so he wandered off alone. It felt like they were on separate vacations.

If Olive were here, we'd park at some cliff overlooking a hundred miles of glorious desolation, we'd play the *Four Last Songs* and we'd feel grand.

She never said she missed me. And she wouldn't say she loves me. Why is it so important that she say the words? She shows it by her actions—she did, after all, risk a call while her husband showered. I should relax. If I seem insecure she'll wonder why she risks so much for such a neurotic weakling. I've got to be fun for her, but I'm losing my sense of humor. Where's my perspective? Where's my irony? I should put things into compartments the way she does.

"Whenever you spend time with your family, you're really mean," Susan said. "They're so thoughtless and selfish, don't you think?"

"How should I answer that?"

"What do you mean?"

"Well, you've just said some very unkind things. Should I agree, or argue, or what?"

She handed him a book. "Maybe you should read this. There's a lot that applies to us." It was pop psychology about triangles among spouses, parents, siblings and lovers. He found nothing germane and wondered what triangles she saw.

Olive/Paul/Alan: Feminine, caring, sensitive, feeling / Masculine, ambitious, upright, unfeeling / Arty, sensitive, successful, virile: Alan's androgyny appeals to Olive; Paul's steadfast predictability to her; her complaisance to Paul, and to Alan; and so on.

Susan/Alan/Olive: Impotently rebellious against female subservience, demanding, bossy / Likes femininity and self-assurance / Career gives her the self-assurance to be happily feminine: Olive likes masculine men; Susan wants to be masculine.

My relationship with Susan has clearly degenerated. Olive asked if I try less with Susan because of her. I said no, but it's probably true. I don't need to build with Susan what Olive gives me. Olive never asks. She gives (blow jobs, lunch, money, time) and I try to give her pleasure in return. Whereas Susan's disappointment and exasperation preclude pleasure. To her I give commiseration. I even solicit her recitals of discontent, since sharing her tribulations shows that I care—though I'm not as good as I was—I grunt with irritation too often. Philip must have learned his complaining about aches and pains from her. I should give him more attention. I should give her more, too.

Her life is a series of problems so all I expect from anyone is complaint. Olive keeps her few problems to herself. Do I still know how to relate to someone without problems? I'm unaccustomed to someone interested in me for myself. Is she really interested in me? Is pleasure all she wants? Well, isn't that enough? What is there in life except birthdays and pleasure? She and Paul might be right.

My relationship style has become based on mutual self-support. I'm crippled, I cry and ask for comfort, I ask do you miss me—no it's not that bad yet, when we're together I'm myself, I'm whole and natural, but when we're apart I doubt my mental health. Stop this. I must relax. Remember, we're consenting adults, no claims, no dependence. Operative word is adult. And Olive is not Susan. Lighten up, Alan. Or you're gonna lose that girl.

Susan asked, "How can we change things between us?"

"Well, maybe we could choose one particular thing to work on, something small, within our power to change."

"What about something big?"

"I'm willing to try, but we seem to have a hard time with big things."

"I have a proposal. I want you to listen and not say anything. What if we let each other spend a night away from the house now and then, with anyone we want. It would be okay for either of us to have affairs."

He was speechless.

"I want you to sleep on it and tell me tomorrow. Now I'm going to bed."

Was she serious? Was she having an affair? Oh, wouldn't that be nice! Did she want to have one? Why did she suggest it? And if it didn't work? Well, could things get any worse? He couldn't sleep soundly and kept mistaking Philip's form beside him in the tent for Olive's. He wanted to tell her at once. Now if something could be done about Paul...

In the morning he said, "Let's try it. There are two rules I'd like to suggest. One, we are each other's number one partner. If one of us needs the other for any reason, illness, I don't know, the plans have to be canceled."

"Okay. What's the other?"

"We don't tell more than the other wants to know."

"Good. I'm glad I don't know any more than I do about your thing. Also, if we don't want to tell, we don't have to."

"Fine."

"This must not become a competition."

"Good lord, no."

He left them watching TV in a motel that night and found a phone. "Here's great news: Susan proposed that she and I can spend time with other people overnight! And she may take the kids away next week. Do you want to spend a night at my house? Tell Paul you're at Fern's. If he calls there, she can say you're in the shower, then call us, and you call him back. Think about it. Now I'll listen to your messages." There were none. He was puzzled. Well, it was only Tuesday. She was probably taking a break, clearing her palate. "No message, you naughty girl. Too bad you're not here. We could paint the landscape, the pure, colorless desert light and the sharp, high altitude mountain sky. From the bristlecone pine forest in Nevada I looked across the valley to the Sierras. It reminded me of a picture in your album and of *Im Abendrot's* vast opening chords, and two larks flying in the twilight…"

They camped again. Susan hiked off while he and the kids played in a stream. He thought about his next message. In the morning he called when he and Philip drove to town for pastry. No messages for him. "Happy five month anniversary. Will you think about our first night during the staff meeting this morning? Have you used our time apart to order your feelings? Have they changed? Mine have not, and I've realized how strong they are. Are everyone's as intense? Are you thinking about what to do with my free time next week? I can't wait to see you Monday. Bye. I love you."

They visited a fishery, swam in a hot spring, looked at rock formations, and though he always liked being outdoors and stretching his eyes to the horizon, solitude and geology didn't suit his mood. The empty space was filled with anxiety about Olive. He'd be better off in a strange city distracted by his own species.

Summer turned to fall with the sunset that day. It got cold. They went to town and visited stores to warm up. He was bored so he went outside. A pay phone tempted him, but Susan could walk out any time. He paced indecisively and then couldn't stand it. He dialed. Still no messages. He spoke. "I'm worried. If you're okay, leave a message."

Susan walked out. "Who are you talking to?"

"Oh, Art Laguna was so worried about a project that he wanted me to check for messages now and then."

She laughed. "Poor Art!"

The van had a flat tire when they checked into a motel in Reno. Alan rolled the tire to a service station and immediately went into the casino next door, got some quarters and found a phone.

"Hi, it's me, finally. Well, it has been an interesting time. I had a chance to examine the whole thing with perspective, without being confused with emotions, passions, all that. My feelings in these two weeks are first of all, I don't have any resentment towards Paul and not much complaints, and think he's okay. You know why? Because I'm not comparing him with you.

"Also, putting how great we match aside, how much fun we have, analyzing that yes, my marriage is eighty/twenty, I really don't think I should make up my unhappy twenty percent by you, or compare your strong point to his weak point, or enjoy in you the things I miss from him. Because by doing that, I'm stepping out with my foot on each boat. Eventually it's not going to work. Either I jump this boat and get onto another, or stay with the first one. Tell the truth, I think it's not fair to you, because—" The recording time limit was reached.

Family at a motel up the street in a strange town. Phenomenal din of slot machines. Phone against shoulder to ear, finger plugging the other. Hand over mouthpiece to cut the noise.

"Well, you should know what I think. I never say it but I love him very much. That's hard to swallow maybe. I have feelings for you too, but he is after all my husband.

"The other thing, it's not fair to him. No matter what fault he has, he basically is a good father and faithful husband. And maybe it's not fair for myself. Because of you I'm not working hundred percent towards my marriage. I should try everything until I just don't love him anymore. Then I get out and start new.

"There will be ups and downs for me because he doesn't share my part about reading, history, music, and even more your basic caring. Even though I feel missing from him on that part, basically I'm contented for the last many years. I do feel clear and pretty feel strongly about this. I have a lot of responsibility with Daniel and my marriage is not that bad, like you. So I want to give it a fair chance.

"Between you and me I don't know what to do yet, but I don't want any more serious passion things. I want to get back to good friends, even we could go out to lunch and—" The limit was reached and she reconnected. "Well, we can still enjoy our interests together, except the passion. I don't know, when you go beyond that stage can you come back to the previous? But anyhow, I still want to be friendly.

"It seems devastating, and especially what you went through with Susan, that's too bad. Ironically you finally get your freedom but you don't need it. But on the other hand you will see this is really much better. At least much better for me. It's very hard, but I really think I've been fair with myself. Anyway, if you put everything aside, you might find I'm not that wonderful. Always like I said, you deserve a hundred percent from somebody as nice as me and can be your wife. That's what you should go look for.

"Sorry about not calling sooner and, uh, sorry to tell you all this. Bye." She kissed the telephone, or sobbed, or something.

One more message. "Well, after all that serious stuff, I just wanted to say cheer up! Don't feel too serious. You know, everything depends on how you look at it. If you treat it sad and serious that's one thing, or you can look at it more upbeat and cheerful way. The whole thing came, to me at least, in a light-hearted casual way, like a French film type of thing, déjà vu or whatever you call it, and it could end that way too. It's not the end of the world.

"I still care about you very, very much. We cannot be lovers, but we can be very close friends. I want to let it go as light-hearted and cheerful just like a French film. That's the good thing about being flexibly and upbeat and different. That's what we should try, anyway. Bye."

Return to motel, change into swim suit, join kids in pool. Go to room, take shower. Cry in shower. This drawing away has happened twice before, but this is probably really it, this time. I just don't have luck with love. Well, what else could have happened? She could have died. She could have ended it. She did.

She's right, it could have been a lark but I got too serious, but I couldn't help that. It was a light French film for her but my marriage was falling apart. What does she mean, no passion? Work this out. Lunch okay, books tapes, paintings. Holding hands not okay. Phone calls in the evening, kissing, not. Oh god she left her message five months to the minute after our first kiss.

What excuse can I give for my despair? He went outside and told Susan he felt terrible. The vacation had been terribly disappointing.

She was not sympathetic. "All this business of happiness is overrated. You just live your life—"

"No! I can't believe that."

"I'm sick of your stupid ideas!"

Tears came to his eyes.

"I'm not responsible for your happiness. You are. You choose to be happy or unhappy." She left to play with the kids. He sat and cried.

At dinner he drank three margaritas and smoked a cigar while they played miniature golf. The kids were having fun and Susan was laughing, so he held himself upright and pretended to smile. Suddenly he thought, there will be life after Olive. He felt better and thought, this is best for her, and best for me, too. The thought trailed off. But oh my god it is painful now.

He left them in the motel watching television and went out for iced tea at the casino. "Hi, Olive. I'm sad, of course, but it's okay. I knew this was too good to last. I know it can't work for you. Without me for comparison you'll do fine with

Paul. I'm happy for you. For my part, you taught me how happy I could be.

"Oh, Olive, thanks for telling me now. It gives me a couple days to get used to it. By the time I see you I'll have my poise back, and it might even be a French comedy. Let's have lunch Monday. You'll do me a favor if you'll listen to my feelings—you're the only one who can. Everything is fine. And we'll do fine together from now on. Goodbye."

On the drive home no one seemed to notice he was blind with pain. On the other hand, he'd been in a daze so long he probably seemed normal. To think he'd thought he was orbiting. He'd been falling, after all. He'd just smashed in the scree.

Susan put Mozart's *Requiem* in the tape player. In a minute she asked, "Why are you crying?"

"This music always makes me cry."

"Why?"

"Death. Finality. The end."

PART 3

CHAPTER 17

Sight askew, Alan sadly went to work wondering what to expect. Olive dropped a note over the partition proposing lunch at Stew's Slocum. Oh, Olive, he sighed, you never will get this language right, will you. He went to the garage the angels had visited, but it was no longer open. You can't do that, he protested, I make love there.

"The garage is closed," was the first thing she said.

"It's like the end of parentheses—while it was open we were in love; now it's closed and we... Aren't we still in love?"

She smiled.

"Here's something for you from Mexico." She kept smiling while she turned the earrings over and over.

He didn't know what to say. He wanted to find out what would be allowed, whether there was any hope. "Will you do something for me? Can we have lunch together for the next couple weeks?"

She sighed. "Yes."

"Do you still want to go skiing?"

"I don't know... I don't think it would be a good idea now."

He didn't ask if she wanted to continue saving for it. "Would you, um, still loan me the pornography?"

She looked away and finally said, "All right, but only if you don't talk to me about it."

"Pretend it's just an interest shared by friends, like history, or books. We are still friends." He hoped. He desperately wanted her to agree to keep seeing him. "Pretend we're old friends with a lovely memory of long ago. That's the trick."

"Basically I'm going to stop comparing Paul to you. Then I won't miss you so much."

"By the way, how did things go with Fern's letter?"

"She gave it with his birthday present to Bob. He said thank you very much, the present is nice, letter is well written, you're very kind. But nothing personal, she couldn't tell positive or negative. Whatever else, he's a real pro. How are you getting along with Susan?"

"Not very well. I have the feeling she doesn't want me around anymore. Maybe we should divorce..."

She looked sympathetic.

"What were you thinking, Olive, when you said maybe I'd find you aren't perfect after all?"

"Maybe I'm too liking material things. But I saw a friend here from Taipei last week who's richly married with a maid and so on, and I didn't feel envy."

"What about me? How can I improve?" Tell me what I did wrong so I don't lose my next love.

"I can't think of anything."

She wasn't saying much, and he hadn't much to say, or rather, nothing he could say would matter much. There was one thing: "Olive, if you ever feel like a one night stand with someone, ask me. You know I'm safe, and I won't get heavy about it." She nodded. "It would hurt to see you with someone if I didn't know. I mean, it'd be fine if we were in love and you fell in love with someone else too, that is, it would have been fine, but now it'd hurt."

She nodded again. They left.

The next days were a miasma as he tried to decide what to do. Not that there was much to be done. He couldn't see straight and he couldn't think straight. He only knew he'd lost her and happiness with Susan seemed remote. He wrote a letter: O Olive I miss you terribly, the joking and planning, the intimate vocabulary of our Chinese lessons, the secret in our glances, the messages that meant you were thinking of me. I miss holding your hand, touching your shoulder, your cheek. But a touch would reopen everything for you, wouldn't it? Your passions rise so quickly along the sweet path from a casual caress to union. I still love you. I can't simply turn it off. Will this pain pass with time? I've got to give you up. I've got to find love somewhere else. And on and on he wrote about the passing of sadness with time and continued writing in his sleep, but he didn't leave the letter for her.

The next time they had lunch she was wearing the earrings. "I was afraid they'd be too heavy for you."

She toyed with one. "I like them."

He wanted to close his mouth around it and take her ear in his mouth. "My sister told me I'm monogamous and won't be happy screwing around. She's right, and now I know what to do—end my marriage. I don't know if I'll be happy, or even less unhappy, or if I'll ever find anyone I care about as much as you, but I do know I can't search while I'm married. I'm sorry it's going to hurt Susan. She'll feel she's been rejected, that she tried but wasn't good enough, that she failed. But it's not her fault; it's that we're not good for each other."

"Paul thinks she is a basically unhappy person."

"I think he's right."

"I hope you will be happy."

"Thank you. The question is whether Claire and Philip will be better off. The tension now can't be good for them, and they know we're suffering and want us to be happy, but what's best in the long run? Of course, they can only consider things from their standpoint. Like me. Am I acting like a child?"

"You'll feel better some day."

"Olive, tell me, is this difficult for you? Just tell me one time only."

"Yes."

"You really did care for me?"

She looked away. "Obviously. I risked everything that matters to me." She paused. "When I came to work after the ski trip I can't concentrate on anything. All day I'm in a daze, and when I found you felt about me the same way…"

"Thank you. It's juvenile, but hearing it makes this easier. To know it isn't easy for you either…"

"Someone who looks from outside could always see the whole thing and this is the way it has to end."

"We were so lucky. Lucky it was you and me, who did it for love, not conquest or pleasure or the sake of bragging about it, lucky we weren't discovered…"

"I always felt God blessed it."

He dared to embrace her when they left and was glad she didn't turn away.

Susan called just as he returned to his desk. "Do you have a minute to talk? Alan, do you want a divorce? I get the feeling you want to get divorced."

He hesitated, surprised and unprepared. He wasn't certain yet. He'd wanted to talk with people who'd been through it. He didn't trust his judgment yet. But as well now as ever. "Well, I have been thinking about it."

"What have you decided?"

"Just a minute, Susan, can I call you back? I want to go someplace I can talk in private."

So this is how tragedy works itself out, an unexpected phone call, a mundane walk to a room with a door, shut the door, dial. "Hi."

"I feel awful but I have to know. You seem so unhappy."

"I have been thinking about it. Have you?"

"I don't have any more hope." She began to cry.

"Susan, what if I come home and we talk?"

"Can you get away from work?"

"This is more important than work."

"Are you sure?"

"I'll be there in fifteen minutes."

He dialed Olive's machine. "I'm going home. Susan called to talk about divorce. Wish me luck."

"I always expected you'd leave one day."

"That's partly it," he tried to say gently. "I never thought you believed in me, always mistrusted me, always suspected me of unfaithfulness—"

"But you were unfaithful!"

"Yes… maybe it was a self-fulfilling prophecy."

"That's bullshit! You chose to be unfaithful."

"Yes, but I didn't mean to hurt you."

"I felt terrible. I feel terrible. I'm worthless."

"Susan, you're a wonderful person—"

"No, I'm not!"

"Don't hold what I've done against yourself. I am a shit-head. I'm sorry."

"I feel like a failure." She began crying.

"I feel like a failure, too. Neither of us is to blame. Though knowing it doesn't help."

"It seems to me you stopped trying after a couple months last spring." They were both crying. "I feel like walking."

They drove to Ocean Beach. In the distance was the Cliff House, another end of parentheses enclosing… Enclosing what? You can't make metaphors out of everything.

"I assume you want the kids with you," he said.

"We'll have joint custody, visitation rights. When are you going to move out?"

"I don't know. I priced apartments. They're steep."

"You already looked?" she said sadly. "Get a nice place so the kids won't visit a dump. I want them to stay at the school during the difficult months ahead. The teachers are kind and the continuity will give them stability."

"Of course."

"I need to know when you'll move out. I can't live with the uncertainty anymore."

"I'll try to find a place this weekend."

A woman who had been at their wedding but they'd barely seen since walked by. Another parenthesis. Everything made a sort of sickening sense: Pedro's call last spring at the first end of the affair, now this woman at the end of the marriage. What a way to meet old friends.

"Do you feel like I'm pushing you into a decision?" Susan asked.

"Yes…"

"Do you mean you're not really sure you want a divorce?"

"Yes, I'm not sure."

"Do you want some more time to think about it?"

He suddenly felt much better. "Yes."

"Oh, good! I'm so glad!"

"Me too!"

"But really, Alan, this uncertainty is hard to live with…"

"I don't want to make it any harder for you, but it'd be nice to have a few more days…"

"Do you think you could decide by the weekend?"

"I'll try."

"I thought you had decided, Alan, and didn't want to say anything that might make you change your mind out of pity."

"Thank you. You are a wonderful person, you know."

"How are you?" Sofia asked cheerfully at his piano lesson. "Did you forget how to play on your vacation?"

"Do you remember how I told you last spring I'd been in love? Well, it only really ended last week. And now, coincidentally, Susan is asking if I want a divorce."

"Does she know?"

"No. That is, she knew something happened then, but not that it continued five months more."

"Are you sure?"

"Who's sure of anything? But Sofia, Susan and I haven't gotten along for years. If it weren't for the children…"

"That's it. If there are no kids you can come and go, meet someone new, no harm. But with kids you cannot."

"I've always suspected that people say divorce is better for the kids as an excuse to ignore their obligations."

"It's the American way. There are unhappy marriages in Russia but people stay together."

"You told me once your parents always fought. Would it have been better for you if they'd divorced?"

"No! It was my greatest fear! There is no fear worse than losing a parent. Alan, even if you made a mistake and you're unhappy, too bad. You cannot put yourself before your children. Go out, play around, that's normal—I'm surprised a man your age hasn't already."

"It's not fair to your family."

She shrugged. "Listen, when they grow up and don't need you any more, go ahead and leave, no one's hurt, but now you must stay."

"Ah, Sofia, you're right!" Things were suddenly clear. "I'll stay. We can find some way to live together until Philip's out of high school."

"Of course you can. And, Alan, don't take this so seriously. These little experiences are unimportant. These women come and go."

"But she's a good person who loves her family. She has good values, she's musical, honest, ethical—"

"Of course she is, or you wouldn't have felt so much."

"Well, it's over, it hurts, I'm sad and lost, but that I can accept. At the same time, falling in love made me realize how bad my marriage is."

"So, that's your problem, not your children's."

"Yes. Well, then, I'll live with it."

"We musicians are fortunate. We have our art. To make music our minds must be absolutely clear, we cannot feel emotion or let ourselves go, we must control ourselves. And this applies to the rest of life, too. Let's play."

"Sofia, my muse, thank you."

She smiled. "Keep your sense of humor, Alan."

Claire and Philip were playing cards and Susan was on the phone when he got home. He smiled at her and said, "I'll stay for eleven years." She nodded and smiled back. Later, while she took a bath, he called Olive's machine. "Well, I've decided not to divorce. Can we have lunch tomorrow?"

He checked later and she'd replied, "Hi, I worry about you and I want to give you everything I can. I'm free for lunch, anything you want, it's up to you. I want you to be happy.

You're such a nice person." There was a sound he hoped was a sob.

At Five Lakes he told her what he'd decided. "But eleven years is a long time."

"You can read a lot of books in eleven years."

He made a face.

After work they had a drink with Jose. "I've been reading some Zen texts," Jose said.

"Who? Watts? Suzuki?"

"D.T. Suzuki, the master. Do you practice Zen?"

"I looked into it when I was younger but I've had other interests lately."

"I didn't know you were religious," Olive said.

"To say I am religious is going too far," said Jose, "but I am convinced there is a power at the bottom of everything. Through Zen, we are able to reach satori with it."

"I never know you're interested in these things."

Jose smirked. "Oh, there is probably much about me you don't know, Olive. What about you, are you religious?"

"Yes, but you'll probably think I have a very simple idea. I talk to God like a friend and ask Him to help me. What about you, Alan?"

"Oh, I think the idea of god must spring from something in our nature. In fact, I wonder if religious rites aren't the expression of instinctual behavior patterns."

"I don't understand."

"Our primitive ancestors evolved behaviors that helped them survive, and the behaviors didn't simply disappear when we developed a complex culture, though their expression changed. Take prayer. We pray when we're confused, depressed, helpless. The mere act of ceasing to move is restful, and since when we're relaxed we have a better chance of seeing a solution or escaping harm, this behavior was selected for. It's animal instinct, but in our arrogance we call it prayer."

"No," said Jose. "You're saying there is nothing beyond ourselves. There is more to it than that. We live in a universe of immense power we can tap into."

"Of course there's something beyond ourselves. It's a powerful and glorious universe, but we can only know it through ourselves."

Jose flicked his hand in dismissal.

Alan didn't mind. None of it mattered. "Boy, I'm just exhausted."

"Why?" said Jose. Olive smiled.

"Oh, I haven't recovered from my camping trip yet."

He walked her to her car. She said, "Use our ski money to pay for this."

"No that's for something for the two of us."

They moved toward each other but she leaned away quickly.

"Goodbye," he said.

"Goodbye, dear," she drawled in low throaty syllables, firm dee descending er.

The fall workday at school closed another parenthesis. He took another can of roofing compound up the ladder, sat down and smoked a cigarette and remembered last spring. He sadly gazed across the flat roof at the featureless sky until he fell asleep.

He stopped at a phone on the way home. "Hello, Olive. The spirit is willing but the flesh is weak." He wondered if she'd know what he meant. "That was hard, yesterday at the bar. Today I worked at the school and tomorrow Susan and the kids are sailing with Steve and Sharon. Well, I just thought I'd let you know things are okay. Don't worry about me." Though he hoped she would.

He had a hard time acting cheerful the next day while Steve enthusiastically described their sail with Olive and Harry, and Susan insisted on anchoring for lunch below the immigration buildings on Angel Island. Later, out of habit, without hope, he checked his messages and had a pleasant thrill to discover one, but increasing disappointment as he listened.

"Well, it's me. I know what you mean. Otherwise I wouldn't call you or check message. I can't help it, still wanting to find out more messages and leave one. It's hard to cut off but gradually we should. We, I, don't want to waste our effort and time. It's probably just gradually decreasing it is fine, right? But. Okay, I'll try not to talk to you anymore. I think by the end of next week we should stop, right? Get back to…" Long pause. "Uh, anyway, that's it. No more. Bye."

Still, it was an excuse to communicate. "I figured out how everything is actually very easy. I'll leave a letter for you tomorrow." Then he played some Bach into the phone. To hear how it sounded, he used the password she'd given him to enter her mailbox, where he found she'd saved his message from the casino. She still cared enough to save it.

Mon amie,
It is very simple to break habits: Simply don't do whatever it is you no longer want to do. It's like quitting smoking. It's okay to think about it all you want, to yearn for it, to tell yourself that one time won't matter, even to dream so hard about it that you're no longer sure if you did it or not–as long as you don't actually light one up.

I know this is hard for you. While I was away it all seemed clear, didn't it? But when you see me you remember and you're tempted. It's hard to ignore something in front of you. But the urge passes. It gets easier.

First you (we) must decide which habits to break. We know we must eliminate physical intimacy. We can think about it (though our spouses may suffer by the comparison) and we can talk about it, but it's this simple: Stay out of each other's pants. And let us not be led into temptation. No wine on *Malta,* stay out of parking garages and private places. Don't you think everything else will be all right?

I suppose we must still pay attention to appearances. Wouldn't it be utterly stupid if someone thinks we're lovers? If after all this we couldn't be friends? Our clear conscience will help us seem normal, but maybe we're doing things you think may arouse curiosity. There's nothing wrong with these messages, but I suppose Paul or Susan might be upset if they were discovered. What do you think?

I'm glad I decided not to divorce. I'm sure (for now) this is right for the kids. (I thought our happiness would make them happy, but now I'll never know.) You'll stay with Paul, I'll stay with Susan. There will never be another you for me so I'll keep on staying. You're more fortunate than I, but I'll do my best, and I've got my fingers crossed.

Maybe, ma chère amie, maybe God did say: Okay, you two have a few blissful months and then if you do things right you can have a dear friend for the rest of your lives, enjoy yourselves, and good luck.

What do you think?

She met him for lunch on *Malta*. "So, what do you think?"

"I do care deeply about you, but I can't talk about it. I'm trying to put those feelings aside. At the B&M party Stella was telling about love affairs on campus, and I start to think what it's like to hear stories about me. I would be mortified if anyone knew."

Ahh, that was the trigger.

She went on, "I never did tell you the depth of my feelings. I had to keep some control, stop going too far out of the right way of acting. I still can't tell you."

"Yeah, I suppose it'll just make it harder."

She took his hand. "The theme of our story is this was seasoning on the food. Now the salt is gone and life isn't as wonderful. But I do feel much more peaceful."

"In an ideal world Paul and Susan would accept that we love each other."

"It won't work. Remember you told me how jealous you'll be if I love a third man? Paul will feel the same way if he knows about you."

It wasn't what he'd said, but it was pointless to explain.

She said sadly, "You and I just aren't the people to have an affair. We're raised to do the right thing. This is the right thing."

"Yes... I know..."

"Fern said you should just get divorced and move on. I said it's different when you have children. She doesn't know what it is. I didn't either, until I had Daniel."

"You should have another."

"No! One is enough! I'm going to think of myself, too."

Steve suggested that Alan move into the empty cubicle next to his, which was opposite Olive's. Before he did, he asked Olive if it was okay with her. She didn't seem to care so he moved that afternoon, sorry that it no longer mattered to be three steps away. At least their heads would be farther apart.

"Hi, it's me. Surprise. I want to tell you it's not I feel sorry for you or pity you. I care for you and don't like to see you feel sad or depressed or unhappy. I know it's hard for you and it's also hard for... Probably I should just say more hard for you than me.

"Um, I want to tell you I wish you're happy like me. You know, every day things move fine and you don't think about other than we're great friends at work. We spend more than forty fifty percent of our life together as a good friend and let's move on like that, so don't expect anything other than that. Still, having that is great, right? I wish you get over me, not to have a hard time, soon.

"I tell you, I still don't think we should continue this telephone conversation. We're giving ourself time and chance to nourish our feelings for each other, and we should really go back to our family. I try very hard to suppress everything else. I'm so bad, I don't have a very good vocabulary, I think of those silly peasant's way of describing things... It's like you want to be eating healthy food, not fattening stuff, and when you're on a diet and eat chocolate, you don't feel so good afterwards, right? I'm not really deserting you, or I'm not really totally don't care about you, it's just this is the right thing to do. You should feel the same way.

"To make this conclusion, I don't think I'll leave you messages very often, once in a while maybe, but probably not most of the time. I'll see you at lunch and we meet at work and treat you as close as Steve plus other feelings, but I do want to clarify this so you understand, uh, so think that way and be happy and uh, enjoy life, as is. That's all."

He was sad. He listened to Shostakovich's quartet of ultimate sadness and briefly felt that the music said: There is life outside yourself, you can be happy somewhere beyond both Olive and Susan. For a moment he felt whole.

To his surprise, Olive invited him to shop for the wine she'd been assigned to bring to Tahoe with Steve and Sharon on the weekend. He was happy to go but it was awkward. They carefully kept on opposite sides of the cart and avoided each other's eyes in the aisles where they'd embraced only four, was it five, weeks ago.

She tried to fill the silence. "I'm afraid their dog will spoil everything. He's so undisciplined he will jump on Daniel. Paul and I had a boxer we could never stop jumping on children. When I got pregnant we even took him to a dog psychologist but he won't change, so we got rid of him."

"You'd rather have a kid than a dog, huh?"

"Paul said we have to choose."

As easy as that. Get rid of a dog, get rid of a lover.

Susan showed him a towel as she folded the laundry. "What is this, blood? It smelled terrible."

"Maybe it's rust. It came from the boat."

"Oh. By the way, would you like a party for your fortieth birthday? We could invite Olive and Paul, and Steve and Sharon, and Harry and Mona. Would you like that?"

Oh Christ. "That's a nice idea. Let's see how things develop."

LETTER TO JACQUES

Habibi,

La commedia è finita and this clown is sad. Mei Li has cut me off to safeguard her crappy marriage. I will be generous and say that she safeguards it for her son. She says it's wise to end before we're discovered. I would continue–it must be possible to have a family and lover both, no?–but I have no choice.

If only we'd met three years ago. It was a question of timing. There are a billion women and one of them no doubt is your ideal mate, but the chance of meeting her is small. You ask a strange woman for directions, she tells you and you go on, but if you had stopped the one you passed seconds earlier, you would have met her. Or you do meet but she has a child and doesn't want to leave her husband.

It seems that during the same week Mei Li was thinking things over, Susan was too. Another case of timing. She asked if I want a divorce. I thought it over and said no, because my suffering is subordinate to my children's needs.

You know Susan. Socially she's kind, courteous and helpful, generous. But nobody reciprocates the way she'd like, so she's always disappointed. And because she expresses disappointment to only her closest acquaintances, I bear the brunt of her many dissatisfactions and as her husband I am supposed to put up with her bad moods. She's come to see intimacy, I think, as little more than constancy in the face of adversity. I think I haven't been very kind to her lately, but I don't think I'm responsible for her unhappiness. But we do share many values and sometimes affection.

She's not easy to live with, but I'm willing to stay until Philip graduates from high school. I'll do my best. I can't think straight, Jacques, but I think it's the right thing to do.

But my god, I hurt. Everything signifies Mei Li–every pay phone reminds me of the calls I made to her; a license plate has the same digits as hers; my stomach churns when "tryst" appears in a crossword puzzle; the kids chant doggerel

about chocolate—I was the forbidden chocolate in her diet;
Susan buys me a jar of olives—I never told you that Olive is
her English name. I try to transfer my yearning for her to
Susan, but I feel unfaithful to her, to my passion, to myself.

Oh my, sometimes life isn't sweet. How do we get used
to it?

Excuse me for not asking about you. I'm too full of myself.
But now and then I think I might recover my sense of humor.
Shostakovich's 15th Quartet helps. I'll write again when I'm
not so unhappy.

His new contact lens didn't fit; his vision was still
unbalanced.

He was smoking outside when Olive parked in the alley.
She glanced at the cigarette. "I'm feeling self-destructive." She
gave him a dismayed, lopsided smile and agreed to meet at
Five Lakes for lunch.

He was surprised to find her already inside; the lot had
been empty. She told him what they'd done at Tahoe and
asked about Susan. They were doing better, he said—she was
being more affectionate and he hoped things would continue
to improve. He dared to say, "I still have strong feelings for
you," hoping she would say she still did too.

But after a moment's silence she said, "How can you feel
like that when you feel good about Susan?"

Did she think transferring emotions from one person to
another was as simple as that? Had she actually done it with
Paul? Was she chastising him and getting him off the subject?
He had a last meager hope of staying close to her: "Will you
loan me the pornography?"

"Why?" she asked flatly.

He cast about for a response. "Um, partly to learn what
your tastes are, partly for fun… Susan is more interested now,
she's buying sexy clothes for us, she seems to genuinely like it."

"Well, I'm glad. I'm doing fine with Paul, too."

"Oh, everything's fine. The trouble is that life just isn't
exciting any more."

She laughed. "Well, with what's happening between you, I'm surprised to hear it."

She was definitely not going to talk about their feelings for each other. He switched to Mediterranean history and offered to loan his copy of the *Odyssey*. She accepted and he was grateful for the chance to maintain some sort of contact.

When they left, he realized she'd parked on the street to avoid being secluded together in the lot.

Though it was true that he and Susan were trying, they weren't connecting. She wanted sex one night but he felt too sad about Olive. Her desire stayed with him the next day, though, so he rented a skin flick for the evening. It happened that she had also rented one, but then she fell asleep while they watched. She apologized in the morning and told him to stay up that evening until the kids went to bed and she got home from work. He stayed up but was so horny that he watched the movie and masturbated, and when she arrived he didn't feel like sex. The timing of everything was off.

Ashes, ashes, all fall down. He sat on the back porch smoking and drinking white wine and staring through the trees in Olive's direction across the bay. He awoke later feeling lost in the darkness, dizzy and upside down, something was utterly not right, something irrevocable and wrong had happened. He groped his way to the living room and called Olive's answering machine. The messages she'd saved were gone.

In the morning he gave her the *Odyssey* and said offhandedly, "You erased my messages."

"How did you know?"

"I went into your answering machine."

"Why?"

"I wanted to listen to the music," he lied.

She didn't reply.

CHAPTER 18

Awaken in the dark night sick and nauseous with the powerless torment of loss you cannot rectify: the death of a child, a death by drowning, a train in the Costa Rican jungle that collided with another and slammed his face into the metal seat ahead: his head snapped back, he held his hand below his nose to catch the rushing blood, lost consciousness and cried for mother and father, for their enveloping tenderness, but they were absent.

Olive was gone.

Her demeanor was now entirely businesslike. In fact, when she saw him heading toward her she took another route. If it was too late to turn, she looked away as they passed. When they met in the presence of someone else she barely spoke to him. She was polite. He was polite. Though it hurt to be treated like anyone else, he hinted at nothing. He had no claim on her. He was awkward. Did she notice? She was awkward too, he thought.

A cold fall morning, low light in a yellow sky and dew on the car windows, a yen for travel and change. The change of season at the start of school always made him itch. A slender girl with long legs and black hair eyed him in the alley and looked back across her shoulder as she walked toward Susan's school, each glance a stratum of emotion, a sedimentary layer in love's geology.

He yearned for a woman, for the private thing, the thing

that happens in secret. He glimpsed a woman leaving a doorway: Walk back with her, ascend the stair, undress in a room overlooking the street, dark hair falling to her breasts, dark pubic hair the secret in the room...

He tried to trick himself to mute the pain: There were other fish in the sea; there was a Shostakovichian world outside this suffering where he could live. But he was duping himself. He couldn't replace her; he couldn't will peace; he must accept things as they were.

Their lives were diverging. She lunched with someone he didn't know. A new lover? He wouldn't mind—if only she told him.

His sister arrived and they sailed to Alameda. The kids played below where Olive had made love to him. He rode above present sadness and past joy, strong and self-contained, with an impulse to hurt her, and then remembered the same anger after a breakup long ago, and then was sad again. He pointed a pair of binoculars from the deck of Berenice's husband's ship at the naval base to his house across the bay. Someone could have watched them like this. He showed the house to Claire and Philip.

"Maybe she's promiscuous," he said to Berenice. "It wouldn't matter as much if she were—a little rubbing of the flesh, as my optometrist says. But she did risk her family for me, of course she loved me."

"She probably feels as bad as you do."

"Most of the time I'm fine. I'm getting over it."

"But you've been saying that for how long now, almost a month? It's obvious you're not."

"Sometimes I scorn her—she isn't suffering like me, her feelings were never as deep as mine."

"You're lucky it wasn't a nasty breakup, but you'd at least have the solace of anger."

Olive talked to Steve and Mike about a ski weekend and suggested the place she'd proposed to Alan. Didn't she remember? Didn't she care? He invited the three of them to sail. Mike declined, Steve accepted, and Olive said she'd think about it.

He sat on the porch in the pale dying dusk drinking wine. All that was left of her was an intemperate taste for white wine. How long would this misery last? Time passed. Life crept its petty pace. It was autumn, colder, days were shorter. He'd followed his god to the end and now how long would it take to return to normal?

Walter Pater said: We are all under sentence of death but with a sort of indefinite reprieve—we have an interval, and then our place knows us no more. Some spend this interval in listlessness, some in high passions for our one chance lies in expanding that interval, in getting as many pulsations as possible into the given time. Great passions, ecstasy and sorrow of love, may give us this quickened, multiplied sense of life.

He gave Olive a copy but she never responded.

Steve asked her, "Are you coming sailing with us?"

"I think I will pass."

He sat with closed eyes listening to her throaty singsong speech as familiar as a wife's, calm and friendly, firm and forward. Its falling inflections reverberated in his gut; he grew aroused; he wanted to enter her slender body. Her laughter was like bubbles in a pond, like the play of a brook over rocks.

Susan wanted to cuddle; he wanted to fuck. He was acerbic, malicious. "You're right, I am oversexed. Maybe I need a girlfriend."

"I knew I shouldn't trust you."

"I'm sorry," he said with sudden remorse. "I'm tired, I guess."

Finally he asked Olive to lunch. She told him to meet her at Dolores Park. He brought a sandwich but she arrived with nothing. The light was cool and yellow. He ate. "I feel awkward around you, and you seem to feel awkward around me."

"I don't want the past to come into what's going on now. I want to forget it."

"It hurts me that you avoid me. You have an easy relationship with Steve and Mike, but you don't talk to me."

"When I joke with Mike, that's all there is, nothing else, but when I talk to you there are deeper meanings that remind me, and I feel guilty about Paul. I want to forget."

"You always felt guilty."

"I did?"

"You talked about it."

She regarded him silently. "I can't believe I did this…"

Her chill made him sick. "I want it to be over, too. But I want to be friends."

"We're on different levels now. We see this very differently."

"Do we?"

"Before, I had the feeling this can be a light French comedy, but my childhood is too strong."

"I thought it could be light, too, but I'd forgotten how much you start caring."

"Don't you feel guilty?"

"No, I feel sad. I miss knowing what you're thinking, what you're doing…"

"It was a lesson for me. I will never do it again."

"Well, I guess I'm lucky it was me who gave you the lesson… I'm sorry, though, that I caused you this pain."

"If it wasn't you maybe it would be someone else."

"Can't we have a friendship now that acknowledges how much we cared for each other?"

"I don't want to remember. I want all links with the past to end."

"The feelings will diminish and the memories will fade, but the fact won't go away. It did happen."

"I want to forget it all. It makes me too guilty." She paused. "I'm just telling you how I feel without trying to think of diplomacy way."

"Thank you. I want to know how you feel." Silence. "This is like mourning, as if someone you love died…" Silence. "Not exactly, of course…" Silence. "I just can't comprehend. You usually understand how you got where you are and where you're going, but I don't understand what happened with us. And what is going to happen?"

"Well, like everything in life, you never know. It's lucky we're busy at work."

"Yes. I hope we get through this soon. It'll be more comfortable. If you feel less awkward…"

"…then you'll feel better…"

"…and we'll get along better."

"I think it's temporary."

"Are you afraid I'll make demands on you?"

"No."

"I'll return your ski money."

"There's no rush."

"Well, it's tied to the past. I'll give it back."

She paused. "Until I get over this awkward feeling, I can't be free with you."

"I want us to be easy with each other. I want us to be friends."

"I'm glad you feel that way. I'm glad we talked. I feel better."

"Me, too. We had to talk. It's been two weeks—"

"Enough. I think I'll leave now, while I feel good."

"Okay. I'll stay here." He sat for a long time gazing over the park and downtown and the bay. It felt like autumn. It felt empty.

Back at the office he erased her last messages and passed her a note: Olive, I hope you will end up with happy memories. If I can do anything (like shut up from now on!), let me know.

She smiled and shook her head.

The pale conversation had dissolved six agitated months in a calm, hopeless finality.

He sealed half of three hundred dollars in an envelope and put it in his jacket.

He called Berenice. "She wants complete separation. She can't even talk to me."

"Well, it may take her a while to get over. I fell in love with a guy even though I knew it would end when his fiancée returned, and it still took months to stop feeling guilty."

"I feel like I've lost a goddess."

"Come on, Alan, she can't be perfect. I hope you can see her faults. It'll help you get over it."

OLIVE'S FAULTS

She lacks the discipline to develop her drawing skills (yet has enough to end a love affair), craves her daily glass or two of wine, treats waiters indifferently and scorns less successful people (doesn't even know the names of the clerical staff), and thinks mastering the trivial rules for success at work was a great accomplishment. She mistakes her tastes for critical thought, which is reinforced by men finding her attractive and laughing at what she says, and others being forced by her position to do her bidding.

She blames victims of injustice for their distress. She is uninterested in politics, volunteers her time to no organization, donates to no charity. She contributes nothing to society. She is generous with her family and friends when it pleases her; otherwise she does her duty.

Her marriage is founded on finance. Her tenderness for her fiancé sprang from his purchase of their house; they overspent to remodel it and the shared debt is a strong connection. They're closest when they discuss major purchases, buy expensive cars, stay at costly resorts. She is materialistic—chic clothes, meals, wine, cars, gracious living—and yet it's an expression of her sensuality (or does sensuality express her selfishness?). Among the financial goals he overheard her list for Steve was enough money to put two children through Stanford (Two! Had she changed her mind so quickly? Did Paul want another? Was she thinking to atone by offering?), a nicer place to live, income property, retirement. She is a consumer.

She will not know herself. Her life is unexamined. She
ignores contradictions—they are unpleasant. She denies what
happened. Passion (love? sensuality?) overcame her scruples
and now she says she'd wanted a French comedy. Had she been
dissembling, then, when she said she cared for him? (Not that
he hadn't dissembled, too, about belief in predestination and
fate, but he'd known when he did, and he'd told her he had,
or tried to.) No, she wouldn't face it. She avoided its ramifi-
cations by pretending it was an amusement more intriguing
than pot or porn, until she started feeling that her lover filled
the role a husband fills. The cinematographic denial which
kept him at a distance broke down, and unable to live loving two real men, she made one imaginary and erased him.

Society's esteem is crucial. She'd wavered until B&M's
party reasserted love's status as gossip in the marketplace. But
she'd been kind for two weeks after the party. Then what?
When had the final denial happened? The weekend in Tahoe
with her family. It was then. Until then she had still been at
the movie. She cast it all away that weekend and rejoined her
tribe. She can't transcend the norms that roll the world along.

But although he saw the banality of her denial, it still
crushed him.

CHAPTER 19

The loss of all they'd planned hurt keenly—the ski trip, the China trip, life together, watching the kids grow up—but he could live with loss, and when he was alone it subsided to an ache he knew would finally fade. But when she swished by with head set straight there was blinding, overwhelming pain without thought, mute and uncomprehending suffering like an injured dog.

He painted the pond she'd copied from a calendar, aching with the memory of life and love bursting in green explosion around their springtime lunch by Stow Lake, his surprise at her acquiescent hand in his, her tenderness. She'd been so tender, she'd still been kind when she wore the earrings, that wasn't long ago but he couldn't remember when it was. What stupid thing had he done? Say he still loved her? Ask for the porn? He wished he knew so he could avoid the topic. On the other hand, since she didn't talk to him, there were no topics to avoid. He should tell her to snap out of it, stop acting like a child. It might work—it's what Paul did.

He told Berenice, "She ignores me totally. I'm terribly disappointed in her, because she promised we'd always be friends whatever happened."

"Well, she obviously cared deeply about you, and now she's trying to suppress her feelings."

"Oh, I understand, but I feel like telling her to relax."

"Don't. Gestures speak louder than words. Be pleasant. Say good morning and smile."

"When I do, she grunts. In fact, she only grunted when I returned her share of the money we'd saved for skiing."

"At least, Alan, we learn something from each love."

"You think so? All I've learned is the feeling of certain emotions."

"Well, that's something, isn't it?"

"Tell you the truth, as she always says, I could live without some of them."

Describing the wound to Berenice and having her sympathy treated the symptoms for a moment but the cure could only be found with Olive. What could a cure possibly consist of? Now and then he would hope to resume the entire affair but immediately put the thought aside—impossible hope would only prolong the pain. Easy friendship then, excluding if she wished any reference to the private things they'd shared. But this too seemed impossible: If Aristotle was right about love being a form of friendship and she denied love, then she denied friendship. If only she'd say hello, smile in the corridor, joke in staff meetings as she did with the others... Somewhere between soaring passion and abysmal denial they could blend a bland, superficial acquaintance into the office fabric, grow some scar tissue over this gaping laceration, this black hole in the cubicle diagonally opposite.

One day she stopped near him and told Mike, "I tell Paul Alan said he bought a wife by making the house down payment in both our names."

"You told him that?" Alan said incredulously. He caught his breath and asked, "How are you liking the *Odyssey?*"

She turned and chatted for a minute. For the first time in weeks she wasn't trying to get away. Later he made a copy of a sonnet he'd come across named *In Praise of Olive* and gave it to her. Her look of displeasure caused immediate regret.

He was on the phone when she walked by on her way out. He hastily hung up and raced to follow. She was outside bending to open the BMW's trunk when he said, "Olive, can't we be friends?"

John Taylor walked up with a case of wine.

"I thought this was your car," Alan said to him.

Taylor stared. "It looks like mine." He put the box in the trunk and straightened quizzically. Alan leaned against the car with folded arms and waited until he left, looking over his shoulder.

"You seem so uncomfortable," Alan said.

"It gets better and worse. It's my problem, not yours."

"Look, I don't want to start anything up again."

"I know."

"You seem so unhappy."

"Now is not a good time to talk about it."

God damn! He smoked furiously to calm down on the way to the kids' school where he had to perform the role of a committee chair.

Late that night he composed a message and read it shakily into the phone. "Hi. If it comes up, I'll tell John I was offering you tickets to an opera lecture.

"Olive, I think you're being too hard on yourself. You should be proud: You decided you were doing something wrong, so you stopped. You shouldn't be remorseful; you should acknowledge your courage. My sister told me it's normal to feel guilty and it may take months to pass. I hope not—I care about you, and I don't like seeing you suffer. You've had some painful things in your life, yet you've overcome them. You'll get over this too. You're a happy person. Be happy.

"I wish I understood better so I can help. Is there anyone you can talk to? It's hard to get over something like this alone. I don't want to come between you and Paul and I don't want to disturb you more than I already have, but I could be a friend for you. Frankly, I don't know what I can do or what you need or what you want, but tell me if there is anything I can do. Lately I've said and done some stupid things. I've been selfish, I was thinking of myself. I apologize."

He listened to her listen to her messages, reschedule a diet clinic appointment, answer calls, speak Chinese to Fern. She left at noon without speaking to him, returned at two, and left for the day at four. He walked by Taylor's office to reassure himself that he hadn't also left, and suddenly remembered her calendar had shown W.P. at noon yesterday (wine party? wine purchase?) and checked Taylor's. There it was: W.P. LO had originated the appointment.

Jealousy twisted him.

Was she consoling herself with other men?

He'd ask Taylor, what are you doing with Olive?

He should forget she existed.

Did she fool me all along? She said she despised Taylor. She knows I don't like Taylor. Did she lie to be agreeable?

What a fall from grand passion to petty poking around her calendar. I've become a common thief.

Forget her. She doesn't like you. You've lost nothing. She was not even a friend before she was a lover.

(Does she blame you for her downfall? Is she still so attracted she's afraid to look at you?)

What did she do with John? Why do I care? Stop caring. It's over. Why does she go out with him? To prove something to me, to herself?

Can I ask him what they were doing? He'd say what is it, are you jealous? And I'd say no, I'm just curious. And he wouldn't answer, to tease me. And then Olive would say get out of my life, leave me alone. And I'd stare at her and walk away.

O! Passion hauls a baggage train of frenzy: The first tentative questions, joyous discovery of similarities, ecstasy of agreement, boundless eternity in the mailcar followed by jealousy, suspicion, the caboose of despair.

My sense of reality is shot. Is she really going to the opera with Dorothy? Mike told me they're going. There's independent confirmation. Or is he in on the alibi? What validates truth? What can I rely upon? My children, too young for the lies based on passion, my wife who lacks it...

Philip called, "Dad? May I have a glass of water?"

Alan went to the sink and the bedroom. "Go back to sleep, honey. It's eleven-thirty."

He called her machine. "What is wrong, why did you go

out with John, I'm not jealous but I can't understand why you bought wine with him but won't talk to me, if you're doing things you don't want me to know, if you don't want me to know what you're thinking, if when you see me it reminds you of things you don't want to remember. You said it's not my problem, it's yours, but it is also my problem, it's like a friend who suddenly won't talk to you. I'm sorry I'm doing this to you but I just don't understand. Do you hate me? Just tell me. Bye."

But he feared her answer in the morning so he left the office to pick up his new contact lens before she arrived. The damn thing still wasn't right and he was still off balance. There was no reply on his machine when he returned and no response during the day. Berenice said Olive sounded guilty, not promiscuous.

"Um, I try to explain," she said that evening. "It might sound harsh but basically that's how I feel so if you ask for it, my gosh, I should just tell you I think it will be difficult to be friends. How do you draw the line between friendship and lingering feelings? Your knowledge of the past which shows in your eyes, wanting to be special friends, it's reminding me of the past. It's hard to clear in my own mind but it's like I explained previously, I want to close the whole thing, freeze it and put it away. Yes, I know you don't want anything more, but even the friendship, it's left over from the past.

"The best way of thinking is to pretend it never happened, just leave it out of your mind. Tell the truth, I really don't want to think about it, so probably it'll be easier for me if you just completely leave it alone. Sorry if this sounds so terrible but I guess this is how this kind of thing ends many times.

"Also when you mention about me going out to buy wine with John, I think that's probably my business." She snorted. "Anyway, it's something I can tell anybody, everybody, not a problem. Bye."

He blushed at that last, but his jealousy abated. Small comfort. He drank wine, smoked and gazed at the bay from the back porch.

He was surprised to find another message in the morning. "Hi, it's me. Sorry to call and ask like this. The question is, Stella's asking me and Paul to donate blood to her kid's surgery. I appreciate if you can tell me a little… you know, you told me everything before but I just didn't pay attention at the time. What she told me basically is the incubation could last ten years, so you could possibly, uh, get it ten years later. Sorry, I don't know how to say this thing better, but I really like to know, even if the chance is one-tenth of one percent. I hope you don't take offensively but I want to know for my own mind, too. Sorry about however it sound, but if you don't mind could you tell me what, which year, I mean, what year, what happened? And please, I appreciate you tell me very, uh, detailed things. Bye."

Oh, poor baby, needed help from one with whom she wanted no intercourse, and help about precisely the most intimate intercourse, and so fastidious she couldn't call it by name. Though he sympathized, he was not inclined to recount his sexual history to an answering machine, and it felt good having her the supplicant for a change. He knew she knew he'd heard the message, so he waited for her to come. The morning passed. He went home to have lunch with Susan.

"You know, I didn't want to divorce," Susan said.

"I didn't either."

"Why did you say you did?"

"I thought you wanted to."

"It was you. You acted so unhappy when we camped."

"I guess I was."

"Why?"

I was worried about Olive. "We weren't getting along."

"Do you want to see the counselor again?"

"No, we're doing fine now."

"She wasn't a lot of help, was she?"

"Well, she got us through the worst last spring."

"I'm so glad we're getting along better now."

"Me too."

"Do you want to make love?"

"Sure!"

Back at the office he decided to get it over with and called Olive's machine. "Tell me when, where, and in what form you want the information, and I'll be happy to tell you."

She came almost immediately and said, "Come have a talk." She led him into a conference room and closed the door. "I don't care about where, I want to know when."

"I would give blood to my own child, that's how safe I think I am."

"I want to know more. What did you do?"

"Four years ago I had unprotected sex five or six times with a woman who was sexually active. When I donated blood that fall it tested negative for AIDS. Last spring, because I was concerned for your sake, I had the test again."

"Did you do anything else in ten years?

"Only with Susan, and I doubt she's done anything."

She smiled at that as she stood. "I'm sorry for asking. I'm very naive about this kind of things."

"It's quite all right."

The next day she told him they wouldn't take her blood because she weighed less than a hundred ten.

LETTER FROM JACQUES

My god! What a horrible story! I feel very bad for you, my dear Alan. I hope things get better and better, at least less and less bad. When I think that you see each other every single day... There must be some mad djinn of suffering in charge of things.

I'm also living a complicated situation with an adorable Moroccan. She wants to leave her ex-fiancé but he owes some reparations for not marrying her. She has to wait for that, then look for a job here or go back to Morocco. Luckily, no one knows what's happened between us. She was at my house for two weeks, her ex-fiancé in the interior on business. I see her all the time but I have to pretend I don't give a damn. When I had her, no problem; now that I don't—for a while? for ever?–it's insupportable. My only consolation is that we were able to maneuver with the discretion necessary in these circles.

Well, habibi, all my encouragement and my friendship. I think you were right to put your children before all else. It takes a lot of strength. In my own case, I think Claude was more tranquil after our separation than always wondering what new horror he was going to see or hear, poor kid. Who can be sure?

P.S. Shostakovich is rather better than whiskey.

When he went to the alley for a cigarette he thought of meeting at her car or his car, or at the boat, or somewhere else to take a single car to a park, or to Fern's... Used condoms always littered the sidewalk, artifacts of some young couple kissing in a car, keenly attentive to approaching footsteps, fondling in the dark, girl pleading no not here not now, boy grasping her wrist to hold her as he unzipped...

Somebody arranged drinks after work as appreciation for the support staff, and Alan's anxiety increased as the date approached. He didn't know how he should act around Olive, he was afraid she would get drunk and flirt, he was afraid she'd leave with someone else. His nerves brought on a cold that afternoon but he drove to the bar, where he met Stella outside and went in with her. Olive was there alone. Thank god for Stella. To his vast relief Olive told her that she had to leave soon. She didn't talk to him. When others arrived she moved to another table.

Harry sat down and talked about friendship. "My step-father, who I thought was nuts, always said, 'You can't trust anybody. If you have two friends when you die, you're lucky.' When I was young I said nah, that ain't the way it is, but though he was a little drastic there's something to it."

"Harry Truman said, 'You want a friend, get a dog.'"

"I wish things were simpler. Sex, for instance, that ought to be simple."

"Yeah, it should be, but it never is."

"For half an hour, it's simply great, but then…"

"Remorse and guilt."

"Sounds like the voices of experience," said Mike.

"But we defer to even more," said Harry. "Tell us what it'll be like in thirty years."

Alan watched John Taylor lecherously watch Olive walk to the bathroom. What layers of desire and knowledge and ignorance, denial and love and compulsion… He said bitterly, "Maybe you just don't give a *fuck* anymore." Harry and Mike looked at him with surprise.

LETTER TO JACQUES

Good lord, habibi, why is this business so hard? The penis, that social member, that pledge of caring for another person—its sole function is to attach us to others, and via that connection to participate, maybe, in the life of the world…

Aeschylus says: "God, whose law it is that he who learns must suffer. And even in our sleep, pain that cannot forget falls drop by drop upon the heart, and in our own despair, against our will, comes wisdom to us by the awful grace of God." As to the wisdom I cannot say, but I know the dripping pain.

The years bring if not wisdom a knowledge of confused passions, and they teach that even decisions made in good faith are made in the impossibility of knowing their effects. We do the best we can, but we never understand. We try to comprehend, act rationally and ethically, and only later are we aware that our choices were made in a fog.

My poor friend, we're all saps. We lead our petty lives in restricted quarters nonetheless feeling the ephemeral intensity of each meaningless moment. We try to live lives of beauty and reason, do our jobs well, fulfill our duties, improve our neighborhood, cope with the daily details of fixing the car and cleaning the house. In spare moments we read a book or listen to music and yearn for a purer life… Sometimes we find an hour or two to paint a picture or cook a nice meal, or love...

I'm ashamed to be so affected. There is fever and abscess and cholera; villages where the desert sand moves monthly closer and women trudge hours for a few gallons of water and the eyes of their children are infested with flies; places where hard nervous men in civilian clothes knock on the door in the night to take away the son and he never returns, and no questions are asked, for no answers are given... What do I have to complain about?

Mei Li wants to forget everything. She won't even look at me. (I hadn't foreseen this, wouldn't have believed she'd deny everything so utterly.) The others don't suspect the passion that was but they do know we're friends (were friends) and someone will realize we no longer speak. How will I answer someone's curiosity? I can't suggest to her that she hide her denial as she hid her bliss—she won't talk to me.

Sometimes I almost seem normal again. At home in the day to day compass of ordinary life it seems that all this couldn't really have happened. But when I see her, when I hear her talking, when I wake in the nighttime hollow, it's horrible.

I find myself shaking numbers by the throat to extract meaning. I buy lottery tickets with our birthdates. Her license number is 666 which is auspicious for the Chinese but *Revelations* tells us the number of the beast is six hundred threescore and six and this is the number of a man: does this mean anything?

Is there a depth corresponding to the height of each passion? Most people live at a mean with minor modulations and so did I until I reached an ecstasy I'm repaying with a despair as great. Suppose you sum all our emotions, the happiness of children, pleasures of grownups, petty interactions with colleagues, sorrow of the starving Saharan, midnight fear of the Salvadorean—what's the mean, where are you and I?

This is impossible. It's an elementary, trite attempt to order the formless passage of time and the moment's endless expanse. It's antique—we can no longer be Pythagoreans.

Alcohol, habibi, I've tried it, it only deepens the suffering.

As its haze closes in, my awareness shrinks to the exact center I want to forget. My usual mood is agitation, insomnia, a quest for tranquility, and alcohol exacerbates the turbulence, clouds my ratiocination, blurs rigor and nuance. It's better to have all my faculties—any chance of escaping this torment lies in surmounting it fully aware. Writing is better. It forces my attention from her and briefly induces a calm lucidity.

Good luck, dear Jacques, in love. So you and your friend must keep it secret. What is this crap? Why are sexual relations so frightening? Society cannot tolerate passion? It's a monkey in the mechanism? People are afraid of the boundless? I am unhappy for you, my poor friend, drenched by shadow in your white Libyan sunlight.

CHAPTER 20

News came from overheard conversations. He learned that the cocktail party hadn't been easy for her either when she told Steve she'd gotten really drunk. He learned Daniel's first word when she told Mike that she'd given him cranberry juice and he asked, "Wine?" He learned she was arranging a lunch when she asked Steve who to invite, and learned he was included when a farewell lunch for somebody showed up on his calendar. He'd be damned if he'd let himself feel bad.

"I'm tired of feeling bad all the time," he told his mother.

"Oh, Alan, I was afraid someone would get hurt. To be honest, I couldn't see a future in it."

"Do you think I was foolish?"

"No, and if some good came of it, if it changed Susan's feelings and made your marriage stronger, then that's even better. And you learned you're capable of passion."

"Well, that's no good if the object of your passion is unattainable."

"It's too bad the way she feels now, but what do you want from her? What do you expect?"

"I ask myself that. It'd be nice to be able to say hello and talk about business, since unless one of us gets another job we're going to be around each other for a long time."

"You know, it sounds like high school when you go out with someone Friday and Monday morning they ignore you."

"Yeah, she is acting silly. Sometimes I feel like telling her to snap out of it."

"Don't do that. Don't refer to it at all. Don't, for instance, send her a valentine on Valentine's Day."

He laughed.

"Your dad wants to say something."

"Alan, have you thought about anti-depressive drugs? There's no shame in it, you know. You seem to be showing the symptoms Berenice and I had."

"Thanks, Dad, but I don't need drugs, I need time."

On what happened to be the seven-month anniversary of the ski trip he finally got a contact lens that worked. For the first time in two months his sight was clear and things felt right. He killed time before a lunchtime piano lesson by strolling through the dense fall air along Stow Lake and savoring the crisp outlines of the red leaves. A young couple was eating lunch on the bench and he considered joining them and telling them about a married man who had sat there with a married woman in the springtime and wishing them better luck, but decided it would only embarrass them. At Sofia's he found that clear vision and a good mood were no substitute for practice, but even clumsy fingers didn't diminish his sense of well-being. On returning to the office he stayed outside for a cigarette and thought he might be able to quit again. As he crossed the alley, Olive drove up. He smiled and mouthed hello.

What Might Have Happened: A sudden wave of resentment swept her. Her vision dimmed, she stepped hard on the accelerator, and the station wagon hopped as it hit him and careened into the street where a pickup slammed into its side. She sat in the driver's seat staring at the corner store, her hands on the wheel. In the silence she quietly started to cry. Two men from the pickup opened her door. She sat, tears falling drop by drop onto her lap.

What Actually Happened: Her face stayed absolutely blank. He entered the office and returned to his chores. The day passed like all the others, slowly, one more day in a succession whose blankness he could only hope would end. Each evening before returning home he had to breathe deeply, look at the sky and forget the pain before re-entering life. He didn't stop smoking.

She still had the music appreciation records and some tapes of Chinese folk songs he'd loaned her. She was listening to his music and she was reading his *Odyssey* but she wasn't speaking to him. How could she borrow something and pretend the lender didn't exist? How rude. He wanted the music back and he wanted to rebuke her thoughtlessness in keeping it, but he didn't want to sound like a whiner. He bought a replacement copy of the *Odyssey* to suggest he'd given up expecting its return and told her, "Philip's class is studying China. I'd like to loan them the tapes. Could you please give them back? Also, you can keep the *Odyssey*. I bought another copy."

"I was planning to buy a backhard, what do you call it, hard…"

"Hardback."

"…for myself. I'm so proud of myself to finish I want a hardback for my library. Can you get them?"

"There was one at the store."

"I'll buy it and give you back your book."

He was disappointed—now his copy wouldn't sit on her shelf as a reproach.

The folk songs appeared on his desk Monday while he was out. When he said, "Thanks for the tapes," she looked up and half-smiled, "Mm, hm."

Tuesday he said good morning as he walked past her at the copier. She looked up and half-smiled, "Mm, hm."

Later, just before five, she walked over. "Stella says I need to talk to you about this contract."

"Can it wait until tomorrow? I have to leave now."

"I wanted to get it done this evening."

So he stayed and did what she wanted.

Wednesday he put her calendar picture and a note on her desk. "Thanks for the use of this. I'm sorry for the paint smudge in the corner." She walked by later and half-smiled,

"Mm, hm." Wow: She'd addressed him first. When he met her on the stairs, he looked at her steadily and smiled. She glanced away, then back and half-smiled, "Mm, hm." That afternoon while she was speaking to Mike, she glanced at him twice. Hell: He was counting the number of times she looked at him.

Susan suggested inviting Steve and Sharon for Thanksgiving "and what about Olive and Paul?"

"No... Olive has cooled off quite a bit."

"Really? She was very friendly to me the other day when I saw her in the alley. What happened?" Philip interrupted with a question. She answered and continued, "Well, that's okay. When I think about having them I get a little nervous, and I want Thanksgiving to be relaxed."

"Sure. Steve and Sharon would be easy."

"What happened with Olive?" The phone rang and he jumped to answer. By the time he hung up, Susan had to leave. The subject was dropped, but what would he say if it came back?

Thursday he heard Olive phone a motel in Sonoma for a room for two. Torment: she was doing things with Paul she once would have done with him. He told her Susan wanted to hear the last of the Mediterranean tapes—would she mind lending them? She nodded without even a half-smile.

Friday was the farewell lunch she had organized. She and Harry were late and she took the last seat at Alan's table, which made him uncomfortable and angry at his discomfort. He moved to Harry's table. Her alto laugh rode above the uproar. When Harry described their sail to Tiburon she called out, "We sailed across half drunk and returned totally drunk!" Were bouts of intoxication the significant events in her life? Or was she still covering up for their near discovery? He glanced at her and she looked away.

On the way back to the office Jose said to Mike, "I couldn't believe you asked Olive if she was pregnant." They all laughed.

"What did you say?" asked Alan.

"Oh, you would've had to be there," they chuckled.

He wanted to ask more but was afraid of revealing his obsessive curiosity. He was angry, agitated, and too drunk to work. He took a skin flick home and masturbated angrily.

That night Susan wanted sex but he didn't. She asked, "Is that what you did all afternoon?"

"Yes, and I just did again."

"You did? I wanted to do it together."

"I had no idea. You have to give me a clue, you know."

He was so angry he couldn't sleep. He'd tell Olive: Keep the *Odyssey.* And give me back my records. What if she returned the earrings too? Well, those belonged to her. Let her throw them away if she didn't want them. He'd say, "Why are you giving me earrings? I don't wear earrings." More likely she'd put them on his desk while he was out. He'd give them back with a note: I don't want these.

In the morning he began remembering scenes from the skin flick and put his arm around Susan but she slept on, so he quietly started the video. She said grumpily, "What are you doing?"

"I'm going to watch a dirty movie." She growled and got out of bed. "You stay," he said. "I'll go." But she slammed out of the room.

He couldn't face a weekend stewing about Olive. Well, no time like the present, he suddenly decided, and went to the office. The Mediterranean tapes were on his desk. His disgust increased. Two fucking months and she was still treating him like this. He took the records from her drawer, the drawer he'd put them in, and wrote a note. "I took my records. You keep the *Odyssey,* or dispose of it. Alan." Then he decided it would be more aloof if typed so he typed it, and then he changed Alan to ADD for a touch of insolence. He left it face up on her desk and hoped she felt bad.

I won't ever look at her again. If she's with someone I need to talk to I won't wait until she leaves, I'll just ignore her and talk. If someone asks why we don't talk, I'll say it's her–ask her. In fact, I'll point out that we don't talk. (On the other hand maybe it's best to remain silent, act nobly.) (What does she say to others about me?) Fight the fire with a preemptive burn. Be acerbic. Be malicious.

If we're in a group and things get bawdy, as they always do with her–jokes about getting it on, everyone does, cheap worldly wisdom, her intimations that she would or she might– I'll hint that she might indeed. I've been discreet out of respect for her scruples but she has none, she flirts as usual. To hell with it. She mistakes my discretion for weakness. She's taking advantage of me. I'll make her squirm a little. She's going to have to suffer, too. I have been weak, I have been uncertain, but I've had enough. It's time to recreate a strong impression. I am strong and I'm going to show my strength.

Enough nostalgia, enough remembering that we did this there and that here and there we met so and so. Over. Ended. Finish with it.

John Taylor hung around waiting for her. He was always around lately. She arrived, they talked, and when John left she handed Alan the note. "How do you know where everything is?"

He didn't reply.

She stood wringing her hands or rubbing lotion on them, he couldn't tell which. "Do I owe you anything else?"

"Since you won't talk to me, I wanted to get my stuff back." She threw up her hands and stepped back into her cubicle. An hour later his resolution wavered and he considered trying to explain, but then reviewed the way she was treating him and decided not to.

The next morning she sat down and typed, walked over and dropped a note on his desk, and returned to her cubicle.

I AM OFFENDED THAT YOU JUST GET RIGHT INTO MY DRAWER AND REMOVE THINGS WITH- OUT ASKING ME FIRST. PLEASE DON'T DO IT AGAIN.

He went to her. "This can't go on."

"This is acting like children. It's like we have a fight, so give back my pencil and I give back your eraser."

"I've been very angry. If I loan you something and you ignore me, it's not right. You're using my things but you're not even talking to me."

"I thought you didn't want the music things back. You said Susan didn't care, you were throwing them out."

"Well, maybe that's my fault."

"These two months are torture for me. I'm thinking about seeing Fern's doctor. My moods change very much. Onc day it's okay and next I'm filled with anger and resentment. I just can't stop to feeling, it was so strong. If only I can go back to the way it was before."

"Try acting politely and courteously, and the feelings will follow."

"That won't work for me. It has to come from inside."

"I'm afraid for you—you want to keep it secret, but sooner or later people are going to notice we don't speak."

"I don't care what people think."

He knew better but said nothing.

She said she hadn't found a hardback of the *Odyssey*. If he did, buy it and she'd repay him; in the meantime, could she keep his?

In the fit of elation that followed, he searched three bookstores. Then he realized her strong feelings did nothing for him except explain her attitude, and then a fleeting hope they might one day be friends passed into the clear knowledge that he still loved her intensely. His sudden absence of anger recalled a shot of Novocain he'd had in an infected finger: After swelling and fever and pervasive torment there was finally relief, thankfulness, and absence of pain: Dolorous still, but the sharp edge was gone.

Dear Olive,

How can I say this? (It's no longer any of my business, but one wants to help.) I don't think it will ever be the way it was before. I'm sorry.

You're trying to suppress your feelings by force of will. If I weren't around it might work, but the trouble is I sit right here reminding you. And maybe it does work sometimes, but generally deep feelings and past actions have to be accepted somehow and lived with. They don't go away just because you want them to.

Do talk with Fern's doctor. Beyond a certain point you're on your own, but talking gets you there faster. Maybe it just takes a long time.

He didn't give it to her. He painted an anguished self-portrait that Claire said looked like a demon.

Sofia told him, "Men get to a certain age when everything is working fine, life is boring, and they fall in love. Sometimes they're even embarrassed about it. But there's nothing wrong with it. As for a plain sexual affair, of course if you have the chance you take it."

"It's absurd. It's chemical. Falling in love releases chemicals the same as chocolate and morphine do, but the euphoria never lasts. My theory is that people divorce when it wears off unless they start producing the endorphins that induce tranquility. Me, I'm in withdrawal."

"It's biological! It's silly, the act is silly, the whole thing is silly, and yet without it life isn't worth living."

"If you don't follow your god to the end, then you haven't loved."

"Of course. At least, it makes going to work interesting for you."

"No, it hurts!"

There was music on the radio he recognized but couldn't place. Its slow stately pace was so sad and beautiful that he parked the car and cried, drop by falling drop. Another achingly familiar movement began, and another, and he listened through its remote nobility to the end. Beethoven's seventh symphony. He turned off the radio and let his feelings dissipate in silence. She would like this music. He dried his tears and went on.

CHAPTER 21

Susan said she was happy to have a family Thanksgiving without guests. Alan wondered what Olive was doing and attacked himself on the back porch with wine and cigarettes, especially cigarettes, assaulting his breath, the core of life.

He took his paintings to the office on the pretext that Steve wanted to see them. Olive stopped and regarded the pond without comment. He pointed to the self-portrait. "This is how I felt a couple weeks ago."

She started. "I would not hang that! People will think you've gone crazy!"

"How was your Thanksgiving?"

"It was terrible. My father had a seizure like the one before. He's still in the hospital."

"I'm very sorry. I hope you're not taking it badly."

"Well," she said to Steve, "I must say we're all used to it now. I have my own family so it's not the end of the world like the first time. Now that I have Daniel, I have other concerns."

The rest of the week passed in silence. She and Jose went out one afternoon for a long time. Alan was jealous and hated himself for it, but told himself it wasn't as bad as it had been. They returned with flowers and Jose told someone they'd bought makings for paella. Alan told himself to assume it was true. He heard her tell Steve that she and Paul had finally arranged a weekend together, but now it had to be canceled because of her father.

Susan occasionally initiated some perfunctory sex. One night they thrashed in the dark until she told him to get off. She finished him by hand. He said angrily, "I agree with you. The whole thing is disgusting, ridiculous, and messy. I don't want to do it anymore."

"Each of us thinks I'm doing everything and you're doing nothing. Maybe there's no point in going on."

"I just don't want sex anymore. Apart from that I'm happy to live with you."

"Why bother?"

"For the children?"

Olive's birthday was nearing. She stopped to chat about Claire one morning, which emboldened him to ask, "Would you accept a birthday present from me?" She wavered but didn't walk away. "Do you have a recording of Beethoven's seventh symphony?"

"Oh, I like that so much! I always told everybody to play it at my funeral."

She had told him that, he recalled. "I used to want Verdi's *Requiem* played at mine. Do you know it?"

"No."

"Well, do you have the *Seventh?*"

"I don't know. I might have a record but not a CD."

"Take a look and let me know."

"Your fortieth birthday is coming up. Are you doing anything?"

"Susan talked about having a party... How's your father?"

"Life is very busy these days visiting him, daycare for Daniel, busy at work."

He heard Mike saying on the phone that Olive was grumpier than usual. He hurried to Jose's cubicle and put his ear to the partition but heard no more. Dare he ask what he'd meant? No, Mike would probably tell her, and then she'd really be upset.

He smoked on the porch and listened to the wind in the trees, the molecules of air and water vapor rushing through leaves, the world as it was now, had been, would be without him, his life such a transitory puff so slow to adjust. Only these past few days was he starting to be able to think of it as something in the past, memories and hopes no longer fresh. But it was hard; he couldn't escape himself: even the effort of avoiding her refreshed the ties and inhibited his adjustment to new conditions at work, the children's school, his marriage.

He cracked a joke at lunch and Olive laughed despite herself. Harry continued, "You know what they say about sex with a Chinese woman. It's like Chinese food—in half a hour you're hungry again."

She smiled.

"We should ask Paul," Harry said.

Or me, Alan thought.

Stella said to him, "You've cut off all your nice hair."

"Yeah, it's thinning and my hairline's receding. I cut it so nobody will think I'm hiding anything."

Olive looked glumly at her plate.

She was indulging herself. She was acting like a brat. Maybe it was tough for her, but that was no excuse.

He'd volunteered to play piano at the departmental Christmas party. "Good," laughed Sofia, "you'll cause emotion in one part of the audience at least!" But as it turned out, Olive stayed home with Daniel, so the emotion was his alone.

Somebody from the facilities group asked one day, "How are things?"

"Work's fine, Randy, but my personal life is rotten. My marriage is falling apart, I had a love affair, it ended, and my ex-lover is so remorseful she won't even talk to me."

"Sounds bad. I know the feeling."

"You do?"

"Yes. You poor guy," Randy said kindly. "Things will get better."

He hoped so. He was tired of this flat and featureless agony, the same vague, undefined sorrow day after day, boring to talk about, boring to hear, nothing to do, no action to take, just wait for time to pass.

Olive told him about her daycare troubles. "Paul's parents have Daniel two days a week, but they never ask us for anything and they're not pleased about it. When I'm late to pick him up they're not at all gracious. I know it's silly, but I resent their attitude to reject their grandson, our son. Daniel's my king."

Yeah, he knew.

A man should always be boss in the home. The wife must be subordinate, and be seen to be subordinate, or he loses face. Thus spake Lee Kuan Yew, prime minister of Singapore.

Lo Mei Li came from that background, and she grew up in a family of women centered on the father, the sovereign, the ruler. (Naturally his poor health caused crises: It threatened the solar system's star.) Mei Li took as husband a man older than herself, and also, as it happened, a slightly older lover. Her sister Mei Ju spent her nubility on an older man. Mei Li wasn't quite as drastic, or she had more sense: her awe of things paternal ebbed, she had a child (the child was male), and her respect transferred from father to spouse and son. (His second hospitalization was less disturbing.) Her Chinese family's regard for her husband's conscientious righteousness reinforced her own, and although his chill dismayed her, she felt he was right. (He responded to a joke she made: "If you're having an affair, that's your problem, isn't it.") But she felt superior to him in ways and rebelled against his smug self-importance. ("Poor Paul," she had said after sex. "He doesn't know what he's missing.") Her lover was the jester who warmed the court's cool black and white morality.

But she had committed treason. For a season of madness

she betrayed her father the benevolent king, her husband the arrogant king, and her son the heir apparent. The illegitimate pretender didn't stand a chance. After his banishment she repledged fealty with a zeal matched only by the throne's ignorance of her crime. The lord, if he thought of it at all, accepted her kowtow as his due, not suspecting why she threw herself at him on weekends, why she was going to ski with him instead of her sister, or that for his suzerainty she'd given up dreaming of a trip to her homeland.

"Randy, if I tell you something, will you keep it to yourself?"

"Sure."

"It was Olive I was in love with."

"I guessed. Last night I was turning over in my mind what you'd said and suddenly I thought, it must be Olive."

"No kidding? Why?"

"I thought, who would he fall in love with? Usually it's someone at work so I thought, who in his office is attractive? He wouldn't fall for a dog and he wouldn't fall for a floozy. Who is there who'd feel remorse afterwards? I bet Olive's the one."

"Good lord, Randy. If it's so obvious, I'd better not even hint at it. She'd die if anyone knew."

"Meanwhile, you feel rotten. I know, it happened to me. I even moved out of the house, although I didn't know if it was the right thing. I still don't."

"You don't, do you? I would've moved out in a minute if Olive had agreed."

"In my case, I'm glad my wife was patient and waited for me to come around. I enjoy her; she has a good sense of humor."

"You're a lucky dog. Mine doesn't. Olive does. Did. Does. I can't believe it's over. We thought it'd go on forever."

"Everyone thinks the same thoughts: This will last forever, we need more time together, kill the spouses."

Alan laughed sadly.

"It'll take time to get over, Alan. There's nothing you can do but wait."

On the nights Susan came home late she slept in Philip's top bunk. Other nights if she was asleep when Alan came to bed, she would move out by morning.

He showed her the box of condoms she'd bought last spring. "Do you want these? I'm not infected and I'm not screwing around."

"I don't sense you care much anymore and I'm not even trying to be affectionate. Do you want to?"

"If you do."

"I've never been so depressed in my life. Do you want to see a counselor after the holidays? I'd like to go weekly, pay money for it, show that we mean it."

"Let's give it a try."

She whined in her sleep when he got into bed that night. Damn it this is my bed too, he thought. She was gone in the morning.

Olive hadn't told him if she had the *Seventh*. The day before her birthday he brought a CD of the *Hammerklavier* sonata instead, but she called in sick so he left it on her desk with a note. "Happy Birthday. May your 38th year be calm and happy like this music. The adagio in particular is at the most divine edge of humanity, beyond language, almost beyond comprehension. All my best."

The envelope stayed unopened all morning. Finally she came over. "Thanks, Alan. I didn't see the song until now."

"Do you have it?"

"No. I'll listen to it."

"It's very pretty."

"Thank you. Your birthday's coming up soon, isn't it?"

"Three days after Christmas."

"What are you going to do?"

"I don't know. Probably sleep."

"Oh, I'm so tired, daycare for Daniel is a day to day thing.

But it looks like you're trying to leave. I'll tell you about it later."

He needed sex. He called a number from a magazine and masturbated while a woman with a Chinese accent talked.

Olive said she'd fallen asleep on the couch listening to the CD after a nice dinner with Paul. Alan was happy she talked to him, and happier when she asked him to edit a memo. She was gone three hours at lunch—Christmas shopping, he assumed, until he noticed Jose was also gone. He felt sick. If she'd do it with me, would she do it with him? And how disappointing she'd choose Jose. But of course they weren't together. And what the hell difference did it make. He had to stop. It was killing him.

He had to talk about her but he couldn't, so he cornered Mike and told him how depressing his marriage was.

"Maybe you need to have an affair," said Mike.

"You think so?"

"Sure. You know who's best? Married women. They don't hang on you expecting more than you can offer."

He smiled ruefully. It had its ups and downs.

The next day she told him about a new daycare place for Daniel. That was good, she was talking, and it was reassuring to see her car stay parked while he played cards with the facilities group at lunch. Then he heard that she'd left with Mike and Jose. Okay, who was where with whom? Mike returned. Uh oh, even worse. Then Jose returned but not Olive. He went outside and saw that her car was gone. Okay, maybe they dropped her after lunch and she went on to campus. He wanted like hell to stop caring. He watched the clock and waited for her return.

Christmas Eve Susan yelled at him for moving a sack of presents when he vacuumed. "I'm sorry," he said. As they put out the stockings she said, "I don't want you to be unhappy. Are you?"

"Yes, but let's wait until after the holidays to talk about it."
Christmas morning he mournfully watched the kids open
presents. Claire looked through a picture album with him,
and none of the images evoked particularly happy memories.
He'd been married fifteen years, alive for forty; five happy
months with Olive into four hundred eighty was barely one
percent. Happy spells with Susan never lasted more than two
or three days.

They went to her aunt's for dinner where her brother-in-
law talked about sailing, her brother talked about Tuscany
(Olive liked Tuscany), her aunt bitched about Italians, and
her sister didn't talk to him. He stood uncomfortably with
each group pretending to have just left another and smoked
alone in the garden thinking about divorce. Long after it all
ended, he would remember Olive as the one who had made
him aware of his connubial misery.

Olive told him she'd worked hard entertaining Steve's
relatives one day and her family the next, but, she made a
face, nothing special for Paul's family on Christmas. He went
home early and called about an apartment for rent. It was
expensive. He framed his paintings and listened to a tenor
recital Susan had received as a gift, and to *Four Last Songs,*
and cried and watched himself in a mirror so he could paint
a crying man someday. He hung a mountain that Claire liked
in her bedroom and hung the pond and self-portrait on the
living room wall. He asked about the rent for the house next
door. Expensive. He called a sex line and masturbated. He
smoked cigarettes on the porch, alone but surviving, peaceful, tired. The weather had warmed. His birthday was in two
days. He wrote. It took an effort to sit down and start each
time, but it had to be done, and it was the only thing that
seemed worthwhile.

"What are you doing for your birthday?" Olive asked.
"Nothing."
"Maybe Susan is having a surprise party for you."

"No, I think not. We're getting along poorly… I don't know if we'll be together much longer."

"For Fern there's no going back, the divorce will come through."

"What's happened with Bob?"

She laughed. "Same as always. They dance, they go out, he's a real pro."

"What is he getting out of it?"

"Friendship. That's good, that's what she needs now. But I thought you and Susan are getting along better."

"We were, but no longer."

"Things might never be ecstasy but they maybe can be acceptable. If you're up here and she's down here, maybe you can see a specialist and work things out."

"We agreed to get counseling after the holidays, but I don't have much hope any more. I feel so bad for the kids. It's going to hurt them."

"Can't you live as just friends, no fights, just make your day to day plans and live that way? It's fighting that's bad for children. Why can't you go back to the way it was at the start of your marriage?"

It never was good. "I don't know…"

"What changed?"

You. You taught me love. "I can't overlook things as much as I did."

"If you want to know what I really think…"

"I do. I'm trying to get some ideas."

"I think you'll keep trying and wondering and finally give up, but you'll feel like you did everything you can. If you don't, you'll always feel bad."

"Do you suppose she and I could live like friends, but with an arrangement to have a… friend… on the side?"

"I don't know." She smiled. "If you don't do it like that, you'll do it secretly. If she expects you to live ten more years like this, she's asking too much."

He smiled, and realized he'd forgotten how much he liked talking to her.

"I really hoped the best for you and her to work it out."

"I know you did."

"Why don't you talk to other men who love their kids and got divorced, find out how they felt."

"Maybe I'll talk to Keith."

"No, he's not... You're not like him."

"Do you know anyone like me?"

"No."

"Mike thinks I should divorce. My sister does too."

"If you do, you'll be at a point where you don't consider the children any more, you'll just know you have to for yourself."

Finally he had nothing else to say. "Well, good night. Thank you for talking."

"You're welcome."

LETTER TO JACQUES

Habibi, I've been in a deep hole. Twenty weeks of rudderless love followed by twenty in a dark cave. First a random world of chance where all was possible (you know how hard the surrealists worked to create their aleatoric moods? I got one for free.); then stark severance from all anticipation, a black lack of potentiality. I think I'm coming out of it. I think so because, instead of undifferentiated suffering, I recognize the desperate monotony I felt before Mei Li loved me. Change is slow and hard to measure, but now and then she seems to have been only a passing perturbation in my crippled marriage, and I think this return to a previous state means I'm getting over her.

Actually, she is still the governing star. She's starting to be friendlier, she seems happy, and therefore I am happier. Thank god. I'm so tired of seeking distractions, tired of writing and painting and piano, tired of reading trashy books to pass an unthinking evening.

You know, normally disillusion cushions a breakup, and it normally sets in when we see the one we've fallen in love with as she is instead of as what we wanted. (And maybe what we

wanted was to find ourself in her, and the disappointment is
with ourself for having been self-centered.) At any rate, she
broke with me before that began, and preoccupation with my
own suffering kept me from learning more about her.

Who is she really? What is she like? I only knew her while
she forgot herself, while she was not herself. I didn't notice
her addiction to stability. She craves attention and excitement but fears change. I see now that she always saw me as
a threat to her stability.

And who am I really? I'm asking this because I suspect
she's self-centered and wonder if I am too. What's important
to me? I try to contribute to the kids' school, to adjudicate
disputes at work with fairness, to consider others' feelings and
needs. So there's some social concern; what about personal
ethics? Would I cause pain to Susan? I have. I do. How far
would I sacrifice my happiness to hers? Not very, it seems. I
would have left her for Olive and I probably would for someone else. I guess I'm a schmuck.

Another question: How long can happiness last, anyway?
Is it always transitory? I do think that a love well begun,
though it change as all things change, can remain happy. My
love with Susan was not well begun. Can it become happy?
I hope so. I'll keep you posted.

Olive handed him an envelope that said Happy Birthday.
He was too overcome to speak. Inside was a gift certificate
for a history of architecture which she'd ordered. An Olive
branch! Friendship! The gods smiled again.

"The clerk said it's a good one. Anyway, it'll be okay since
you haven't read much about architecture."

He wanted to thank her for all it represented—acknowl-
edgement of the past, the search for a meaningful gift, an
acceptance of future delivery which indicated this was not a
momentary impulse but would endure, a tender of reconcili-
ation, the end of the drought, the return of the future—but he
was afraid of saying anything that would overstep the line.
"How thoughtful. Thank you. Say, Susan got something for

Christmas you'd love, a recital by three marvelous tenors in Rome last summer."

"Oh, I think I would. Give me the label information so I can buy it."

She went to her desk and he fondled the certificate. O joy! He couldn't work. He wanted something to happen at once. I'll go home and read the label. No, better, I'll go to a store and get the CD. He was back in an hour. "Here, Olive."

"What is this?"

"It's the recital. I bought it for you."

She reached for her purse. "How much do I owe?"

"You just keep it."

"No, I ask you to buy it for me. This is not a gift."

He'd overstepped the line. He took the money with a shrug he hoped would show it didn't matter as much as it did. "My favorite is *E Lucevan le Stelle.*"

"I'm happy I recognize some songs now. When I saw my first opera *Tosca* I thought it's pretty but I don't know these songs."

She'd told him *Rosenkavalier* was her first. It didn't matter. What mattered was that she was friendly, she was ready to get along.

On his birthday Susan asked if he wanted to do anything special. He said no. She said they'd probably get divorced. He asked her to wait for the counselor. She said, "Can you try to have a nice day for the kids' sake?" They went bowling and had cake and presents at home. The kids, at least, enjoyed themselves.

On New Year's Day he stopped smoking.

Olive seemed to be avoiding him.

He got a haircut.

Mike sat talking to Olive and Steve before the weekend. Alan went back and forth wanting to be included but uneasy about staying. Jose told an off-color joke. Olive was staring at her computer screen and said, "I would like to know why you keep cutting your hair so short."

I'm barely held together, it's one of the few things I can control these days, I'm trying to keep my trim. And why do you ask? You were upset at that lunch, too—do you think I'm cutting it for you? "It's the bald Mike Trumbull look." She didn't join the laughter.

Susan sounded hopeless when they met the new counselor, and he didn't know how to react when she talked that eve ning about the things she was going to miss when he moved out. "Can you hold on a couple more weeks?" he encouraged. "Things can only get better."

Olive silently accepted an article about Lebanon he thought she and Paul might like, but when he returned from lunch a manila envelope on his desk held it, the *Hammerklavier* CD, and a note.

I am very angry inside again.

I need to have my peace back but don't have the time to sort it out yet.

Sorry to be blunt.

In general, I regret everything that happened and don't want any special feelings lingering.

So, I don't think us exchanging gifts is appropriate.

Sorry, my mistake.

The office sounds faded into silence. He put the note in his pocket and walked outside. Susan was parking her car in the alley. He said hello and she told him about a job interview she'd had that morning and he told her he thought they'd work things out and she said she thought sex would be good again someday. They said goodbye and he went to the corner store and bought a pack of cigarettes.

He drove to campus and invited Randy for a cup of coffee and showed him the note. "This is pretty final," Randy said. "Obviously she wants to end everything. The best thing for you is to forget it. Put it behind you. Get on with your life. She may be afraid of starting up again or something, but whatever the reason, she wants it to end."

"Yup. That's what I thought. I just needed someone else to say so."

He called her. "Hi, this is Alan."

Silence.

"I'm sorry, too."

Silence.

"Would you like the book back when it comes in?"

"I will take care of that."

"You'll call the bookstore?"

"Yes."

"Okay."

Silence.

"Sorry."

"Okay."

"Goodbye."

Later he wished he'd told her how cruel she was.

He woke up dreaming about writing a note on the gift certificate: Be sure you see a shrink, you need help, you need to grow up. He fell asleep again and dreamed he'd moved into her cubicle and she'd moved into his. He sat in a red office chair talking to Steve and a pretty young woman in a dark green dress who resembled someone he knew in college. Olive walked up silently, wanting everyone to go away so she could sit down. He noticed a glimmer in her hair and said, "Your hair really does have brown highlights." She smiled and said, "No, it's black." He wondered if she tinted it but wasn't telling him. She stepped to face the computer with her back to him in a familiar gesture of exclusion but he made no move to leave. She stepped on his foot with her high heel. It hurt, but rather than move his foot he reached down to push hers away. She moved it and then rubbed his hand with her other foot. He ran his hand up the inside of her thigh, under her dress, then stood and pulled her shoulders from behind to force her into the chair. She turned. He seized her and kissed her on the lips; she was compliant but not responsive. He said, "I feel like killing you." She smiled.

CHAPTER 22

No, it wasn't that I didn't love Susan when I married her. I trusted her. I wanted a family, and a marriage founded on passion was too risky. I was like the Greek chorus who sees passion destroy the protagonist and says, 'Heaven preserve me from this kind of love.'"

"Maybe she worried that if you ever became as passionate about someone else as she was about you, you'd leave," said the counselor.

"That's right, and it almost happened," said Susan, "and I'm still worried. Is it really over, Alan?"

"Oh, yes. It's over." He sighed. "We get along fine except for sex. She doesn't like it and I need it. I don't expect ecstasy, and I can be reconciled to less than I'd want, but there has to be some. It's part of intimacy."

"Sex is based on trust," said the counselor. "First we need to establish trust."

"That's right," said Susan.

"You never trusted me, did you?"

"And why should I?"

The next week she said he controlled his feelings to such an extent he couldn't express them. He laughed painfully at how much he was concealing for her sake and how open he'd been with Olive. "If that's true, I'll never find intimacy with anyone unless I change, and I might as well change with you. Please give me the chance."

The concert two years ago with Olive—had it been Beethoven's *Seventh?* He got the old schedules Susan kept. It had been. That's when she talked about her funeral, and that's why his hearing it the other week had so moved him. And the concert had been exactly a year before the ski trip. The sheer perfection of all this damned coincidence was nauseating.

Dear Susan,
The only feelings I've concealed are the ones I'm ashamed of or think would hurt you. Do you want them all? You're welcome to them, to the whole unanalyzed intensely felt slew of impressions that pass through me.
I have always loved you.
I have always wanted the best for you.
I have always respected your opinions. I don't know anyone with reactions so similar to mine.
I want to be closer to you. I want your warm friendliness and I want you to accept mine.
I don't care about excitement, passion, erotic desire. That is fun, no doubt, but as you say, it doubtless wanes.
Which is not to say I will or can live happily without sex. I cannot help biological compulsion. Though I can control its expression and prevent its realization, I cannot control its existence or intensity, as you cannot control your menstrual cycle.
Please excuse my clumsiness. I'm trying to show by sharing a few thoughts that I care about our continued life together.

She kissed him and joined him in bed. "Would you like a blow job?" But he was nervous, it didn't work, and she felt bad.

She showed him the phone bill. "What are these charges?"
"They're pornographic phone calls."
She surprised him by saying merely, "Oh. Expensive, isn't it?"
He used his ski money to pay the bill.

The ordinary face was an unexamined surface, but Olive's had been transfigured by sexual excitement and love and was imbued with meaning. He watched her during a staff meeting. She pretended irony to deflect attention from statements she feared were inept or erroneous, narrowed her eyes in amusement, opened them charmingly wide, dressed, scented, and made herself up with care. There was always calculation in her apparent frankness. He had the sensation of a moral problem, a vague ethical question, and tracked it to a memory of her asking him if she'd been right to reveal why an architect hadn't been selected for a job. She was insecure.

"Boy, these cubicles are tiny," Randy said. "You sure don't have much privacy."

"This would be a lousy place for a love affair."

They went outside and Randy asked, "How are you feeling these days?"

"I'm sorry she won't be friendly, but I don't really care anymore. She's chosen to constrict her life by excluding me; so much the worse for her, she can stew in her own juices. I can't let myself suffer because she can't cope with her guilt."

"It's too bad she doesn't just say okay, it's over, I made a mistake. Why make everybody miserable?"

"She's putting off the day she'll have to face it. She might suppress this, but one day she's going to meet another guy and bang, the whole thing over again."

"The worst thing must be working so close to her."

"It does hurt. She's cold as ice. She won't even look at me when we pass in the hall, but I'm getting used to it. It was a lovely fling, but it's over."

"Is she afraid she'll fall for you again?"

"Since she won't talk to me, I don't know, but I think she's angry with herself. Tough."

"Sounds like you're a bit angry."

"I suppose so. I overheard her saying she'd been asked to find another daycare because her bratty son was beating up another kid, and I was glad he's giving her trouble. I've got to get over this."

"It'll eat you up."

"I'm trying to tell myself that you like some people, some you don't, and some you never speak to."

"Sometimes you think everything's okay, wake up in the morning and think ah, I'm over it, and later you start feeling bad again."

"I feel bad all the time."

"Affairs are just no good—the woman's usually a floozy."

"And if she's not, you want more time together, want to spend the night, live together. You're never happy."

"Except maybe in the beginning."

"Oh, the beginning… I stood there wondering if I dared to go into her room… I did, in the dark, in the silence, and woke her up…"

"She must have been coming on to you before."

"No, she was really surprised by what happened. Well, maybe unconsciously, but she only realized it after we made love."

"Hm."

"It was wonderful! The wonder, the excitement, the tenderness—it was glorious!"

Randy nodded. "It's the only thing that replaces the feeling you had as a kid on Christmas morning—a new piece of ass. Not to be crude."

Susan was upset. "Who screwed up the closet?"

"I straightened out the boxes."

"It's all messed up."

He lost patience. "I thought about how I could screw it up the worst possible way and then I did."

"What's wrong?" Claire asked.

Susan shouted, "These boxes are all mixed up."

"I'm sorry," said Claire.

"I'm not sorry," said Alan.

"You're nasty. You're so bossy and authoritarian."

"Wait, time out, as the counselor says to say. I was nasty, but what did I say that's bossy and authoritarian?"

She didn't answer.

"If you don't want to talk, say so and we'll drop it."

She didn't reply.

"Susan, sit down. Why won't you talk to me?"

"I didn't hear what you were saying."

LETTER FROM JACQUES

All my best for the new year. May it be a year when peace returns. I'm speaking, of course, of your personal situation. As for the international situation, I'm scared! If Saddam is wiped out it's war with all Islam, and it's no better if he appears victorious—the Arabs will think they're better than they are. They already do, the idiots! They don't listen to the few reasonable men among them, they murder them.

I'm well situated, alas, to know the blind archaic nature of Muslim Arabs. My girlfriend is in a horrible situation—obligated to leave Libya where she can't stay without working and where she can't live with me, a Christian. I would happily marry her, but she could not tell her family—her brother would kill her (this is not a joke). I would have to convert to Islam, but I don't care, that's no problem. And she will need papers she has to get in Morocco and without a job contract she'll have trouble returning. They don't let single women enter, even adult. You see the shitty situation.

I'm in France. I got malaria so they sent me to a hospital in Paris. I return to Tripoli next week so I can see her before she leaves. This forces me to give up a week with Claude. Another problem. Life is less and less easy.

What kind of future is there? It's impossible for me—even baptized a Muslim—to ask for her hand. The brother is fanatically religious and the mother, a little crazy, understands nothing but the shitpot Koran. All the doors are closing one after another. Trust in God, however. (I'm starting to talk like the Arabs. Lord!)

All my affection. I hope you're in better shape than I am. Best wishes to Susan and the children.

Siegfried's funeral march came on the radio and he pulled over to listen, remembered waiting for Olive somewhere, anticipating the instant she'd come into view, her familiar stance, her walk, his heart's rapturous movement outward, the smile and joy at the smile returned, the embrace, the kiss. The invasion of tenderness angered him—he wanted to be scornful and ironic, but his body cheated him by furnishing gladness and sorrow.

He felt incomplete and driven to get to the heart of something. His emotions were woven into a network of thoughts, memories, sensations. Nothing was purely itself—everything was part of the same thing. One world, one life, one self. But he was separated from the sharp outlines of things, the atmosphere didn't quite touch his skin, a homogeneous haze clouded his perception, he was the background and the forefront was an intense, diffused blur like the near approach of meaning. He could not understand.

He felt miserable, rented a skin flick and went home, put it on and realized he'd seen it before—it was the one he and Susan had watched. The soundtrack changed to the second movement of the *Seventh*. Jesus Christ. He was sick of reminders, sick of pain, sick of his obsession with something that was gone.

LETTER TO JACQUES

Habibi Jacques, what a horrible situation. My problems pale beside yours. How you must have suffered in Paris, feverish, distraught by her absence, puzzling out what would come next, the choice between her and Claude. Like you I would choose her—Claude will always be there. One assumes.

Yourcenar says love carries us into a different world where we cease to belong when the ardor is spent or the ecstasy subsides. Well, the pain of its loss is yet another world. How does one person become so important? Why does one single person's rejection hurt so much?

I always fall for unattainable women, capricious bitchy demanding flirtatious little girls. Or maybe I pick situations where total intimacy is impossible. I knew she was right when she said it couldn't work, but I was too passionate to imagine anything but passion.

I've been on a jury, a squalid case, childhood beatings and fraternal rape, misconstrued testimony, statements out of context, a tawdry piece of theater. The trial took two weeks and covered so little of a life, and we the jury took fifteen minutes to decide. How quickly we judge another's anguish. How quickly would my own be judged?

I do my job. I'm no longer in the clique. I find my own rewards and enjoy my clients, which I haven't been able to do for months, but there is a lack, a need to connect with something, without knowing what. I'm smoking a lot.

Susan says I think about sex more than other people. Maybe so. How much of my life have I spent on it? Half an hour a day, I suppose.

Well, good luck to you. May things soon improve.

He heard a Strauss tone poem he'd loved twenty years earlier and was pleasantly surprised by how much more meaning it now held. Two more decades would add another quantum of appreciation, and one twenty-year beat after that he'd be hearing it for the last time—paltry steps toward insight culminating in an old man of small understanding. Life was such a brief flash.

Would he understand Olive in forty years? Would he understand himself?

The uncontrolled acts of a fool were apparent, though it shouldn't have mattered—love forgives stupidity. Was she ashamed of him because he'd acted foolishly? Ashamed of falling for a fool? Ashamed now, cold sense of propriety recovered, for having acted a fool herself?

His manic intensity had probably frightened her. If he'd

been less passionate, less demonstrative, if he'd held back, hadn't revealed the extent of his insanity, been cool, calm, debonair—would she have continued? A light French comedy. An occasional mouthful of chocolate. Was that really all she'd ever wanted? So that shallow fop Taylor, or stuck-up Jose, somebody like that would have been a better partner. But would she have cared as much if he'd been lighter? And would he have wanted anything less? Well, mere sex would've been okay. Inconsequential sex. It might have worked. Sex and love had been inseparable, but when she brought up pornography the possibility of meeting in the realm of mere sensation arose. Things could have lightened up. But by then he'd followed his god too far; it was too late. He could have acted no differently. He'd tried to be true to himself and honest with her without reservation. There was nothing to regret.

Strauss sang: Life is spacious and wonderful and melancholy because everything has an end. She was probably back to a normal suburban life, husband faithful and true, a small circle of friends, an easy flirtation now and then, membership in a swim club, evenings at the opera, books on tape, small pleasures. (Did she still give herself completely to music or was she inhibited by the memory of how far she had let herself go?)

All he regretted was her bad faith. She hadn't kept her end of the bargain that they were consenting adults who could call it off and stay friends. Well, he'd keep the new bargain. The cold shoulder. If she came to chat he'd ignore her. If she wanted information he'd give it laconically.

He had a chance to snub her one day when Mike asked about something and she asked Alan, "Yes, what is all this about design-build contracts?" He stared at her a moment considering how best to offend. Then the phone rang and he picked it up without a word. Small pleasures.

Over the din at a party their boss gave for them and their spouses, he asked Steve, "Where's Paul?"

"He and Daniel weren't feeling well so they stayed home."

"Oh, that's too bad. Say, I'm sailing on Sunday. Want to come?"

He and Olive didn't speak, but she talked with Susan for a long time. He sensed her looking toward him but didn't turn. Only once, while she danced with Jose, her eyes defiantly met his. She was a poor sap.

Susan said afterwards, "I think Olive has a hard time with Paul, but no relationship is perfect, she'll stick it out. She told me she wants another baby but first they're going to remodel their house. Actually, I think they're full of themselves. Do you know what she said? One of their neighbors objects to having their view blocked and she said, well, we're both architects, what if we move and they get somebody who isn't as tasteful?"

"Pretty self-centered, isn't it?"

"Very selfish. Well, she'd better not wait too long for another baby. She's already thirty-six."

Good lord, all this time I thought she was thirty-seven. I've been playing the wrong lottery number.

Berenice asked, "How are you and Susan getting along?"

"We see our therapist weekly and we're growing closer. I enjoy talking to her. The only thing is sex. As usual. I'm keeping my eye open for other possibilities. I know a few tricks for having an affair."

"Alan, come on. Haven't you learned?"

"Oh, you're right, I won't. Claire and Philip are happier now that I joke and play around again. I'm happy they're happy."

"Are you still writing?"

"Yeah, it helps distance me from my feelings, but I have no illusions about its literary worth. Maybe the kids can read it someday and understand why a particular year was so rocky. Maybe I can."

"That's good. Maybe you're getting over it."

"I think I'm just waiting for something else to come and take control of me."

"You're always going to the basement to paint or sitting on the back porch writing," said Susan. "You never pay attention to me and the kids."

"I'm sorry, but there's nowhere else to do it. What if I look for a studio to work in?"

"At least you wouldn't be around here dragging everybody down."

"I heard of a room a few blocks away."

"You did? You're looking? We can't afford it. You'll have to move your boat to a cheaper place."

"That's fine. I'd rather have a studio than a boat. Actually, I've been thinking of selling it."

"Why do you want a room? Probably for another love affair."

"Oh Susan, no. Look, forget it. If you're worried about that, I'd rather not. I'll paint in the basement and write in the library."

"Why do you all of a sudden want to write and paint?"

"I always have, you know. I just decided to start."

"Oh, go ahead and see the room."

He did, but he didn't take it because it didn't have a private entrance, just in case he did meet someone.

Randy asked how things were going.

"It's so cold the glaciers are calving and falling into the sea."

"What? What are you talking about?"

"Me and my ex."

"Silent treatment?"

"Yes. For example, I was talking to Taylor and she marched up, took him by the arm, and started talking as if I wasn't there. I want an apology. I'll only talk to her if she apologizes."

"For what?"

"For anything. I've apologized to her for taking things from her desk, for hurting her, for having caused her suffering, but I've never heard her apologize to anyone for anything except her poor English, and that's only to forestall criticism."

"Doesn't she ever feel she's wronged anyone?"

"Nah, she doesn't think about others—her only concern is how she appears."

"Is she insecure?"

"Sure, aren't we all? She doesn't like it."

"Who does?"

"But most people are decent despite it."

He dreamed feverishly that he was trying to solve a puzzle, was searching for some combination of insights or wishes or memories that would rearrange the past to produce a different outcome, an altered world in which she still loved him. They were standing near the reception desk and started talking. She was upset about something, probably Paul. He moved closer. She apologized. They embraced. He was tender and warm, all bitterness gone.

It was too painful. He put it out of his mind so thoroughly he couldn't recall it later.

Mike wanted him to work with Olive on a plan to enlarge their cubicles.

"Olive doesn't talk to me anymore."

"Why not?" Mike asked, surprised.

"You'd have to ask her."

He met her in the alley. "Would you like a truce?"

"What's a truce?"

"A cease-fire."

"My feelings go up and down. Sometimes it's okay and sometimes it's not."

"I'd like to be able to be courteous to each other."

"The next time I start to feel angry, maybe I should talk to you. This is the fourth time…"

Fourth time of what. "I wish you would."

"I can't act a way I don't feel. It's the way I am."

"If you act a certain way, it pisses me off. I don't really

want to talk about it. I just want to get along."

"Me too. I want it to be smooth. How do you feel?"

Why in the hell was she asking that? To be cruel? Did she really want to hear about it? Should he tell her? Naw. He told her how his work was going.

He thought all day and all night, rose early and wrote a letter.

Excuse me for writing. I want to say clearly one time what I said so clumsily yesterday.

I don't like this cold war we are having. I'm not the kind of person who takes pleasure in being cut and cutting back. I'm amicable and I can put up with quite a bit, but I am not a saint. After a while I start reacting.

It doesn't matter to me who you are or how we got to this point. Perhaps you feel that I caused your unpleasant feelings. We have the right to feel as we feel; indeed, we cannot do otherwise. However, we all have an obligation to act in a civil manner, even to people we don't like. And our actions, past and present and future, are our own responsibility. We cannot blame anyone else for them.

Nor is it fair to choose a scapegoat for our feelings. I understand that you treat me according to how you feel, and I'm sure you don't care how I react. That is certainly your prerogative. Although I would prefer indifference to a state of hostility, I will get along regardless.

Please excuse the personal nature of this note. I can't see how to reestablish a normal working relationship without alluding in some depth to feelings. The main thing is this: I'm sick and I'm tired of the silent war that's been going on, and I'm proposing that we forget it. Let the past be the past. Let's get along. Let me know if you accept.

She led him to a conference room. "I must begin by saying that some of the things in this letter made me mad. First, I am a grownup person. I take responsibility for my actions. I am not a child." She referred to some notes she'd made.

"Second, I can't act other than I feel. I can't just say hello. Also, I thought about when you said maybe people will notice we're not talking. First, I don't think they'll notice. I don't say hello to Wanda Steiner or Jerry Diamond and it's not remarked. Second, when you said that, it made me think about the whole thing again. I don't want to."

"Since you haven't talked to me, I don't know whether you're treating me badly on purpose or because it's the only way you can cope."

"Maybe I should. When I hold it inside I lose my proportion, and when I talk to you I see things are normal."

"You know, I was so glad we were getting along at Christmas that I wanted to do a favor for you, so I got you the CD." She started to interrupt but he continued. "I probably did too much. After you gave back the birthday present, I thought you may have thought I wanted to start something again."

She shook her head. "It's not you."

"When something happens it affects what happens next. I'm not giving advice; I'm just telling you what I think. We cannot totally erase the past."

"Maybe I am different. I think I can."

"The past created the present. Each time you see me, you're going to remember."

"Sometimes I don't."

"This is the last time I'll refer to anything except work. I won't talk about my family; I don't want to hear about yours."

"Maybe that's best. Try that for a couple of months. Maybe afterwards…"

"I wrote the letter to try to get along better. I don't like working with someone I don't get along with."

"I don't mind you wrote the letter. I just don't like what it says." She was getting restless. "Maybe I should talk to you. Things don't build up that way."

"Yes."

She stood. "I must tell you too, when I hear you typing your book in the morning it makes me upset."

He would have responded but her hand was on the

doorknob. "Good luck to us both," he said.

She nodded and left.

When she left at the end of the day, she said goodbye with a small smile.

The spring wind crashed through the eucalyptus by the porch, and the vaporous air was the same as the day of a seminar before the ski trip. They'd shopped for clothes at lunch before that seminar and he'd sensed a tentative response to his feelers. He wore the pants he'd bought then to this year's seminar and took a seat behind her. Such thick, shiny hair. She ran her hands up into it, fingertips stretched upward from her ears without disturbing the glossy, still surface until a wave appeared and her fingers emerged like dolphins from the sea, bones close to the taut brown skin like the hands of a monkey, hands he'd held wonderingly in his.

He finally understood her casino message. She would miss him, she would miss the passion, but her marriage was more important. Well, she'd said it clearly enough and he was dismayed at taking so long to see that her marriage was a possession like her house, her career, her clothes and cars, her operas and books, nothing more. Nothing wrong with that, but he'd believed there was some depth behind those prideful looks, believed, for instance, that because they were both aware of the deception they practiced, they also both recognized that nothing is as it seems, that all is open to question. But there were no questions for her, no reality to be teased from appearances—what you saw was what you got.

Her allure came from the favor she granted to melt her haughtiness into a smile of complicity, a facile facial contortion which concealed vacuity and meant nothing. Acuity with a V for Olive. She'd suggested that he might grow disillusioned, but he'd always planned to avoid it by accepting that no one is perfect, and the intimate pressure of her lips had further clouded his perception. How clever of her to break off when she had.

He glimpsed the swell of her breast and remembered his

desirous curiosity a year ago, remembered too that full breast clad in a beige brassiere, and its brown nipple bare beneath his hand, and her full belly softening with age, and the cesarian scar. He had possessed her. She smiled and men wondered, does she? Would she? He alone knew what she would do, had done, knew the colors of her passion and the inchoate expression of her flesh, but his knowledge of that language was confined to a sealed dictionary.

She said hello as he walked past.

She asked his opinion of the seminar and they talked about their projects.

She asked again about the new type of contract he was using.

She told him she was organizing a lunch.

Mike returned from vacation and asked in a concerned low voice, "You said that Olive is mad at you?"

"She doesn't seem to be anymore. It's okay now." He only smiled when Mike raised his eyebrows curiously.

"You know what you have to do to her, just put your hand on her ass and tell her to knock it off!"

He laughed. That was just the problem—too much hand on her ass.

He overheard her arrange a ski trip with Steve and Mike and wondered if she'd noticed it would be exactly a year after theirs.

He sold three shares in *Malta* to reduce the cost of slip rental.

By the end of the week she was barely talking to him again. She told Steve she was getting bronchitis and was afraid it would ruin their weekend. Alan suggested, "Why don't you get some antibiotics?"

"Why?"

"So you can take them if you keep getting sicker."

She didn't reply.

He inquired about a job he'd seen advertised. The thought of some distance from her and a complete change of scenery was appealing. Funny, he'd overheard her asking about jobs. She must be feeling the same, or else Paul was out of work again.

Susan felt ill. "I haven't been sick since I had pneumonia a year ago. It's the anniversary of your breakup, isn't it?"

Caught totally by surprise, he almost corrected her. "What do you mean?"

She replied with a smile. "You know what I mean."

He smiled and said nothing, but their silence was not uncomfortable.

The last of the ski money paid for pornographic calls, money always intended for sex, though in the end used for a pleasure rather thinner than planned. Another parenthesis closed.

Athena commanded the earth to bring forth the olive tree, her gift was adjudged good, so the city was named Athens. He smoked in an alcoholic daze under the tree in his yard, toying with the idea of painting its portrait. Above was Orion, the same as he'd seen it for forty years, the same as it had been for millennia—it hadn't changed a whit. The view from Sirius, yes, a question of focus, of the duration chosen for the background. Some afternoons with Olive had been eternal, but when measured against the stars life vanished the instant it began, and from another galaxy Sirius probably flickered just as fast. Things changed with unimaginable speed although adaption took forever.

Philip came out and said, "I took a picture of the olive tree with my new camera. Do you think I wasted the picture?"

Alan started. "No, anything is a good subject."

"But it's not a picture of you or Mom or Claire."

"Oh, sweetheart, we didn't give it to you just for pictures of us. It's for you to have fun with."

"When you finish your cigarette and your wine, will you play a game with me?"

"Yes, let's." They went inside together.

CHAPTER 23

For three nights running, just before he fell asleep, the image of the right rear end of a bronze BMW appeared accompanied by a diffuse erotic yearning and the certitude that it would not be fulfilled. Then he began noticing BMWs on the street. Their glistening firm lines, like those of a woman wearing lingerie in a glossy photograph, reminded him of Olive. At first he shuddered and glanced away but soon he was actively searching them out and eventually he could recognize model and year at a glimpse.

Returning with Susan from a counseling session one afternoon, he saw John Taylor parking his BMW near Union Street. The combination of Taylor, car and place created such a strong impression of Olive's milieu that he clenched his teeth to keep from groaning. He wanted to own one, to enter her world and recover her, so he visited a dealer and learned that they cost far beyond his means but also discovered that she and Paul had the very cheapest model, the least expensive prestige money could buy, like their house just inside the Piedmont border.

It was a relief when the mania waned and driving was again a means of getting from here to there.

Susan stopped moving while making love. "This is no fun. It doesn't feel good. What's the point? Why do people make such a big deal out of it?"

"Right. If you don't like it, why do it?"

"You know, it would be better if you shaved first."

"My skin breaks out if I shave more than once a day. Maybe I could try an electric razor."

"Try it."

He moved his hand to caress her but she told him to quit so he lay still until he came.

"Women can't be friends after a love affair," said Randy. "Sex is so mixed up with their emotions that in order to stop they have to wall off the possibility of friendship too."

"I've always claimed that men and women are basically similar, but maybe we're one of the species who only get together for mating and split up as soon as it's over. Or maybe you're right about women; men do seem to be able to have sex with less involvement. But it's got to be possible to surmount the differences. We only have to accept that nothing's perfect."

"It sounds like you're starting to let go of this."

"Hah, I wish! It's not me who can let go, it's whether it will let go of me."

That evening he craved that weird conjunction of two sacks of flesh and feelings, two minds and souls, love and friendship and sex. The counselor had suggested that he was to ask freely and Susan was free to refuse. She refused. He accepted cheerfully but felt lonely and got drunk.

"Why are you drinking? Are you unhappy?"

He didn't want to dissemble, but the truth that he was would only make her feel bad, and the reason, that he wanted to fuck and anyone would do, especially Olive, couldn't be told, so he said he was overworked.

He'd begun to notice a complicity among Olive, Mike, Jose and Steve to claim they were working harder than they actually were, and Olive's late arrivals, long lunches and excursions for personal chores particularly offended him. When their boss suggested assigning her one of his projects, he was pleased to think she might have to start working eight hours a day, but nothing came of it.

She surprised him by asking his opinion of two architects, but then he overheard her calling the one he had recommended against. All her actions lately seemed designed to spite him. He retaliated by interrupting discussions she was having, but it didn't seem to affect her and he found it was no charm against his unhappiness.

She snorted when they passed in the corridor. Two paces later, he snorted loudly in reply. When they next passed, he took the initiative and snorted first.

A week later, she walked by and said shortly, "Hi."

"She speaks."

On her return she said, "I speak."

"Just not to me."

She walked on by.

One day he joined the group for lunch. She stared at him and pointedly rode in another car. Harry met them at the restaurant and laughed as he sat down. "I dreamed of you last night, Olive."

"Uh oh!"

"It was good! Great! It was so good I told Karen about it." He smiled broadly and everyone laughed. "Are you blushing? You should be."

She shook her head.

"Do you have an electric razor?"

"No, but Paul has a hand razor."

"No cordless razor you use for certain places?"

General laughter. She said coyly, "We will invite you and Karen to come swimming with us. You'll like it, we don't wear much clothes."

Mike said, "Speaking of that, you know the woman who lives with John Taylor? Are they sleeping together?"

"Oh, no," said Alan. "It's platonic."

"Not anymore," said Olive.

"How do you know?" asked Jose.

"John told me."

"That doesn't prove anything," said Mike. "He'd like you

to think you finally scored."

"I'd like to know," said Jose.

"Me too," said Olive. "I am so interested in who's having an affair." She ignored Alan's glance.

"A friend of mine just had a baby," said Harry. "They named him Baxter."

She made a face and turned to Steve. "I don't like that name. It sounds like bastard." When her comment went unnoticed she continued, "For a foreigner the names all sound the same, you know." Alan was pleased that nobody replied.

As they broke up after lunch Harry said, "I'll tell you about my dream sometime."

She laughed throatily. "We should have a drink together," she simpered, and gave him an ostentatious hug and kiss while staring past his shoulder at Alan's glare.

She was taunting him. They'd been in love, and now she was acting like it was a gossip item. If that's how she felt, if it was all only a little titillation, why shouldn't he just go and brag about it? He'd kept her secret but now by god talk about kiss and tell, he'd tell on a grand scale. He'd finish his book. The whole world would see.

"I'm angry," he told his mother. "Not that she flirts—she's always flirted with this guy Harry. What upsets me is doing it in front of me."

"Maybe she did it to get under your skin. At the very least, she's being thoughtless, or maybe she did it to divert attention from you and her. But don't let her know how deeply you still feel. If she's at all designing, she could use it to manipulate you."

"And sniggering about affairs. It's not fair—she flirts around and I'm supposed to keep quiet. I feel like telling everyone so they can see how hypocritical she is."

"Be careful, Alan. You don't want it to backfire and lose your job for sexual harassment."

He told Berenice, "The affair was our own business, and her reaction is her business, but the estrangement is social. I should let the office know we don't get along. By keeping it to myself, I'm participating in the group under false pretenses. I'm covering up for her and not being true to myself."

"Alan, I don't know if you should."

"I'll only feel whole again when it's public knowledge that she doesn't speak to me. I want people to know it isn't my fault."

"What will you say if she asks why you're telling?"

"I'll ask whether it's true or not. I'm just acknowledging a fact."

He asked Harry to lunch. "I want to ask you a question, and then I'll tell you a story."

"Sounds interesting."

"It'll knock your socks off."

A few minutes later he heard Olive laugh. "Oh, but it's your dream, not mine." Then, "So I was the instigator and you had nothing to do with it?" A pause, then more formally but still friendly, "I am flattered that you would dream about me. It's very sweet of you."

Well, well, I'd better warn him about dreams. Rather, I should tell him it's a trick I used, maybe it'll work again. I should bet he can't get her into bed. It'd be worth a hundred bucks. How would he prove it? Let's see, he'll have to describe the color of her pussy and what he finds on her belly. The cesarian scar. What if he tells her and she comes to me furious? I'll say it's like the bet in *Cosi Fan Tutte*. As an opera fan, she ought to get a kick out of that.

"Harry, tell me if I'm paranoid. I'm not getting along with the other PMs and I wondered if you've heard anything."

"No, I haven't. What do you mean?"

"It's a general impression. Jose misquoted me the other day to cover up a mistake he made and he implied I can't control my contractors."

"He's extremely self-serving. I can see how he'd sacrifice you to cover his ass."

"Mike seems to be snubbing me, too. He told me to go

ahead and have my contractor clean up a mess of his, but now he won't talk about reimbursement. And Steve's avoiding me. And my relationship with Olive has deteriorated."

"They're a pretty tight group. You know how exclusive they can be."

"Are they saying anything about me?"

"Jose's remarked about how reclusive you are."

"Has Olive said anything?"

"No. Why would she?"

He swallowed. "How close have you come to making love to her?"

"Never. Did you?"

"Yes."

"I figured it out."

"What? How?"

"You asked if I'd change desks with you. I wondered, but I thought well, they're friends, they want to sit next to each other. Then Mike told me you made a lot of noise the night you stayed at his house."

"He couldn't have heard! We were quiet like mice and there was a bathroom in between."

"He said there was noise all night long, doors opening and closing."

"I thought he was joking because he was sure there was nothing."

"I figured if there was nothing, he wouldn't have said anything."

"Well, well."

"I wondered how it'd turn out, if you'd end up divorcing and marrying each other."

"It was this close." He held his thumb and index together.

Harry laughed. "Where would you have lived? Piedmont?"

"Yeah, I figured Paul would move out. Harry, remember when we all sailed to Tiburon? Afterwards you and Steve and I went to the bathroom."

"Off the boat?"

"No, the one on shore."

"I think so..."

"Do you remember following Steve out of the bathroom and seeing Olive and me leaning against the fence?"

"No..."

"Well, that answers something I've wondered about for a long time." Harry looked puzzled. "Olive and I were kissing and we always wondered if you guys saw."

Harry threw his head back and laughed. "No, I didn't see and Steve never said anything."

"He never hinted?"

"No, I don't think anybody suspected. If they had, they would have told me."

"I always heard that the first rule of love affairs is don't do it in the office. You can't believe how painful it is when it ends."

He laughed again. "Well, I'm sorry for the pain, but I suppose you have to expect it."

"Oh, yeah, I'm a big boy, I can't complain. The worst is she's treating me like dirt and I can't say anything. She only talks to me if someone else is there, to give the impression things are normal. She took back a birthday present she gave me, returned mine, doesn't deliver messages people ask her to give me, flirts with you in front of me."

"Well, she's definitely overreacting. You know, she flirts with Jose, too."

"And she doesn't even like him." Harry looked surprised. "She told me she doesn't trust him."

"Hm."

"I mostly wanted to know if she really does screw around."

"It sounds like she doesn't, and she doesn't know how to handle it. When somebody screws around, they just write it off, they don't care, no big deal. She's a very insecure person, you know."

"Listen, I was thinking about betting that you couldn't go to bed with her. What if I offered a hundred bucks to make love to her within, say, two years."

"I don't think so. Maybe, if it was handed to me on a silver platter and there was no way Paul would find out."

"He wouldn't find out."

"Yeah, he lets her go out by herself all the time, doesn't he? Nope. I wouldn't do it. What's the point? A few minutes of pleasure, and then all the trouble. It's not worth it. There've been plenty of chances, but there'd have to be a lot more involved than just screwing."

"That's for sure. There was more than that for me, but I still don't know if it was worth the trouble. Say, do you know if electric razors are better than straight razors?"

"No, why do you ask?"

Alan told him.

Harry laughed and said, "Let me tell you about my dream."

He stopped at a church on the way home for some quiet in order to assimilate what he'd just done. It was frightening to have revealed a secret involving someone else's honor, and he tried to gauge its effect on Harry. He was almost able to see her through Harry's eyes—a confused little girl who joined cliques to bolster her self-esteem—and himself—a poor sap crushed when he got less than he'd expected—before the janitor asked him to leave so they could lock up for the afternoon.

CHAPTER 24

The next winter Slocum Stew's closed for remodeling and he read in the paper that the restaurant where they'd eaten after the symphony had been sold. More parentheses closed.

Three evenings a week he drove Claire across town and sat writing in the back of a theater while she rehearsed a play. One evening he finished the story. The end. He walked outside, sat on a bench, and tested his sorrow against the lights of Tiburon across the bay, spoke her name aloud. Lo. The short phoneme died in the air like the meaningless tone of a gong.

The world outside had reappeared. People were people again instead of cartoon characters who appeared, spoke and vanished in isolated instants like shards of crystal.

He had moved beyond her set of friends to a new group from Facilities who were less chic, less arrogant, less concerned with their status, and interested in simply making things work. Dull but dependable. Well, so he'd lost a few friends. But it hadn't really been friendship—everything began and ended with the affair and had been wrapped in it. All he'd lost was a certain loose office camaraderie.

He saw that she'd never been frank. Though he'd always sensed that she withheld things, he'd attributed the anxiety it caused to his own insecurity. Friday the Thirteenth, for example: He'd been so worried about losing her that he hadn't seen that she'd actually been stringing him along until she decided between the risk and the fun. He'd missed the hints: I've been thinking differently since I met Susan, she said, but she hadn't shared the thoughts and he hadn't asked. Maybe she hadn't known them herself—she was so good at self-denial—or maybe she was trying not to hurt him, though she probably didn't know that lack of candor can be as hurtful as a lie. The closest she came to telling him was saying it wasn't fair to him, and even that concession was an offhand corollary to her justification to ending it. Well, she'd probably done the best she could. His falsehoods were no better. It was impossible to understand everything and even harder to put into words.

"Well, it's getting better," he told Randy.

"Yeah, eventually it does fade away."

"Funny thing, sometimes I see her as she'll look when she's old. Other times she looks like a little girl, the way she did when we made love. It still hurts a little then."

Randy laughed. "You were just in love with her body."

"Have you seen those pictures of Chinese banquets? You know, successful old businessman with a smiling young beauty queen whose only role is to look pretty. That's her type. Empty-headed vain cutie trying to marry a rich man."

"And you weren't rich enough."

"Yup."

"You're looking chipper," Stella said one morning. "You look so much better than you did for a while. Were you having a hard time?"

"Was it so evident? How did I look?"

"I don't know. Frustrated."

"Well," he drawled, "I wasn't getting along with some of the project managers."

She looked surprised.

"Olive doesn't talk to me any more."

"Really? Why?"

"She's decided she doesn't like me, I guess."

Stella nodded. "You know, she used to talk to me but if John Taylor came by she'd walk off and pretend she hadn't been talking to me at all, like she was ashamed of me. It hurt my feelings until I realized she's like that."

"She must have been afraid he'd think she was gossiping on office time."

"Yes, she's afraid of what people think of her."

He considered telling Stella why she'd canceled a lunch. The morning of the lunch someone else asked her out and she told Steve she didn't know what to do—she wanted to go out, but she did owe Stella a lunch, but Stella would always be there… She had left a phone message that a meeting had suddenly come up, though she could have walked a few steps and told her face to face. What a liar and coward. Love affairs may not come naturally, but lying does. I'm a blinder fool than I thought.

After two years he and Susan agreed they could make it without counseling and replaced the sessions with a standing dinner date. One week she held out an envelope just before they left. "I found this in your drawer. They're pictures of what's her name, that little Chinese woman you work with, Olive Lo. There are negatives, too."

"They must be the pictures I took at the office."

"What are they doing in your drawer?"

He couldn't think of anything to say. "I forgot about them."

The sitter came and they left. "I must say," she said, "I suspected the worst when I saw those pictures."

"All right, I'll tell you. Olive helped me work out the plot of the novel I was writing back then. I told her about you and me, and she told me about problems she was having with her husband."

"Did that make her see the bad things in her marriage?"

"I think so. He's very insensitive."

"I know. He didn't talk to me at all that time at Art's, and he got up and left me with the kids as soon as he finished eating. He's rude."

"For a while she confided in me but then I think she got scared about making a change, felt guilty about talking behind his back and was embarrassed about telling me so much, so she cut me and made up with him."

"Maybe she told him about you, blamed it on you, and that's why he doesn't like you."

"Maybe so."

"I'll bet Steve Naglee knows. You could talk to him."

"The pictures. Remember when the office moved three years ago? I took extras of her because we were such good friends, but I kept them separate so people wouldn't think there was anything more. I see how you felt. You saw them and it all came back, the anxiety, the resentment."

"So many things point to her... Was it her?"

"No."

"Would you tell me if it were?"

"You said you didn't want to know."

"You said I didn't know whoever it was."

"You don't."

"I just thought maybe we should get it over with, get it all out and be done with it."

But from her tone he knew she was relieved not to know.

"Remember when you went to San Diego with the kids?" she asked. "I'd been trying to please you all summer and constantly worried you'd leave because I wasn't. When you were gone, I got mad at you for causing all that grief. By the time we met I was very angry, and it took several days to get over. I always used to react by withdrawing."

"You know, until that spring I really tried to get along, tried to talk to you, communicate. Then I did withdraw, and then I met this woman. Of course, I could have chosen not to—we're not beasts in the grip of instinct."

"Yes."

"What I got from her was support, encouragement, uncritical admiration. That's why I did it."

"Was writing the book a form of therapy?"

"I guess. You know I always wanted to write, and things were so unsettled... It gave me a goal."

"Did you ever finish it?"

"I pretty much gave it up."

"Why?"

"It wasn't much good. I'm not a writer after all."

"But you worked so hard on it."

"It doesn't seem as important now. What's important is being happy with you and the kids, enjoying our lives, and contributing a little to society."

"That's what I've always said."

"You're right. You've been so patient with me."

"Well, we all have to do what we have to, don't we?"

"I love you."

"I love you, too."

He sold his last share in the boat since the kids had never taken to it, Susan never went out, and he hadn't gone in months. He took the spare sails from the garage and Susan waited in the car while he walked out the pier for the last time. He opened the hatch and threw them in, then lay down on the mattress, surprised at how small it was, wondering how two bodies had fit. Ciao, he said silently, and locked the hatch and left.

"Well, that's that," he said.

"Are you sorry?"

"Sort of. It was fun."

"You know, I'm sad for you but not really sorry. I'm glad it's gone—it had too many emotions."

"What do you mean?"

"You know, your love affair."

"Hmm?" He hesitated. "I bought it afterwards, after it was over."

"Oh, Alan, I know you used to go there at lunch and make love."

He smiled and looked out the window.

After a moment she talked about something else.

LETTER TO JACQUES

Congratulations, Habibi! I'm so glad you finally completed the marriage. Three years is a long time to wait.

Is the wonder of the beginning still alive? I hope so. I hope it lasts all your lives. Me, I've learned to be happy with compromise. I wanted six children and Susan wanted none; we're both happy with two. Same thing with love—I'm approaching her outlook: Less grand passion and more small demonstrations of caring by cleaning the house or doing the laundry. Well, well, life without passion is still worth living. Of course, if it comes you're a fool not to try to prolong it. It leaves soon enough without our help.

I could never keep my balance. It was like skiing—you fling yourself over the top and react to the forces with rigorous attention and yet a certain lightness of attitude. (Like playing piano, or raising children, or being married.) When your reactions aren't quick enough you fall. It happens all the time. You learn to fall gracefully, get up, dust yourself off and continue, but the object, after all, is staying on your feet. I knew all along rushing down the hill that I was barely upright. I did the best I could, but when I look back it seems I never was in control—I was forced by my passion where the forces willed. And then I fell like I've never fallen before. A caterwauling, windmilling sprawl of despair.

My piano teacher told me to keep my sense of humor. Good advice. What it means: Step back. Be objective. Laugh. Mei Li and I laughed about various ironies. For instance, we'd both learned as children to keep our mouths shut to conceal our ignorance; during our affair we kept them shut to conceal our knowledge. We were ironic spectators of a play where the other actors didn't know the plot. But Sofia meant the higher irony of watching ourselves act knowing we won't ever know the plot either and laughing at our own clumsy ignorance.

I went to China for the building dedication. They asked me to deliver their greetings to Mei Li and I said I would, but I won't. She hasn't spoken to me for two years. As they drove us to the airport through a small valley jammed with filthy brick buildings and corrugated metal roofs jumbled on the hillside, black smoke spewing into the cold gray rain, utterly foreign symbols painted on disintegrating fences, dirty people moving randomly on muddy footpaths choked with rubble, I asked where am I? Where am I in the world, where on earth am I? I don't even know if this is life. Have I died and gone to hell? Then I thought, I've been here and know this place but can't remember where, like early childhood visits to unknown places, uncomprehended visions of chaos; then I knew the place was China, those are Chinese characters on the crumbling walls. I have travelled far, I am beginning my journey home. I've lost touch with the world and its people. I am solitary. But then I told myself not to be so hyperbolic; I chatted with my companions and gazed at the fields as the outskirts gave way to countryside; and I wondered why I fall in love with places so far from home.

Claire and Philip's favorite music happens to be a disk Mei Li gave me. The other night they played it to accompany a skit they put on and I wondered, can I keep from crying? Don't, I told myself, it'll just make them feel bad about their morose father. Don't burden them with your past. So I didn't.

I've regained my balance. My skis are back on.

It's all for the best—I wouldn't have been happy with her. Listen to this: She'd planned a trip to Disneyland, and when the riots in LA broke out she blithely assured everyone she'd go anyway—she'd had too many trips canceled because of one thing or another. Only when somebody told her she might be pulled from her car and beaten to death did she change her mind, and she thought it was quite inconsiderate of the rioters to spoil her weekend.

And this: She has proposed her husband for a job vacancy in our office. I don't know if she's convinced I'd swallow it, or wants to rub my face in it (she's pleased to see people she dislikes suffer, though she's careful to not gloat openly), or doesn't care, or is desperate to get him a job, or what. But talk about callous!

Susan and I share our values, our volunteer work, our love of the arts, our children, our past. We have grown very close. Our sex life is good. (Thank god that particular fury has diminished.) We're slowly falling in love.

And that is the solution. Tenderness and love. Their lack cased the whole thing, and their presence, my dear Jacques, is the only meaning in life.

I hope so much that the two of you stay tender and accepting. It's very simple, but such a damned struggle sometimes. You have all my love.

He sealed the letter and sighed, opened his drawer and took out the pictures. She was a pretty woman with a pleasant smile. He put them in his pocket and went down to the garage.

From a box he took the manila envelope which held the letters and cards they'd given each other and turned it over unopened. Notes from Olive. Once he had read and reread them to understand each nuance and savor each pleasure. They had meant he was on her mind—she was thinking of him and anticipated his reply. Now they were passionless stains left on a beach by an ebbing tide.

Another envelope held the tablets of paper he'd spent hours writing, describing love and sorrow, splendor and sadness, trying to save something from oblivion. He'd written the book he'd promised her, but she no longer cared.

May as well move the cortege along. He put it all in the car and drove to the top of the tallest hill in town. The city and the bay and the sea calmly spread beneath another hazy fall sky.

We live, we die. Events seem so important, but in the long run it all means nothing. We think we're at the center of the world, but the world doesn't even know we're here. He gently pushed open the lid of a trash can and dropped everything inside. It fell with a rustle.

He turned slowly and fully around, feeling the vast, empty space above the world.

It might all have happened to someone else. It could have

been a story contained between the covers of a small book due at the library. It was no tragedy. No one died, no lives were destroyed, no marriages dissolved. No one drunk to death, no ruined careers. Passion and bliss and pain all faded with the simple passage of time.

All in all, it was all quite ordinary.

www.ingramcontent.com/pod-product-compliance
Lightning Source LLC
Chambersburg PA
CBHW020742250626
47155CB00003B/882